TOWNIES
AND OTHER STORIES
OF SOUTHERN MISCHIEF

TOWNIES
AND OTHER STORIES
OF SOUTHERN MISCHIEF

ERYK PRUITT

The following is a work of fiction. Names, characters, places, events and incidents are either the product of the author's imagination or used in an entirely fictitious manner. Any resemblance to actual persons, living or dead, is entirely coincidental.

Copyright © 2018 by Eryk Pruitt
Cover design and jacket photography by Brian Phelps
Interior designed and formatted by E.M. Tippetts Book Designs

ISBN 978-1-947993-35-8
eISBN 978-1-947993-50-1
Library of Congress Control Number: 2018955317

First trade paperback publication October 2018 by Polis Books, LLC
221 River St., 9th Fl., #9070
Hoboken, NJ 07030
www.PolisBooks.com

POLIS BOOKS

ALSO BY
ERYK PRUITT

Dirtbags

Hashtag

What We Reckon

For Lana

"First you make a roux…"

-Commandment of Southern Cuisine

"I shall try to tell the truth, but the result will be fiction."

-Katherine Anne Porter

"This is how it's always been.
This is how we do things in the country."

-Slim Cessna's Auto Club

TABLE OF CONTENTS

PART ONE

LUFKIN

NOVEMBER

For what seemed a long time, there weren't no place further from Dallas than the Piney Woods of Lufkin. That November—the one in sixty-three—all us Texans suddenly got lumped together. Everybody liked to have a story of what happened that day, where they were, what they done. I reckon I have one as well, even though I never told it to nobody and never planned on it.

We saw it on the television, like everybody else. They had a box in Tucker Danville's office, in back of his restaurant. He had the place done up like his own living room so he could relax when he wasn't yelling at waiters or telling folks they was crazy, their steaks weren't undercooked. He'd keep a bottle of good whiskey back there, as well as a bottle of bad whiskey. You always knew where you stood with Tucker.

Anyway, we were eating the lunch special that day, same as half of Lufkin. Tucker'd put a sign up earlier advertising how folks could get the very same lunch the president expected in Dallas, and since the pope said it was okay for the president to eat steak, then it must be okay for all Catholics to eat steak. Father White from up the road drove down and raised a stink on account of Tucker's sign, saying his lunch special was heresy and blasphemy and a bunch of other sinfulness and we was dispatched to make sure things stayed calm.

Tucker felt obliged and told me and Rufus to stick around, have something to eat. Weren't none of us Catholic, so we thanked him and took a seat.

I wasn't halfway through my Dr Pepper when Tucker's wife come out, told us all the president had been shot.

Me and Rufus went to the back office with Tucker and sat on the divan against the far wall. On the news was Walter Cronkite, his voice flat and grave. Folks in the dining room got antsy again and Rufus went to calm them down.

"This ain't good," said Tucker. "This ain't good at all."

"Folks are bound to get grumpy," I said.

"It's going to be a long day," said Tucker. He handed me a glass of whiskey and held open his door, as if waiting for me to leave. I gulped it down and handed him back his glass.

It tasted like shit.

They'd already formed a posse by the time we got to the station, about a dozen men with sticks and Louisville sluggers and maybe a shovel or two. At the head of it was Roland Marshall, who didn't have so much a drop of Catholic blood in him, but what blood he had was good and riled. He pointed his finger this way and that and caused such a ruckus that there weren't no use in trying to calm folks down.

"We best go along with them," said Rufus. "Make sure don't nothing get out of hand."

I agreed and he hopped into the bed of John David's pickup, me riding shotgun. During the ride out, John David said he never once agreed with the president, especially in the case of the blacks and what he reckoned was done in Cuba with the Bay of Pigs.

"Communist or no Communist," said John David, "we can't have folks shooting our president."

I agreed, but didn't say nothing the rest of the way. Let John David do all the talking.

We come up on the train yard round about three thirty. The president was long dead by then, though couldn't nobody remember how we heard it. Radio, maybe. Train was probably five minutes off. Rufus put his hand to the track, but we could hear it just over yonder. I took one last stab at keeping folks calm.

"All y'all know I ain't got no sympathies for the president," I told as many of them would listen. "But we got to keep our heads. Ain't no sense in doing nothing we're going to regret. Especially in the name of no-count Kennedy."

Some grumbled, some didn't. Regardless, up came Rufus of all people and told me to let it go, just let it go.

"They just blowing off steam," said Rufus. He'd been deputy for going on fifteen years, eight longer than me. "It's high time."

It was true. The baseball team had won State that year, but Texas being as it was, didn't nobody give a shit about baseball when the football team had a losing season. The last loss—a gut-wrencher against Diboll—put a dark cloud over everybody's head all week. Folks knew if they didn't have a big game later that evening, there would be no festive spirit come Thanksgiving.

I was one man in a mob of plenty, I always told myself. Wouldn't be nothing I could do, even if I felt it needed doing. I explained to Rufus and Tucker and even John David that perhaps I should go wait in the truck. But along came the train whistle and for some reason I stayed right where I was.

It hadn't come to a full stop yet when a few fellas climbed into one of the freight cars, one with the cargo door open. There was a commotion inside and out they came. Hobos. Bums. Each of them hitting the ground running, and a good thing too, because we was waiting for them. Gray Tollett played for the baseball team back in fifty-six and he hadn't lost none of his old swing. Showed when he ran his bat along the back of a hobo's head.

John David got him one in the stomach with his shovel, then took it around across his back. That one went down and John David figured he'd stay on him instead of running out to fetch another. He kept pounding on that hobo's back and carrying on about how they picked the wrong train. Wrong train and the wrong town to ride through on it.

They scattered. Everyone gave chase. Everyone except me, on account of I felt I'd seen enough. I didn't like Rufus carrying his gun with him, but he was long gone, giving chase across a spread of pasture alongside the train yard. Him and a mess of others, all determined to catch them one. Soon enough, it was just me. Me and a couple fellas couldn't get up and run after they'd been beat like they had.

Then, in the freight car: a ruckus. It wasn't until I saw Bill Olsen from down at the hardware shop that I realized I'd never seen him come out of the freight car. There he stood, clutching his belly like he'd had some bad chicken and he reached his hand out to me and said some shit I couldn't make sense of.

"Come on out of that freight car," I told him. "Let me have a look at you."

He came out all right. He fell to the ground, face first into the rock bed along the tracks. He didn't move and plenty of blood, red and purple and black, come out of him and got to puddling. At first, I wasn't thinking. I ran to him and rolled him over, and no sooner had I seen he'd more than likely been stabbed that I realized I'd turned my back to the freight car and whatever'd done the stabbing. I rolled over on my back not a second too late.

Two fellas come out of the car. Both in dirty, stinky jackets. One of them was Mexican or something like it, the other white. Neither looked to be in the mood to talk. I fumbled a bit for my sidearm but couldn't get at it quick enough and they were up on me. I got kicked, I got punched and I covered my head with my arms and soon enough all the world was a scream—high pitched and total—until I heard the gunshot.

First I thought it was me got shot. Weren't nobody kicking me anymore so I rolled and rolled until I was good and under the train where I resumed to fishing my revolver from the holster. The gun was my daddy's and he'd used it to shoot at Bonnie and Clyde and I'd yet to point it at anybody. Those days were over as I peeked out from behind one of the wheels and saw the Mexican dead on the ground, the other one with his hands up, reaching for the sky. Rufus calling for me to come out, everything's under control, come on out.

We liked to never get that fella back to the police station. Everybody wanted a piece of him. Rufus and me loaded him into John David's truck and told John David he could ride in the back or hitch a ride with somebody else. He said he'd ride in the back so long as he could punch the fella in the face once and we told him no, but he climbed anyway into the truck bed.

Sheriff made a stink about us heading out to the train yard, but understood why we did it and told us not to talk no more about it. He had the fella in a jail cell and told Rufus to watch the door, make sure none of those boys came back for him. He looked the guy up and down, then called for me to follow him into his office.

"Which train y'all roust him from?" he asked.

"The Mo-Pac," I told him. "The one blows through after three thirty. Why?"

"Where's that one come out of?"

"Come out of?" I scratched my head. "I don't know, sir. I know it runs southeast to Houston. Perhaps through Corsicana or thereabouts."

"What about Dallas?"

I shrugged. "Maybe."

"And about how many others was with him?"

I counted in my head. "I remember about eight or nine of them come running after Billy Olsen and the others flushed them out. This one stayed inside though."

"He stayed inside alone? All by himself?"

"No sir," I said. "He had company. A Mexican."

"Where is the Mexican?" asked the sheriff.

"Lying dead in the rock bed by the train. That's the one Rufus got."

TOWNIES

The sheriff sat on the edge of his desk. He was an old man. In his younger days, he'd been full of fire and brimstone, but that had long run out. Used to, he'd be at the front of a gang of guys out to make sure weren't nobody jacking with the ballots on election day, or if a Negro had to be lynched, that folks didn't get out of hand, chop off parts or set him on fire and such. These days, Sheriff rarely went out anymore. Took dinners at home instead of up at Danville's or even the Dairy Mart out by the highway. He didn't even campaign during the last election and proved he didn't have to. Didn't nobody but himself seem to want him to step down.

But he was still sharp as a whip. The skin around his eyes crinkled and he pursed his lips, same as he always did when he thought something out. He pulled on the whiskers below his lower lip and then stood again and put both his hands on both my shoulders.

"Let me ask you something," he said. I nodded and he said: "Was the other fella—the Mexican—was he dressed like that one in there?"

"He was dressed like a hobo," said I. "But they all was. Every one of them."

"Shoes too?" He pointed at his own dusty boots. "I need you to think about it real hard."

"I don't follow, Sheriff."

"The Mexican fella. What kind of shoes was he wearing?"

I shook my head. "I couldn't tell you, sir. I didn't pay no attention to what kind of shoes he was wearing."

Sheriff grabbed my arm and walked me back into the tank. There we stood at the bars and he pointed in at the fella. Nobody said nothing, the fella just sitting there in the cell, staring back at us while the sheriff waited. Waited until I took the time to first notice what he was getting at.

"That shitting thing in yonder is dressed like a bum, sure enough," said the sheriff, "but tell me what kind of guy rides the rails in hundred-dollar leather shoes."

I opened my mouth to speak, but sure enough closed it again.

"I need you to get out to the train yard and find out if there's enough left of that Mexican for us to take a look at."

The girl come to visit him the next morning, bright and early. She liked to have stopped traffic, as hadn't anybody in Lufkin seen a girl the likes of her. She was painted and lit up like a theater marquee, hair blonder than any other I seen before or since. She walked on heels so high she liked to float, but in she came and with her about a half-dozen fellas been following her since the parking lot.

"Everybody calm down, calm down," said the sheriff. He pointed out that more than enough of them had wives and the rest of them had their own business to mind. No sooner had he shooed them out of the police station than he turned his attention on her, asked how he could help her.

"You've got a friend of mine," she said. "I aim to see him."

He played dumb, but didn't anyone have to guess who was her friend. Sheriff instructed her to take a seat while he tended to a couple things and she did. Crossed her legs and chewed bubblegum.

She was a pip. Lips red as a Coke can and made up for a night on the town. She probably had about six different colors on her whole body. *Technicolors*, I think we were calling it at the movie house. She didn't seem bothered by anything, not even me pretending not to be watching her, until the sheriff came around and said she could see him, first she needs to sign some papers.

He looked over her forms and said, "You're a long way from Dallas, Miss…" He looked over the tops of his glasses at the paperwork. "… Velvet. That's an unusual name."

"I'm an unusual girl," she told him.

"What do you do back in Dallas?"

"I have fun," she said. "And I'm good at it." She winked at him and walked to the door, stood there until he opened it for her.

"Right this way," said the sheriff, and she was gone. Sheriff closed the door and sat at the edge of the desk, stroked the whiskers under his lip.

"You ever seen a girl looked like that?" I asked. "All made up like a comic book?"

Sheriff didn't say nothing for a minute or two, and when he did, it was to ask me didn't I have something better to do.

When she come out, she put a cigarette between her lips and stood still, waiting for somebody to light it. Didn't nobody move, so I fished a pack of matches out of a desk, struck one, and held it out until she lit her cigarette. She took a drag and looked up at me. Thanked me. Exhaled into my face.

"I need to arrange to have my friend out on bail," she said.

"No can do," said the sheriff. "Your friend struck one of my officers. We're holding him until the judge can see him and that won't be until Monday. He'll have to wait in the cell."

"I see," she said. She stepped closer to the sheriff. "What if I tell you I can get you enough money to cover any possible bail your judge might come up with?"

"Bail for a man striking one of my police will be mighty high," said the sheriff.

"We'll cover it."

Sheriff wouldn't budge. She stared at him and he met it, didn't flinch. He swatted away a fly which may or may not have been there, then walked back round her to the front door.

"Sheriff," she called after him, "may I ask you something?"

"I reckon so."

"Which of these here officers was struck by my friend?"

I felt my stomach trouble up and I didn't move. Nobody said nothing, but she must have sensed something because she turned and got a good look at me. Smiled. She took her sweet time walking my way.

"What if I apologized to the officer?" she said. Those red, red lips puckered up sweet and juicy. She squeezed her arms together and her goods fluffed up nice and round, nearly peeking out of her blouse. She batted her eyelashes and I felt every drop of blood go either to my face or down somewhere below and I hoped to high heaven folks saw neither one. "How far would that get me?"

"Look, I got one man dead, stuck in the gut from this whole incident," said the sheriff. "Your man ain't getting out of that cell."

"We told you the other fella done that," she said.

"The Mexican?" Sheriff shook his head. "He done it?"

"The Mexican, yeah." She smiled as if she were in on something weren't nobody else in on.

"Well, the Mexican ain't here to answer for it, so your friend will have to do." The sheriff held open the door for her. "Webb will take you to the motor court. It's close enough to the courthouse, should you want to stick around for the judge come Monday. But it's right on the highway, just in case you don't, and think you better get on back to Dallas."

She held his gaze a bit. Then turned back to me.

"You Webb?" she asked.

"Yes, ma'am," I said.

She smiled, nodded, and said no more as she walked out the door.

"What are you waiting for?" barked the sheriff, and I realized there wasn't nothing, nothing at all worth waiting for and high-tailed it out after her.

Halfway out of downtown, she'd already started in on me, coos and come-ons, laughing at my jokes. Only I hadn't said any jokes and wasn't likely to, given the situation. I had no wife, nor any prospects, and simply the smell of her drove me plum out of my senses. I'd have better luck chasing a gum tree out of the ground than I would that image of her in my head with her goods bunched up.

"Your boss don't like me," she said.

"He don't care too much for me none either," I told her.

She laughed more than I felt necessary, then said: "What about you? Are you mad at me?"

"Mad at you? I don't see what for."

"You said my friend hit you."

I nodded. "Oh, that." I hung a left out of downtown, knowing full well it was the long way to the motor court. I thought of every possible side street and stop sign between us and there and ran calculations. "I don't reckon it's any of your fault, ma'am."

She giggled. "Still, I hate that it happened to you. You seem like a nice guy. Do you mind if I smoke?" She put a cigarette again to her lips and I pushed in the car lighter. "Where did he hit you?"

"I'm fine," I told her.

"Show me."

I kept my eyes on the road. I pointed to my ribs. That's where she put her hand. Soft, so as not to aggravate the bruising that had sprung up. She ran an ivory-white hand up and down my ribcage and I wondered could she feel my heart slamming against the side of it.

"Where else?"

My hand shook, but it found the gumption to point at my thigh. She ran her hand down yonder way and we nearly crashed the squad car into a utility pole.

The lighter snapped to and I collected it quick and touched it to her cigarette, kept it there until it was good and burning.

"What do you want from me?" I asked her.

She smiled. "Just a ride someplace I can rest for the night. I got to figure out what to do." She sat forward in her seat and didn't try nothing cute the rest of the trip. Once she got her a room and got settled, she asked me would I like to come in, look a few things over. I asked her what kind of things.

"Things," was how she answered. "Ones that need looking over."

"Ain't a good idea," I told her.

"Why not? Because of your boss?" I nodded and she said, "I got a boss too. And my boss wants my friend out of that cell. And he needs that to happen pretty quick."

I nodded. "Ain't nothing I can do about that," I told her.

"Sure there is," she said. She took hold of my collar and led me into the room. "You're a sweet boy. All you got to do is stay sweet."

Inside that room was mighty dark. Best I can remember, didn't nobody ever turn on the lights.

So when folks ask where I was, there's never any point going into the whole story. Plenty people asked for quite a while after. When I made it back to the police station and everyone was in a fit because the sheriff was dead and the fella from the train yard was long gone, an explanation was demanded from me and I had nothing worth a shit to tell them. So I kept quiet. I kept quiet a long time.

They say the fella must have wrestled the sheriff's gun free from him. They say Sheriff had lost a step the past few years as it was, and it wouldn't have been difficult. Not in the least. They say he must have shot him, fished the keys to the cell out of his pocket, and went along his way. I knew the sheriff kept the cell keys on the wall in yonder, that no prisoner could ever reach them on their own, but that ain't what nobody wanted to hear back then. What they wanted to hear was two words: case closed. So that's what I told them.

No sooner had I shook loose of everybody asking questions, than I ran back out to the highway, back to the motor court. She wasn't there. She wasn't there and I wondered what in high heaven led me to believe that she might be.

Time passed and they needed somebody to pick up where the sheriff left off. Naturally, they asked me if I cared to have a go at it. I told them no, I'm not one to get mixed up in things. Don't care to make much noise. They thought those among my better qualities and had me elected immediately. I got a new badge, but still carried my daddy's gun. The one he drew on Bonnie and Clyde way back when.

I had no plans to be like my predecessor. Not yet, anyway. I went up to Danville's the first night after being elected and ordered myself a steak, well done. Tucker came out and invited me back to his office. We talked this, we talked that, we talked about what life would be like now that a Texan was in the White House.

"You know what kind of folks don't get bit by black snakes?" asked Tucker. He poured us each a drink and held it up.

"Them who don't jack with them, I reckon," said I. We touched our glasses and each took it in one gulp.

Not since that night at the motor court had I tasted something so good.

THE HOODOO OF SWEET MAMA ROSA

Had Old Poke Billet not been so fond of the Risen Christ, he would have swore up a storm. Instead, he spit sideways, as he was known to do, and dropped the screwdriver back into the toolkit.

"I'll be," was all he said. He removed his cap and wiped at his sweaty bald head with his hand, then replaced the cap. "I'll be."

For the past two weeks, he couldn't get nothing to work. First his weedwhacker wouldn't fire. He fussed and fiddled with it for two days, then had to take it in. It took them two more days and twenty dollars to get her to whacking again. Then went his edger. He'd taken to giving excuses to people on why he couldn't finish their yard straightaway, something he was not known to do. So when his mower blade wouldn't stay put, his faith had become tested.

In his younger days, Poke Billet ran with a temper, which was not a good thing to accompany a black man in deep East Texas. He took

15

to liquor and dancing and anything to keep his mind off work done in the fields in the hot afternoon sun. That Poke Billet would have kicked the mower and thrown it down into the shoals, watched with glee as it busted up over the rocks. That Poke Billet went to the prison work farm for all of his thirties. No, this Poke Billet took to Jesus now and saw no point in striking out at his machinery. He'd just dirty his good pair of work boots.

So he knelt to pray and asked God why his equipment wouldn't function. For all three of these pieces to go out on him so soon after the other must mean he wasn't living right, and he didn't wish to anger his Lord. He closed his eyes tight and his lips moved but spoke nothing as he asked forgiveness, retribution, and maybe for a little help.

And no sooner did wander up the Sinclair boy—the older of the two—his face full of wonder at what an old black man would be doing on his knees out in his work shed. Poke had known the Sinclairs ever since they moved into the neighborhood back when their oldest hadn't been a year old. Poke had been mowing all the yards for years by then, and had no problem adding the new family to his route. This one here got old enough to push the mower himself and Poke took it as no offense to be relieved of his duty. Now he reckoned he'd grown up some more.

"What are you doing?" asked the boy.

"I'm saying my prayers," answered Poke. "You say your prayers, don't you, boy?"

"Don't call me *boy*. My name is George." The boy stood straight. "And my mom doesn't make me pray anymore. I'm thirteen now."

Poke nodded. He got up from his knees and dusted at them with the backs of his hands. He squinted and said nothing at the boy.

"What are you praying for?"

"You ain't always got to be praying for something," said Poke. "Sometimes I just like to talk to God. He's the one who's always with me, so he's the one I talk to."

"My daddy said you was a crazy old man," said George Sinclair.

"I reckon so."

The boy kicked a clod of dirt and it skittered intact into the work shed. He waited to see if Poke would pick it up, since everything else had its place. Poke chewed imaginary sunflower seeds, his lips and teeth running back and forth in crazy kissing motions, a habit he'd picked up somewhere long ago.

"I come by to tell you that you been cursed," said the boy. "I thought you had a right to know. Sweet Mama Rosa put a hex on you and your shop and I figured you ought to know about it, that's all."

The old man watched the boy a moment. Poke shook his head and smiled. "I ain't got time to mess with curses and hexes and that stuff. It ain't Christian." He waved the boy away and returned to the mower, upside down and hoisted between two sawhorses. For the life of him, he couldn't figure how the blade wouldn't stay put.

"It don't matter if you ain't got time for a curse, you been cursed. A curse don't give a whip if you got time for it. And it don't care if it is or ain't Christian, neither." George didn't appreciate not having all of Poke's attention, so he spoke louder, almost to a shout. "If a curse is put on you, you done been cursed and there ain't a single thing you can do except be cursed. So maybe you better move on."

Poke's hands stayed at his side. The kid urged him, pushed him. *To what end*, Poke wondered. He spit sideways and turned the mower blade slowly. *Why did the blade keep slipping?* He studied it, mostly because he reckoned if he looked at the boy, he'd end up saying all the things he fought to keep inside his mouth. The world had come a long way over the past few decades, but not far enough that a black fella could tell a white boy how the world works and not expect a talking-to.

When Poke turned from the mower, the kid had gone. He saw tufts of red on the back of his head bobbing and weaving through the nettles and Johnson grass, back across the field from whence he'd come, off to his own part of the world. Poke watched after him and thought, not for the first time, about how strange it was that the boy would travel so far out of his way just to tell him a tale as ridiculous as the one about curses and Sweet Mama Rosa and whatnot.

And then he set back to wondering what the devil had been happening to his machinery.

George Sinclair walked the block for the third time and double-checked his notes. The Flemings lived in 316, the Pierces across the street at 317, and down the road Charlie Whitfill at 410. Nobody's weeds were whacked, and skinny strands of St. Augustine stretched out from the ends of the pavement. He straightened his tee shirt, which did nothing for the wrinkles, and made for the Flemings.

The wife answered the door. "Hello, George," she said. "How are your mother and father?"

"Just fine, I guess," he answered. "I was stopping by to see if I could take a crack at mowing your yard. It looks like it could use a little bit of help and I aim to be the one to help it."

"I appreciate it, but like I told you before, we've been letting old Poke Billet for years and we're generally pretty happy with what he does for us."

George considered this and looked back at the yard to let her consider it as well. "When's the last time Mr. Billet's been by to tend to it?" She bit her lip and tried to remember. She couldn't. "Been a while, I imagine," he figured. "Same story up the hill at the Meske place. He ain't been after them weeds for a week. Maybe he's too busy to make it over here."

"I doubt that's the problem," she smiled. "Poke's been tending to these yards since as long as I can remember. Listen, I'm truly grateful for your offer, but I imagine Poke will be by shortly."

George's face darkened. He wanted to grab her by the shoulders and shake a bit of sense into her, if it were at all possible. *Can't you people see that Old Man Billet ain't coming no more? Can't you people see I'm here to do this work?* All that and more he wanted to shout into her face, Mrs. Meske's face—hell, all their damned faces—but he tried like hell to remember his manners or what passed for manners and smiled as big as he could.

"You please give me a telephone call if Mr. Billet don't stop by before them weeds get too tall, you hear?" He extended his hand. Mrs. Fleming took her time accepting it, but did and promised that yes, if Poke didn't return, she'd certainly call.

You better, thought George Sinclair. He went on down the road to the next house.

Had Poke Billet been outside, he'd have spit sideways. Instead, he looked Virgil in the eye real square and asked him to repeat himself.

"I don't like being the one to have to tell you, Poke," Virgil said, "but all that sand in your fuel tank has done a number. It's wrecked your fuel filter, your pump, and gone straight for your carburetor. It ain't the end of the world, but on an old truck like this, it's going to cost you a pretty penny."

Poke stared at the truck. His uncle gave it to him when Poke left jail, and before he had a place to live, he'd had the truck. He'd slept in the bed, he'd used it to get around, and he started his lawn-tending business out of it. He kept it clean, oiled, and fine-tuned. Never had he had so much as an oil leak.

And now this.

"Where's your johnnie?" Poke asked Virgil. Virgil pointed around back. "Can you excuse me for a minute?"

Once inside, Poke locked the door, tested the knob, then dropped straight to his knees. He prayed feverishly, those lips mouthing the words but silent. He pleaded and praised and made all sorts of deals. When he satisfied himself, he stood up and looked into the mirror.

"Ain't no curses," he said. He said it again, but this time mostly to convince himself. "Ain't no such thing."

George Sinclair had been watching her for a week before he'd gotten the nerve to approach her. Never had he seen anyone like her. Sweet Mama Rosa appeared to be in perpetual mourning: always wearing black, swinging a rosary, draping a veil across her face when outdoors. Her skin, dark and sun-kissed, even well into winter. She sported a well-known habit of lapsing into a broken foreign language during emotional outbursts, where her cadence could explode with indecipherable, fricative bursts of unknown vocabulary. She wore jewelry that George thought could be from another planet.

George found her leaving the burger stand with a grease-bottomed sack and a soda, her sucking at the straw through her veil as she waddled down the street towards the Mexican part of town. He followed behind at the distance of about a block, just as he had for the past couple of days. Before he knew what he was doing, the distance had closed some. Before long, as if she could sense him, she turned around.

"You're Rosa, ain't you?"

"I'm Sweet Mama Rosa," she said.

"Yes, ma'am. Mama Rosa."

"No. It's *Sweet* Mama Rosa. Now tell me how I can help you."

He licked his lips. "Is it true you can put a curse on a fella?"

She laughed. George bristled and his face furrowed. Sweet Mama Rosa watched him and let her laughter die.

"You hear too many ghost stories," she said. "People think I am gypsy or magic or even a witch. They no want to know the truth that I am only a Catholic." She laughed some more. "And even so, there is no such thing as a curse."

George squinted his eyes so tight she wondered if he could even see through them. He tilted his head sideways, as if he were looking into a funhouse mirror. A car drove past slowly with music bumping deep bass from its stereo speakers. Sweet Mama Rosa wondered how the boy was getting home.

"I don't need you to tell me no secrets or read my fortune or nothing," he said, "but I need this done for me real bad. And I need it done real quick. So are you going to give me my curse or not?"

"You listen to me," Sweet Mama Rosa growled. She gripped the paper sack full of burgers tighter. "I've had it up to here with *pinche gringos* and their crazy superstitions. There are no such things as curses, and if there are, I don't know anything about them."

George stuffed a fist into his pocket and withdrew a wad of dollar bills. He stomped across the asphalt and, in less than three steps, brought himself to Sweet Mama Rosa's face. He showed her the money.

"I'll give you twenty bucks."

"Follow me to my house," she replied. "I know just what you need."

Old Poke Billet gripped his cap in his hand and kept his eyes down at the *Welcome* mat, took it like a man. The Whitfill woman gave it to him real good and he couldn't blame her none. All the while with her shouting at him, he wanted to speak up and tell her it wasn't his fault, that his truck done quit on him, that at different times of the week, his machinery'd been acting up, but he knew she wasn't hearing it. She probably also wouldn't take into consideration the fact that he'd been regular as rain with their lawn since the mid-eighties. No, he reckoned she enjoyed herself plenty standing out on the front porch and talking to him like a dog.

"I'm real sorry, Ms. Whitfill," Poke said again and again.

"I'm real sorry too, Poke," she said. "Real sorry. But Charlie works so much and it stresses him out to see the yard like this. We've had a boy come round for about a week or so now looking to tend to it. I'm going to give the job to the boy, Poke. You hear me?"

Poke started to protest. She put up a hand. He knew better. By God, did he know better.

"Now you've been a real good help these years," she said. "But if we can't depend on you, maybe we ought to let the neighbor boy crack at it. Look it, you don't even have your weedeater."

"I'm going to come round with it tomorrow. You'll see. You can depend on me, Ms. Whitfill," Poke said. "I promise."

She looked at him and at the yard and at the mower he'd wheeled across town and then back at him. "We'll see, I reckon," she said, and stepped back into the house.

Poke hopped to it. He said a quick prayer before he pulled the start cord and said another after it started. "Thank you, Jesus. Thank you, thank you, Jesus." Then he wasted no more time and got to mowing, as he would need to roll that mower a half-mile to make it to the Gavin house by two.

The next day, Poke noticed, not for the first time, that the Sinclair boy watched him as the old man went about his business. And his business was jogging all across town with the weedwhacker to finish the job he'd started the day before. Sweat ran rivulets down from under his cap and his shirt clung damp to his wire-thin body. Earlier he'd noticed him sitting in a tree while he worked a yard about a mile off. Now as he headed toward the Bandrow house, little George sat on the curb, tossing rocks at a stop sign. He stopped a moment and realized suddenly how out of breath he actually was.

"Why you keep following me, boy?" he asked between gasps for air.

"You ain't never going to make it in this heat, Mr. Billet," said George. Poke wondered if he'd ever seen the boy smile like such. He wondered if he'd ever seen anyone smile like such. "You keep running that weedwhacker about town like that and you'll plum fall over. You'll just see."

"I'll reckon I'll be fine."

The boy launched another stone at the stop sign. "You may reckon wrong. If I was you, I'd take me a little spell under a tree or back at your work bench."

"I'll see to it."

"Maybe let someone else mow these here yards for a while." The boy started to toss another rock, but stopped. He looked it over, turning it in his hand a bit, before placing it in his pocket. He threw the next one. "Since you ain't got your truck, maybe you let somebody else carry the weight for a bit. Let somebody else work these yards for oncet."

Poke couldn't work up any moisture in his mouth, so when he spit sideways, nothing came out but air. "I can't do that, boy. My truck'll get fixed here directly and then I'd just have to let him go. I wouldn't be able to keep him on."

"It don't matter no ways!" George fired the next rock wild, sailing right of the sign and off into the scrub brush. "You been cursed and you ain't going to mow yards with cursed lawn mowers and cursed weedeaters and cursed whatnot! You're going to run yourself silly and get yourself in a fix and then you won't be able to mow yards no how."

"What I tell you about them curses?" asked Poke, but he wished he hadn't. Arguing with a little white boy would do no one any favors, so he figured it best to shuffle on, which he did. As he jogged away with his weedwhacker, he could hear the boy calling:

"You can't outrun this curse! I hear Sweet Mama Rosa came over from Arabia with a tribe of gypsies and some fella killed the rest of them and she had him turned into a dog. Then he got picked up by the dogcatcher and was put to sleep or adopted by some other fella that liked to beat on dogs, one or another. But you got cursed and you better get out of town or else!"

Poke paid him no mind, or tried not to. All day, as he whacked at the weeds or jogged to the next house, he couldn't stop his mind from drifting over to the boy and his wicked premonitions. Poke had no idea why that Sweet Mama Rosa would put a curse on him but he'd seen her. He'd seen her once at the filling station and had quickly looked away. He knew his God did not want his eyes upon her, her with those mysticisms and divinations. Could it have been that he'd offended her and this was his penance?

But he tried harder than anything else not to think about it, going so far as to stop every few moments when he caught himself with it on his mind and dropping to his knees to ask God what should he do, what should he do? Before long, he'd caught himself up in a frenzy and the sun beat down on him hard enough that he fell to the ground.

He laid there for who knows how long, face upward. He opened his eyes and the sun threatened to burn them clean out. His mouth gasped for water. He put his hand over his eyes, then took them off again. He stared into the sun.

"Yes, sir," he said after a moment. "I got cursed."

Far off, the wind rushed through the shaggy sycamores, lifted the poplar leaves, and went on its way.

"No, sir, that ain't the Christian way," said Poke into the sky. He licked his lips.

"I reckon I can see to that for ye."

And with that, he stood up and dusted off his britches. He looked down the road until his eyes adjusted. He left his weedwhacker behind and went into town to tend to God's business.

Sweet Mama Rosa came to the door complete with her veil, rosary, and what most folks would call funeral clothes. "Why do you keep pounding on my door?" she wanted to know. "If I wanted to talk to you, I would have answered the first time you knocked. Now go away!"

"Listen here, Mama," the boy growled. "I done paid you twenty dollars to put a hex on that old man so he couldn't mow no more yards and it's been two weeks and he's still mowing them. How on earth am I supposed to make any money around here if that old man is still mowing all the damn yards?"

"I'm not your mama, *mijo*," she said. "I'm your Sweet Mama *Rosa*. And maybe the curse takes a little longer to work. I don't know."

"What do you mean you don't know?"

"I told you that I don't know nothing about curses. I believe I told you that several times."

"But you took my money!" he said.

"That I did," she said. She saw she did his disposition no favors. "Listen, give it some time. These old curses and spells aren't as strong as they used to be. Just give it a little while."

"I ain't got a little while," snapped George. "The season ain't going to last forever. I ain't got time to waste waiting for your stupid curse!"

And he stormed away from Sweet Mama Rosa's house, stamping down first his left foot then his right, hands stuffed in his pockets all the way back to his own part of town where he knew he had some decisions to make. Before long, he found himself at Poke Billet's work shed and the evening sun well on its way down. George smelled the motor oil and the fresh scent of newly cut grass and knew the equipment had only recently been put away. Careful so as not to set a door to squeaking, George opened the door and slipped inside.

Everything was pristine. George reckoned he'd never seen anyone take such good care of their things. He saw tools from another time, hanging proper on the wall and looking new as yesterday. A calendar full of names he recognized hung on the wall. It advertised motor oil made out in Ohio. George clenched his fists and wanted to knock everything in that shed to high heaven, but made himself breathe deeper until he gathered his wits.

"I ain't got no time to waste waiting for a curse to work," he muttered. Outside, a whippoorwill did its thing and he froze, waiting to hear the ruckus Poke Billet would be making, rushing outside to see what the hell was going on. Nothing happened. Nothing happened and George got to breathing again and looked around the shed. Moving slowly and as quietly as he could so as not to disturb the night's peace, he set about wreaking havoc on Poke Billet's things.

Once he was through, he slipped out the work shed and, on his way back to the field from whence he came, he looked to the old man's truck, just as pristine and well-tended as every damn thing else. George glowered, balled up his fists, and grabbed as much sand as he could carry.

"No, sir," he whispered. "No time at all."

THEM RIDERS

Wilbur Turgow dropped the dew-soaked newspaper and stared hell-fire toward the neighbor's yard. Not a split second later he stomped across the rust-stained patch of lawn separating their houses. He hoped to high heaven they heard his footsteps shouting across the way long before he made the front door, but felt vindicated when he had to ring the bell anyway. And ring he did. Over and over and over until—

"Mr. Turgow," said Rhonda. Turgow wished the man had answered, as he never liked delivering fire and brimstone to a woman. But this weren't no ordinary woman.

"I think I done asked you folks to mind them weeds, didn't I?" he growled. "I done said time and time again to your husband to look after your yard."

"I beg your pardon, Mr. Turgow," she began, but there never was any reaching him when he took this way.

"I done told you," he stammered. "See how them weeds grow up over my property, shitting seed and pollen all over my grass? I pay good money to take care of my side, I'll have you know."

"I suppose you do," she said, lowering her eyes.

Still, he would have none of it. "I reckon that neighborhood you moved from nobody gave nary a lick about the condition of their yard. Not the ilk running about those neighborhoods, do they? Well, I tell you, around here it's a different world. A much different world."

She didn't bother asking him to explain. There was no mystery. To a man like Turgow, she and her husband could have been aliens, for all he cared. She fancied any black family would have the same issue in this corner of the world.

"You can get uppity all you want," he said. He thought to say more, but something far away caught his attention, if only for a moment. He listened, head cocked to the side like a mongrel dog catching a faint whiff of feline or something lame. He slowly turned his head to her and smiled, smiled as if suddenly blessed. She thought she'd sick up her lunch.

"Mr. Turgow?" she asked.

"They'll come," he whispered. "They always do."

"I beg your—" She clutched her apron and wished Wendell would come walking up the way. "Who'll come, Mr. Turgow?"

He flung brown juice from his lips, specked the edge of her front step. He didn't bother to stamp it with his foot.

"They like things a certain way in this town, you hear?" Behind him, bronzed beech leaves rattled like bones. He leaned closer. "They always did. They run out them big tobacco companies once. They run out the priest feller who took to boys. And they going to run you folks out, plain and simple. They watch this town and they make sure don't nothing improper set foot in here. And if it do, they weed it out."

Her face caught fire and she cursed her eyes for burning, for betraying her in front of this man. She wished she could be strong and put the fear of something into him, wished to heaven Wendell would never find out. Wished she could take care of it. It'd been her who pushed Wendell to move here, her who insisted they leave that trash-strewn lot across town. They'd moved. They'd settled. And then Wilbur Turgow.

"Mr. Turgow," she said evenly, "I'm going to ask you to step off my property. Do you hear me?"

He smiled that sick smile and again her stomach lurched. "I hear you good and proper," he said. He took a step back, then another. "You tell your husband what I said about them weeds. And you think about what I said about them riders. Because folks know when this town gets threatened, they come. You hear?"

He left and Rhonda let go of her apron for the first time in who knew how long.

Rhonda went down to the Minyard's for some milk and things; not the old one out on six-oh-one, but the newer one just put in by the hardware shop and the five-and-ten. She tramped up and down the aisles with a list of things in her head, but picked up nary an item because she was lost in the words of Wilbur Turgow. She'd run over in her head a few dozen times the deal about the riders before she heard Suzanne Warren crowing away in her ear.

"You deaf or something?" Suzanne smiled. "I asked if you was okay?"

Rhonda nodded. "I'm so sorry," she said. "I must've been off in my own world. What was you saying?"

"I was saying that the way you carried on in the aisle here, you must be from another planet." Suzanne tinkered with her child in the front of her shopping cart, set the kid to, kept him from fidgeting through the basket of soup cans and toilet paper and boxes of ready-meals. "Heck, I bet you and me could have been talking an hour and you'd have never heard a word I said."

Rhonda's lips tightened at the edges and she waved her hand. *From another planet...* She hugged her groceries. Across the aisle, Bob Parson's wife looked through the cereal.

"I have had a horrible day," Rhonda said.

"Oh dear," said Suzanne. "Wendell's all right, ain't he?"

"Yes," said Rhonda. "Wendell's fine. Neighbor trouble. Wilbur Turgow."

"Ahh." Suzanne closed her eyes and nodded. She looked down the aisle. Bob Parson's wife moved along. "Never you mind him. He comes from another time. A time when folks like you and folks like me weren't supposed to shop in the same grocery. He's harmless. He can get agitated, sure, but he's harmless."

"Agitated is one thing," said Rhonda. "But Turgow is a mess. He said there was riders out there would tell me and Wendell what for."

Suzanne wiped the corners of her mouth with her thumb and forefinger. Her eyes darted to and fro. She opened her mouth to speak, but thought better of it. Bob Parson's wife made her way back onto the aisle, still eyeballing cereal boxes, or pretending to. Suzanne made a smile, or what Rhonda hoped was a smile, and touched her shoulder lightly. "Neighborhoods are like an Almond Joy, sweetheart:

there's a nut in every cluster." She squeezed Rhonda's bicep tight and pushed the cart along, young one and all. Rhonda thought a moment before drawing her next breath.

Tears stinging her eyes, she paid for her groceries and shoved her own cart out the electric doors. This was not why she moved here. Kelman's had shops up and down the coast and she could have taken her pick, but she'd jumped at the chance to work at one so close to her mother, one smack dab in the middle of the new shopping center in town. Any town with a Kelman's was a town on the rise. Or so she told herself.

She stopped shy of lifting the trunk lid, let her head rest at her wrist a moment. She took it all in. Across the road were jackhammers, but on this side were robins, wrens, and the sound of children. Kids asking for candy or begging Mom to ride in the front seat or even kids on the mechanical horse out front only cost a quarter. She thought about Wendell and what they could or couldn't do and where they may or may not be allowed to do it.

She thought about Kelman's and where the other shops were, and Suzanne came up from behind and put a hand on her elbow.

"Them riders ain't nothing but ghost stories," she whispered.

"I beg pardon?"

"Ain't nothing but boogeyman talk they tell to keep folks in line," she said. Suzanne looked around the lot, made sure to keep the cart holding her boy at a straight-arm's length. She kept her voice low. "Sure, oncet a few men ran about making sure tobacco buyers was kept in line. Maybe later they chased out a few Germans or some Japs. I've heard stories about…I've heard stories. But that's what they are: stories."

"Wilbur Turgow ain't no story," said Rhonda, and she meant it.

"I've dealt with Wilbur Turgows my entire life."

"We all have," said Suzanne. "They come with the territory."

Rhonda wanted to tell her, "Then pity the territory," but instead opened the trunk of her car and began stacking groceries. Suzanne pushed her own shopping cart back a step and leaned into Rhonda.

"Don't say no more about them riders," she whispered.

"What's that?"

"Them riders," hissed Suzanne. "You don't need to say no more about them. It won't do you no good."

Rhonda lowered her head. What more did anyone need to say? Suzanne squeezed her forearm as if to say all was okay, then went back to her child and her shopping cart full of whatnots and wheeled off to her parking spot. Rhonda, when finished packing, slammed the trunk shut and got in the car.

"Ain't no use," she grumbled before turning the key in the ignition. Across the street, jackhammers chattered. "Not around here and not around nowhere. Ain't no use whatsoever."

She said nothing to Wendell that night. They went to bed after dinner, him none the wiser, and she'd let herself forget, but came around suddenly well past midnight when the sound of hoofbeats and hell-fire brought her to.

"What's that?" screamed Wendell. He threw himself from bed and into his slippers and fussed around the nightstand for his spectacles.

"Dear Wendell," she moaned. "It's them riders!"

Wendell knew nothing about it and meant to demand explanations but the noise outside drove him to hysterics. Lightning spit and pissed down from the heavens and thunder with it, screams as long as the night ran in and out of every window and wall until Wendell found himself down on the floor along with her, him long without his bathrobe and baying about how he loved her and hoped and prayed this wasn't the last time for him to hold her.

"Them riders!" she cried. "They've come! We should never have moved here."

Wendell held her tight. Tales from childhood ran through her head but, never one for ghost stories, she'd dismissed them. But now...

He held her closer. Outside, the wind howled and moaned and raised such a ruckus they reckoned more than just their house would be laid to waste. Her shouts and cries mingled with the din and he must have figured he didn't want to hear them anyway, would rather just hold her. He fell over her and hoped it all to be quick.

And outside, all the while, hoof beats and wind whipping and men laughing. Men laughing.

"I love you, Rhonda," he said so many times it tasted like air. "I love you so much."

And an orange glow floated at the bottom corner of the window, then the bottom half, then it looked like all of outside had been colored bright orange and Rhonda shut her eyes tight until all she saw was black, but heard the crackling and snapping and couldn't be fooled into believing that everything was not afire outside the window.

Where men had once been laughing, she heard someone half-intoning a church hymn or something like it, barely trying to keep in tune. "God is a-fore us, yes he is," he, whoever he was, kept singing. He had no other words to the song, just kept at that single lyric, but kept at it proud. "God is a-fore us, yes he is, yes he is."

"I have to go out there," Wendell said. "Somebody could be in trouble."

She clutched him and fingers like iron wouldn't loose him for nothing. He screamed for her fingernails. "You get yourself right back down here, Wendell Penn," she cried. "Don't you leave me, do you understand?"

"There might be trouble in the neighborhood," he said. "Someone might need my help."

"Sit you back down here with me," she cried. "I need your help. Do you hear me? It's us! It's us they're after!"

And Wendell, having never heard fear tinge his wife's voice like so, forsook all other duty as extraneous and returned her back to his arms where she stayed until the orange glow at the window gave way to sun up and no more were the cracklings and snappings, but birds, birds carrying on outside. The branch from the old gum tree scraping across the roof's shingles due to a breeze. Wendell rolled off his woman and, for the first time, let her breathe.

He put a hand to Rhonda's shoulder and gave her a shake.

"We're dead," she moaned. "We're dead and I'm fine with it. I hate this street."

"We ain't dead," he said. He smiled and checked her for cuts and bruises and looked deep into her eyes to make sure everything was still ticking, then hefted himself to his knees and dusted his palms on the thighs of his long johns. He looked about the room and, using the nightstand for support, brought himself to his feet.

"You heard them horses last night, didn't you?" Rhonda asked from below.

"I don't know what I heard," said Wendell. "It sounded like a storm. I'm going to check the kitchen." He waved a hand in front of him as if surprised to see everything still intact, then made his way through the house. But each room—kitchen, living room, hallway—had been left to it and he found himself standing at the front door, scratching his head.

"You heard it well as I did," said Rhonda, and he wondered how long she'd stood behind him. "It weren't no storm. It was horses. Men on horses. That's who made that noise."

"That weren't no horses, Rhonda," said Wendell. "Sounded more like a storm. A big one at that. I best head outside and check on the neighbors, make sure everybody's okay."

She rushed to him and grabbed his bathrobe by the belt. "No, Wendell. Don't go out there. Stay inside. If anything's wrong, somebody else will come and tend to it. It ain't our problem no how."

"Now, now," he said, holding her. "Everything's fine, baby. There ain't nothing to be afraid of no more. Storm's passed."

"No, it ain't," she pleaded. "This storm ain't never going to pass. It started well before us and it'll keep blowing and blasting long after we're gone. There ain't never going to be an end to it, and if there is, we'll be long dead. Please don't go out that door, Wendell. I know you heard me."

He tried to smile. He put both hands on her arm and softly moved her aside. "Honey," he said, "we need to check on our neighbors. They might not have been as lucky." She started to say more, but he didn't want to hear it. "It's our duty now." He stepped from her and opened the door.

Rhonda fell to a heap and choked on her own sobs. She didn't tell him because he was a good man. She knew Wendell would kick up a fuss if he caught wind of Wilbur Turgow and his ilk, hassling her and others like her. Wendell meant well, she figured, but he'd never accept their lot. He'd go out fighting and screaming, and then where would she be? Where then?

She put her head in her arms and figured she'd rather suffocate herself with her own bathrobe than watch Wendell destroy himself, when she heard him shouting. She poked up her head and listened to be certain.

"Rhonda," he hollered. "Rhonda honey, call the police!"

She leapt to her feet. Rather than track down the cordless, she raced outside. Wendell saw her coming and moved to tackle her, the entire time pointing and screaming and ordering her back inside.

"What's the matter?" she cried. "What is it, Wendell?" She doubted she could take much more. She lifted her eyes to the sky with full intention of asking what kind of God could allow this to continue for as long as it has when she saw it, raised up high in the shagbark hickory at the edge of her yard. Her mouth opened to scream, but nothing pushed forth. Faraway were chainsaws.

"Go back inside, honey," said Wendell. He put his arms around her and blocked her view of the tree. "You don't need to see this."

She raised a crooked finger to the top of the hickory. "Wha—?"

"It's Mr. Turgow," he whispered. "We'll need to call somebody to help cut him down."

She put her head to his chest and he rushed his wife into the house, hoping to high heaven that she'd erase that and all other painful images from her mind. Hoping she could go on knowing nothing about what a terrible world in which they sometimes lived.

KNOCKOUT

A person's phone tells you a lot about them.

The easiest thing to discover about someone once you have their phone is their contact information. Their home address. Where they work, if they work. Their friends and family.

But these days, phones carry so much more information. Say they're on Facebook, then you can find out what interests they have. Dreams. The discussions they have with their friends.

Get into their text messages, and you discover even more. What kind of lover they are. How they talk to their mother or their father or their co-worker or even that secret little thing they keep on the side. Some text messages they save, like the one from an older brother that's dated over two years ago. The one that said the cancer wasn't going away. Said he couldn't wait to see him one last time, but he better hurry.

That one.

Thumb through that phone and you find all sorts of treasures. Photos. Passwords. Apps to stupid games you could care less about and so should anyone else. Reminders throughout the calendar that make a pleasant little ringing sound when it's the birthday of someone special.

And videos.

Lots of videos.

Like the one where the guy is trying to rap. It's a neat song. A lot of fricative rhyming about how much he loves his son and wants to be a good father. How he doesn't want the cycle to continue, how he's going to break the chain / ain't going to be the same / going to stay until it's done / he's going to be there for his son.

That one kind of moves you some.

The next one is better. It's a video of the rapper and his girlfriend on a date. She blows out a single candle at some restaurant in the city. She can't believe how lucky she is. She thinks he's the best person she's ever met. He turns the camera phone towards them both as he leans in for a kiss.

This is called a selfie.

Everything about the next video is familiar. It's the parking lot of the Winn-Dixie around the corner from your house. A cloudless summer day that you remember all too well. The camera behind you, but getting closer. You can't watch the video without wanting to shout at yourself in the screen to turn around, watch out. They're coming.

Two other guys approaching you, hoods up. You're loading groceries into the trunk of your car. Your wife will be cooking stroganoff tonight and you said you'd pick up things on the way home from work. You've got a bag to go when they come along behind you and ask you something that you think is directions to the stadium but you don't so much as turn around before—

Yeah, they got you good. It's right there on video. Right there on some bastard's camera phone. You feel it the same as you felt it when they socked you good and proper but it wasn't the punch to the face that did the most damage. Sure, that punch destroyed your trust in all of mankind, but it was bouncing off the bumper of your own car that destroyed your cheekbone. The landing on the pavement that broke that thing in your head. You call it your right-and-wrong lever. The thing that keeps you from setting fire to anything and everything you see fit.

That's what they broke. And they broke it to pieces.

It broke when you fell to the ground and reached out for anything you could but all you could grab was that asshole's sneakers and he fell too and dropped his phone. Unlike you, he got up. He ran.

He left his phone.

Other things you find on it: a text message about the only thing he's afraid of is snakes. He ain't got time for no snakes, he texted someone. So you bought three cane-break rattlers from a guy you know. A guy you would never have spoken to in the past but hey, that's the past.

A text message from his baby momma saying he needs to be home, watching their son this weekend until seven, so she can work her job at the local fried fish joint.

The calendar that rings a pleasant little sound telling you it's time for him to pick up the boy.

And like you said earlier: his address.

You hold that phone with one hand and the sack of rattlers in the other as you make your way up his front steps, that motherfucker.

HOUSTON

Kate didn't take five minutes fooling around down there before my rocks were good and gotten off. She rose from the floorboard, adjusted her shirt, then hollered out the window at Bunk to let him know she was finished, he could come back to the car. I'd barely slipped myself back into my pants before the interior light clicked on and Bunk threw himself into the backseat where he said not a word, just stared out the window.

If it were me, I'd have been grinning and making jokes about the whole thing. We'd still be laughing, all the way back to Nacogdoches. I'd have likely never let it go. But it wasn't me, and I'd never been in that situation, and therefore, had no idea what I was talking about.

It was my first time in a lot of situations.

"Sorry I yelled at you like that," I told Bunk. I watched him through the rearview. He didn't look up. "I was just a little stressed out. I had no right."

Bunk muttered something, but still would not look up.

"Promise me you ain't sore no more," I said.

Bunk nodded, his eyes still out the window.

I said, "Tell me it's all good and we don't have to think no more about it." When answered with only more silence, I said, "Say the words, Bunk."

"It's all good," he said with a sigh. "We don't have to think no more about it."

I started the car and merged back into midnight traffic. The roads from Houston to East Texas grew thicker with pine as the traffic thinned to the occasional trickle. It wasn't for a while of this before finally Bunk said:

"You ain't been yourself lately, Deke."

"What's that supposed to mean?"

"Maybe we change the subject," said Kate. She fiddled with the buttons on the radio, but could only find talk stations and shit classic rock.

"No, let him talk." I tilted the rearview toward him for a better view. "What do you mean, I ain't been myself, Bunk?"

"You just ain't the same person," he said.

Kate turned in her seat. "Bunk, why don't you take a nap? You seem a touch cranky."

Bunk was older than Kate, but she knew how to put him in his place. He hung around the two of us for drugs, sure, but everybody knew he was waiting for me to be finished with Kate. His plan—I reckoned—was to swoop in and rescue her, but then what? A girl like Kate would eat alive a boy like Bunk. She'd give him something to cry about. All the beat poetry in the world could offer him little respite after she'd leave him crumpled, broken, and neutered.

I wanted a front row seat, but for now…

"I'd really like to hear what you have to say, Bunk." I turned down the radio, then cast the reminder of my cigarette from the window. "I ain't the same person, you said. What did you mean by that?"

I didn't have to look at her to know Kate delivered him the stink-eye. Her message sent, she spun in her seat and watched the road. Folded her arms across her chest. She'd gone to all that trouble—bless her heart—to calm me down and here was Bunk, stirring the pot.

"Forget it," he said.

"I'd like to hear it, Floor Boy," I said. Floor Boy is what we called him because there were never enough seats for him. No matter where he went, he seemed to always find his way to the carpet. He'd yet to cotton to the nickname, so I reckoned it as good a way as any to get him riled up.

"I'm just saying you've turned into an asshole, that's all," he said. "When I first met you, I thought you were cool. We talked about comic books. Baseball cards. But then…" He shut his mouth, then thought better of it. "But then, look what happened to you."

"And what, pray tell, has happened to me?"

"You turned into *this*, is what."

"And what is *this*?"

"The kind of guy who does shit like this," he said. "The kind of guy I can't stand."

"And you're such a stand-up guy?"

Kate put a hand to my shoulder. She kept her eyes on the road. "Deke…"

I didn't care to hear it. "What do you think would happen, Floor Boy, if we turned these almighty powers of perception around on you? What kind of character would we expose there? You think I don't know why you hang around Kate, reading her your poetry?"

Bunk opened his mouth. He closed it.

I kept on: "You think I don't know why you're sitting in the backseat with your fists clenched, dreaming all the ways to tell me to go fuck myself, just because of our little pit stop back there?"

Kate took her hand off my shoulder. A lot of good it had done.

"It wasn't even my idea," I told them both. "I'm the one who said we needed to get back to Nacogdoches, the quicker the better. *I'm* the one who said we got no time for riff-raff. It was Kate who said pull over and told you to take a walk in the woods while she—"

"That's not what I'm talking about!" Bunk shouted from the backseat. "That's not anywhere near the top of my list."

The silence swallowed up his words and we rode a good while before I felt cool with breaking it.

"Then what are you talking about?" I asked him.

"Shut up, Bunk," growled Kate.

But I wanted to hear it.

"I'm talking about the guy in the trunk," he said.

Oh yeah.

And then there's that.

The guy in the trunk.

We rode the rest of the way to Nacogdoches in silence.

Only hours earlier, I had given Kyle Karver one specific instruction: "Do not take your eyes off the money until you have the weed."

"You're being paranoid," is what he told me. "These guys are cool. Trust me."

"I don't give a shit," I said. "You are to stick with either the weed or the money at all times. Nod if you understand." He laughed it off, so I repeated myself while putting my hands on both his shoulders. I let him know I wouldn't let go until I was satisfied.

"Fine," he said. "I understand."

And with that, I let go of the money and watched him disappear out the restaurant's front door. I went back to the table where Kate and Bunk waited. The waitress had just popped over with another order of mozzarella sticks and I asked if she would fetch me another cup of coffee.

"Refills ain't free," she said. "This is a sports bar, it ain't Waffle House."

I told her I didn't care, just bring me the fucking coffee, then I sat down to wait. Kate tried to pass the time with a funny story, and Bunk did what he could to distract me, but nothing took. In no time, my leg got to shaking and I could hear nothing coming from either of their mouths, only the million different thoughts rattling throughout my head, each of them starting with, "I should never have let Kyle out the door with all that money."

Not that Kyle was shady. Not that he wasn't either because, to be honest, he was shady. He was also an idiot. Kyle once quit his job because a co-worker gave him a map to a mysterious field of kind bud hidden deep within the East Texas thicket. He needed to focus on finding the weed, he said, when he returned home unemployed from his pizza job. He promised to cut us all in when he found it and, day after day, he marched out to the Piney Woods of Angelina County, armed with a map, machete, and a box of trash bags. Every day, he returned home: dirty, sweaty, and smelling quite the fright, but insisting he'd find it tomorrow—oh, he'd get that weed tomorrow.

You could count on Kyle to take too much acid and paint his room and furniture purple. You could count on Kyle to pick a fight with the biggest and most connected guy in the room, then disappear after his friends get involved. Kyle was the kind of guy who got girls pregnant and never chipped in for more than half on the abortion.

Kyle was not the guy you gave three thousand dollars to buy drugs and expect everything to go right.

The panic started in my leg. It shook so much that it rocked the tabletop, then knocked the salt shaker to the floor. That panic worked its way up to my stomach where I reckoned I could puke, then to my eyes, which twitch when I get antsy. It rocked my insides so hard that I could neither see, hear, think, nor smell anything but regret and was on the verge of tossing the tables after only three minutes of seeing Kyle quit the restaurant, when he reentered the room and took a seat next to me.

"Are you going to eat all those?" he asked as he plucked a cheese stick from the basket.

"What are you doing?"

He dipped the stick into marinara, then popped the entire thing into his mouth. "I haven't seen you guys in over two months. I'll be damned if I'm going to spend tonight riding around in a car with five other guys." He wiped his hands on his shirt. "I'm having a beer with the three of you so we can catch up."

"But the money—"

"Don't worry about the money," said Kyle. "They'll be back in forty-five minutes tops. They only have to go a few blocks."

My entire body broke into fever. I balled my hands to fists and dug fingernails into my palms until I heard the skin pop. Kate leaned across the table.

"Kyle," she said in a voice firmer than I was accustomed to hearing from her. "Where is the money?"

"I gave it to the guys. They'll be back in forty-five minutes."

"You gave them all the money?" she asked.

Kyle shrugged and reached for another cheese stick.

"What did I tell you?" I growled. "I gave you one fucking instruction. What was it?"

Kate said: "Where did they go? Who are these guys? How well do you know them?"

Kyle laughed it off. "Don't worry about them," he said. "They're straight up. They're fine. Besides, I have their cell number. I'll hit them up if they don't come back. Nobody leaves someone their cell if they're planning to rip them off."

I knew, deep down inside, that Kyle believed that. I knew ill will was probably the furthest thing from his mind. But I also knew it wasn't me Kyle needed to convince. He could talk from here to Sunday about good intentions paving the road to wherever, but it mattered not a hill of beans unless he could somehow sway Gumm and Little John.

I also knew he had little intention of leaving Houston to do so, which is why I insisted he ride back to Nacogdoches in the trunk.

For those who liked to party, Little John and Gumm ran things in East Texas. They could get weed, which meant, at one time or another, they saw damn near everyone in town who liked to smoke it. Before long, if you wanted your car fixed, you called Little John and Gumm, who sold weed to a mechanic outside of town. If you got a DWI, Little John and Gumm knew a lawyer who could get it dropped to public intoxication. Coke, pills, god forbid a gun…I never asked about it, but rumor had it that Little John and Gumm once got a guy a kidney. A *kidney.*

Somehow or another, the weed you smoked in East Texas came from Little John and Gumm. Folks all over town would name it. One guy might sell something called Sherpa—*"You get so high, it's like you're in the mountains, man."*—while another guy sells the same stuff to hippies in Nacogdoches and called it Purple Haze. No matter the name, all of it came out the door of Little John's apartment and it got there via Highway 59 out of Houston, driven by guys like me.

Gumm took me the first time, to show me the ropes. He listened to shitty country music and smoked blunts, drank tallboys from a paper sack. He introduced me to his guy and told him I'd be driving from now on. The guy: a Mexican teenager. The kid's *abuela* watched television in the living room with a smattering of children in tow. On the way back, Gumm sat eleven pounds of Nuevo Laredo skunk in a backpack on the bench seat between us.

"You ain't going to hide that some?" I asked him.

"Hell no," he said. "If I see cops, I'll throw it out the window. I can't get rid of it if it's hidden somewhere. If they got me, they got me, but it's getting out of the truck."

I had no idea if that rationalization worked or not, but I would adopt a different approach for my sojourns down south. I bought a pup tent. When I bought the shit from the Mexican kid, I stuffed it into the bag which held the stakes. Then I wrapped that bag inside the tent. Then I stuffed the tent inside it's bag, and that bag inside the tent's box. All of that would be stuffed inside the bottom of my trunk, beneath enough garbage and other detritus to discourage anyone from further checking, which meant if they were checking, the gig was most likely already up.

Gumm and I saw things different. He didn't care where I stashed the shit. He also didn't care if I pinched because, as he explained, *everybody pinches*. He didn't even care if I took a girl with me, so sometimes I brought Kate. But he had one rule and demanded it not to be broken.

"Never monkey with the supply."

He said it enough times he could have been punching me in the face while saying it.

"Never monkey with the supply." Sometimes I'd tell him I was running late to pick up the money from them. I'd catch an earful, him telling me I'm monkeying with the supply because I'd told the Mexican kid I'd be there at five and—goddammit—I better be there at five. If someone went to the trouble of securing pounds upon pounds of Mexican schwag into their tiny Houston apartment, Gumm told me I better do everything in my power to get it the hell out of there.

"Never monkey with the supply."

It was Kyle's idea to undercut the supply. In effect, to monkey with it. Kyle always had an angle. He'd up and left East Texas a few months previous and fancied himself somewhat cosmopolitan and connected now that he lived in the big city. *The mean streets of Houston*, he often called them. Every time he phoned back to Lufkin, it was this or that about some night club or another, or the greatest damn Indian food or taco truck or something presenting Houston as a great paradise, a mecca to which all East Texans should aspire to migrate.

This was the guy who suggested we go with the guys who had the better deal. The guys he'd only met a few days earlier, in a bar. Those guys were the type to salivate over guys like him. *Guys like him...*

What about me?

I'd had big plans too. Every one of them tossed like cigarettes out the car window as we drove the long, dark highway back from Houston. Sure, I'd monkeyed with the supply, but with the money I skimmed by going with the better deal, I could have afforded a QP of my own, maybe even a half pound. I could have sold sacks around town—same as usual—but undercutting Gumm and Little John. Soon enough, I reckoned, I could have wrangled a couple pounds of my own, could have kids driving back and forth to Houston for me, could have started my own empire...

Once again, I pictured Kyle's hand-drawn map through the forests of East Texas and reckoned the only difference between him and me was I rode in the front seat of the Chevy Lumina, while he was in the trunk.

I had been due back at Gumm and Little John's apartment hours earlier. As the sun set over the Angelina river, I imagined them pacing the floor, loading up on guns and powdering their rifles. Perhaps assembling a search team or, more likely, a posse. I circled their street a couple times but did not stop the car. One by one, the street lights clicked off and the sky tinted from purple to blue.

"You don't mind if I get out here?" asked Bunk. "I can hitch a ride back to the dorms."

I expected Kate to tell him no, that's ridiculous. Instead, I found her studying my face. She put a hand to my elbow. I pulled to the side of the road, but did not let go of the steering wheel. I liked her hand there and thought for more than a moment about asking her to never remove it. All those times, I'd considered telling her we were through, that one of those other girls meant more to me. That wasn't that moment, though. That very moment, I could marry her. Have babies with her. Grow old together, like some people do.

Bunk took that moment and broke it to pieces. He said something or another, then kicked open the back door. Whatever he said, he was still saying it as he slammed the door and stomped feet down the road, away from the car.

We watched him grow smaller and smaller a bit before I turned to her and asked, "Would you like to eat donuts with me?"

She nodded and said yes. "If that's what you want," she said. "Donuts will be fine."

The cell phone rang three times while we had at it. Three times it rang and vibrated both, sending it scuttling across the nightstand, then crashing onto the hardwood floors. I was too busy having my head fucked into the headboard to hear it, or even give a shit if I did. Kate hated for me to be stressed. She hated it like the dickens.

Then rang the landline. Nobody ever called the landline.

It went to the dusty machine beneath my desk and I could hear Gumm's voice. He sounded concerned. "Deke," he said, his voice faraway, but still closer than I could handle. "I *need* you to call me *right away*. It's very *important*. No one has *heard* from you. You never *showed up* in Houston *last night*. Please *call* us as *soon* as *possible*."

All the wind left my sails. That dick of mine went limp. Kate, bless her heart, bounced up and down in my lap. She was never one to give up without a fight. She grunted and kicked like a buck hog, expecting it to magically reappear and get back to work inside her, but instead it regressed to a stubby, floppy thing, as useless as a fart. She hopped off and went face first to my crotch. She had gumption. She had fight.

"Baby," I said. I'd come to embrace it.

"No," she panted. Her mouth made it worse, somewhat more embarrassing. I let her have at it a minute, then tried again to stop her. "Not now," she said. "Not yet."

But Elvis had left the building. As if I didn't have enough to worry about. I had the two biggest drug dealers in four counties trying to track me down, unawares as of yet that they'd been jacked. I had a guy in the trunk of my car, parked three blocks away so no one would know I was home. I'd lost the respect of Bunk, and I had a girl beating the shit out of my limp pecker because it had gone AWOL. I put one hand over my eyes and let the other fumble about for a pack of smokes.

"What are you going to do?" asked Kate. She'd surrendered, but kept her head on my milky white thighs. She was sad, pouty-lipped. Stationed there, so if the situation were to change, she'd be the first to know.

I'd thought on it some. I could run, I reckoned. I didn't have much worth keeping. I could be on the road to Louisiana in no time. I fancied myself resourceful and able to start over. Or I could jimmy a busted lip and a couple bruises, then tell Gumm and Little John a couple black guys jumped me. But, I remembered, Kyle and Bunk knew the truth and would hardly keep quiet on their own. Maybe, I thought, I could knock over a gas station or the Kroger on North Street and get enough money to hold everybody at bay.

Or I could even tell the truth…

"I don't know," I told her. She fingered the cigarette from my hand, took a drag, then passed it back. She lay there, staring at my pecker like a long lost love.

We got dressed and she found me pacing a storm in the kitchen. She stood in the doorway and appeared to have her own decisions to mind. I couldn't blame her. Kate was young and she liked to party. She liked to score, and a stunt like this could put her future in jeopardy. She'd already totted up all the parties she'd no longer be invited to thanks to her involvement with me.

"If I ran," I said, "would you come with me?"

She laughed before she could stop herself. When she collected herself, she said, "And go where, Deacon?"

I shrugged. "Somewhere. Louisiana. Dallas, even." Nowhere did her eyes light up. They could barely meet mine. "Mexico, maybe. I don't care. Anywhere. Is there somewhere you want to go?"

"Yes," she said, after a moment. "I want to go lots of places. That's why I'm in school." Then, after a moment more: "I'm not dropping out of school."

I opened my mouth to say something. I thought better of it. That happened a couple of times before I closed it for good.

The cellphone rang again. Then the landline. I squatted, the backs of my thighs on the balls of my heels. I put my head in my hands and rubbed fastidiously at the temples.

Ring. Ring. Ring.

Ring.

Then—finally—it stopped.

"I'm going to have to run," I told her.

"You should talk to them," she said. "Gumm and Little John have a lot of money. Maybe everything will be okay."

She said it like she believed it. Like *I* should believe it. She put her hands in her pockets and stared at the floor. Cheap kitchen linoleum with designs that meant nothing, but meant nothing over and over and over, across the floor of the kitchen. I held my breath so long I wanted to say fuck it, I don't need you anyway, or something that might cut equally deep, then kick her out on her ass. Over and over in my head, I ran through each and every one of her defects and flaws and called good intention to remark aloud on them all, item by item, when suddenly I felt a twitching and stirring in my pants.

Wasting no time, I took her by the hand. I maneuvered her against the wall. My mouth covered as much of her as possible and I was fumbling like a teenager with her belt when she removed my mouth, my hands, my body, from the entirety of her.

"No," she said. "Not until you get back."

"What if I don't get back?"

She blinked.

"Then the last time," she said, "was the last time. Get your keys."

We walked three blocks to where I'd parked the car. I had no idea what to expect when we reached it. I'd parked in the shade, on Kyle's behalf, and felt immediately relieved to find it not surrounded by cops or paramedics, or worse: do-gooders. The car sat alone and quiet. Kyle Karver did not beat on the trunk from the inside. He did not scream for help or revenge. He made no sound at all.

Kate stopped on the sidewalk, a good ways from the car. I reached for her hand, but she would not take it. Instead, we stood there, arms at our side in idiot fashion until finally I mustered the words that did not need saying.

"You're not going with me, are you?"

Behind her, a breeze lifted the branches of a poplar. A cat crossed the street. All the world carried on, same as it did yesterday. Same as it would tomorrow.

"I got class in a half hour..."

I nodded.

"Besides," she said, "I'd just get in the way."

"You'd send me to Gumm and Little John's alone?"

I reached for her hand. She put hers in her pocket. At that moment, I wanted her more than I'd ever wanted anything. How long had she been so beautiful? How long had I not noticed? I promised if I could have but one more chance, I would never waste another moment of our life together. I'd take her up against my shitty Lumina and then in the backseat, then in every rest stop between here and Louisiana or wherever the hell she wanted to go.

"You're not going alone," she said after what felt like ten forevers. She kissed me on the cheek. She took two steps backward. "You're taking Kyle with you."

KNACKER

Some things you can't never get used to.

Like how it could rain on a sunny day in Ireland and there still not be a cloud in the sky. The entire ride to Wicklow, I pressed my face to the glass in absolute marvel to watch the downpour and reckon from where all it came.

I counted that among the many mysteries I'd embraced upon leaving the States. Like the chocolate trace of a creamy Guinness sliding down the gullet. Or the slap on the nose from malt vinegar poured into a bag of fries...er, *chips*. The brace of hash mixed with shit tobacco, and the dirty sear it scratched against the tonsils.

And evermore: the language. Yes, the words shat forth from young men such as my traveling companions, Mike, Padraig, and Nathan—and their like—was pure delight, a respite from the tired, lazy euphemisms of my own dulled culture.

For instance, instead of balls, they said *bollocks*. Rather than *whacking off*, an Irishman was *tossing*. One never grew *tired*, one grew *knackered*. They had a million ways to say they were drunk. Cigarettes were *fags*, anybody brown was a *Paki*, and everywhere you looked, you found cunts.

Cunts.

Your friends were cunts. Your enemies were cunts. Strangers, even, were cunts. You referred to an old man as "that age-old cunt," and the youngster, a "cunt yet." Women were cunts, sure, but most likely it was a man. A slow guy, a fast guy, a skinny fella, or a fat one. Your parents, they were cunts. The Guard? You bet your ass the Guard were cunts. The priest. The barman. The French dude on a bicycle. That big cunt. This wee cunt. All of them: cunts. Cunt, cunt, cunt.

Cunt.

And instead of traveling by foot, they *legged it*. Mike suggested we *leg it* from the bus stop to the warehouse and we did, taking a good fifteen minutes to get there. Walking up and down suburban streets until we came to the most unimposing of structures: a storage facility.

"This is it?"

"Shhh." Mike put a finger to his lips. "Wait and see, brother."

Any and all walls inside that building had been torn asunder, leaving one long warehouse, dark and dusty. What scant light there was came from two twin bulbs on lamps set in the middle of the room and left plenty of space for shadows. Among those shadows operated one of the shortest men in all of Ireland, shirt sleeves rolled near to his elbows as he barked orders to a gaggle of bedraggled hobos. The poor wretches stood shirtless and surly in yonder corner and looked not to know what to make of the little fella before them. He paused, mid-harangue, to remark on our entry and his eyes liked to pop out of his head.

"Jaysus, Mike," he said as he approached. "Your man's fucking huge."

Two fat men in bowler hats sat in chairs along a far wall. They nodded in my direction and exchanged whispered shit talk.

"And he's really a Texan?"

"Have a look at his boots."

He did, but was yet to be sold.

"How do I know you're not having me on? Slapped a pair of boots on a BIFFO?"

"What's a BIFFO?" I asked.

Said them all: "Big Ignorant Fucker From Offaly."

"We're not the type to have you on, Notter." Mike slipped an arm around my neck. Inched that wily eyebrow of his ever upward. "Deke, my boy. Why don't you share with Notter here your thoughts on the Irish?"

"As a whole?" I asked. Mike nodded, so I told him. "I got no ill will toward your people. Not a lick. Way I heard it, you folks took just as much issue as we did with the British, and you earned your way into my heart when twelve or so of you fought and died at the Alamo. I think it's a horrible shame the way you were treated while building railroads across America and I believe it's damn near impossible to hate a group of people with so many inventive and innovative ways to handle a potato."

Notter scratched the bottom of his chin. He stepped in a circle around me, sizing me up. Dollar signs riverdanced in those beady little eyes of his. He bit his lip.

"They tell me I'm going up against a man named Ballsy." I pointed into the crowd of yonder hobos and asked, "Which one of them is Ballsy?"

"Have you not seen a photo of Ballsy?"

I shook my head.

That expression on his face turned out to be his smile. He said, "Ballsy will arrive shortly, mate. You're the main event."

I feared the constant and unexpected stream of flattery I'd received as of late would turn me soft. I told them, "Perhaps it's best if I go stand among the hobos, so as to remind myself what it was once like to be hungry."

If I'd have remembered my hat, I'd have tipped it. Instead, I swaggered toward the hobos. *My people.* Why, not long ago, we'd have battled each other for a warm, dry doorway beneath which to lay our heads. Raced the setting sun to that spot below the steps on Lower Leeson, or maybe beneath the patio table at the joint down by the Canal. Helped one another over the wall surrounding the Green. Or ran point for an outfit nicking tips from the hats and guitar cases of buskers along Grafton.

I reminded myself it was only yesterday morning that I, too, had awoken in the gutter.

"Hey," I told them, "my name's Deke."

"We know who you are," said the short one up front. "You're the Yank with the space-age sleeping bag."

"I told you hobos plenty times before," I snarled. "I ain't a Yank. I'm a Texan."

"That's right," said another. "You're the dodgy tosser from Texas, and I'll claim those boots once Ballsy's done with the likes of ye."

"I can take any man on this island," I said. "I stand a good two, three heads taller than the lot of you. What's that all about? Some of these bathrooms around here, I got to step out of just to turn around. I ain't sure if it's all the potatoes to blame, or if it's because you turn to drink so early, but I'll have no problem licking any one of you hobos and making sure you stay licked."

The bums swapped glances with each other. The meanest one, he turned to me and said:

"To be clear, you've never laid eyes on Ballsy before, have ye?"

To which dropped them all again into laughter, which sent me to fidgets. I puffed my chest and arched my back, then lit into them.

With a finger to their faces, I told them, "Laugh all you want, but ain't a single one of y'all what they call *a money maker*. They got all kinds of notions I can break records when it comes to selling knacker fight DVDs because folks want to see an asshole get beat on. Maybe they found out a bit late that it takes a Texan to see it done, but they found out all the same and you jack-offs will find yourself out of a job once again."

To shutter any and all thoughts about throwing further shade my direction, I took my leave. I nearly slammed into Padraig, who pointed a camcorder in my direction.

"State your name, mate," he said. "For the camera."

"I've been thinking about that," I said. "What would you say to a nickname?"

"A nickname?"

"Something flashy," I suggested. "Like Death Out of Dallas, or the Texas Twister."

Padraig lowered the camcorder. "Better if you state your full name, and where your family can be located, should anything unfortunate take place."

I promised I would, but shortly after, settled in to watch the fights. Leaned against the wall alongside Mike as the first two knackers stepped to the center of the room, near the twin lamps, then went at it. All the while, Padraig kept the camera pointed toward the fighters, never taking the lens off them. Not when some asshole from Cork split the cheek of a skinny kid out of Dublin. Not when some redhead broke his hand over the nose of a Kerry-born fella. And not after they wheeled in a British guy, then an angry boyo from the North had him pulled off him after breaking both the limey's arms.

Never once did he take the camera off the action in the center of the room, not until they'd run through all the fighters and he turned that sucker again in my direction.

"Your turn, Deke."

I looked around. Said, "But where's Ballsy?"

To answer my question, all the air sucked clean out of the room.

"Holy..."

He was flanked by six guys in black t-shirts. Muscular men who walked on the balls of their feet, so as to keep at the ready.

He was a big man. A good three, four heads over the rest of his countrymen. All of him, one bulging muscle. His head, shaved clean but shaved with something dull and rusty, as it was nothing but a riot of nicks and scrapes. With each lumbering footfall, he let fire a hollow yelp, as if he were a lunatic drill sergeant, or a rabid mental patient.

Stomp...*yelp*. Stomp...*yelp*. Stomp...*yelp*.

Likely, the latter, because so crazy was he, only one eye worked. The other lolled and set to wander while the good one burned hellfire. So insane, he marked up every inch of himself with jailhouse tattoos—from stem to stern—and even some up the length of his neck. So batshit nuts was this guy that he held in one hand a half-drank pint of piss-yellow ale, and in the other…well, in the other he held a leather strap tethered to a chimpanzee.

Yes. A *chimpanzee.*

Not a wee monkey, but damn near a giant ape, a mere head shorter than its massive keeper. It had hair bristled as Brillo pads. It had shoulders broad as a Pinto. It had the temper of a thousand angry hornets and teeth the size of my middle finger.

It followed its keeper at the length of the black leather strap.

Stomp…*yelp.* Stomp…*yelp.* Stomp…*yelp.*

Then: silence. All fell quiet as the big man halted his horrible march and turned that mess of a head like a turret to face me. That wild good eye of his like a conflagration, that grin like a junkie, that inked-up sausage of a finger pointing my way.

"Dear Christ," I managed. "Is that Ballsy?"

Behind him, the chimp had yet to notice his keeper stop his march. So preoccupied had it been with this, that, or the other, that it walked plum into the back of him and that pint of beer sloshed across the chimpanzee's thick fur.

You could have heard a nun fart—and then you couldn't—because up from that chimpanzee came a fury as it let fly a terrible frenzy, drowning that warehouse with high-pitched wails of terrible protest, then the dull thudding of its mighty fists as he worked to beat the meat off its keeper's face.

The big guys in black tees jumped to action. One tried to take him high while the other went for the chimp's knees. Neither made it, only to be stopped by the monkey's vise-like grip before he cast them aside with little thought. That's when two of the others made their move. One with an electric cattle prod which was quickly snatched and the chimpanzee broke over his knee. The other with a snare pole and he struggled like mad to slip the noose around the neck of the chimp while the other two wrestled it mightily to the ground.

"No, mate," said Mike, "*that's* Ballsy."

Not a word from me as my jaw hung limp as a weary pecker. In fact, in the whole of the warehouse, all could be heard was a piteous moan from the monkey's keeper as the boyos in black shirts dragged his broken body to safety.

Said I, "I'm not fighting Ballsy, guys."

"Now's your chance, man," said Notter. "He's bollixed from scrapping with the lads."

"I'm not fighting a monkey."

"If it's any consolation," said Nathan, "it won't be much of a fight."

I repeated myself. Then again, but with greater volume.

Michael slipped his arm around me. "It's not as bad as you think. The best part is, you'll be unconscious for the majority of it. A nice, dreamy sleep, and when you wake, you'll be a hundred Euro the richer."

"I thought it was eighty Euro."

"Turns out," said Mike, "a lot of people will pay good quid to see a Yank get beat on by a chimpanzee."

The monkey had finally been restrained. They led him by snare poles to the center of the room.

"Look at it this way..." Nathan nodded to the fat cats in bowler hats sitting in the shadows against the far wall. "Do you really suppose those rich cunts will let you out of this warehouse without fighting the monkey?"

Notter shoved me further to the center of the room. Closer still to the monkey.

"Try and get a couple licks in, if you can."

Ballsy no longer struggled against the restraints. No longer sent fury to the rafters. The only sounds from the beast was the labored rhythm of angry breaths. His chest and shoulders heaved, but nothing else bothered to move. His feet remained planted, his fists kept taut, and his eyes never once wavered…

…*from me.*

"We need your name," whispered Padraig. His camera lens doubled in size.

I took a deep breath.

"My name is Deacon Easter," I said, "and I'm from Dallas, Texas. My mother's name is—"

And that's the last of it I remember. Like many nights of a terrible bender, I'd lost it all to the ages. Because everything after that, I had to find out by watching it on DVD like the rest of Ireland.

TOWN AND GOWN

Horace Moncrief had mown clear up one end of his yard and down the other, then was ready to go after the patch on the side when he saw the dog get hit by the car. Old blue dog, one he'd seen before, and a gold four-door, which he hadn't. The dog whirled like a helicopter, completing a few axels, before landing on its back, where it then somersaulted into the deep ditch at the front of his lawn. The four-door bothered only to tap its brake lights after doing its damage, then tapped them no more before speeding into yonder.

Horace thought more than twice about chasing after it, perhaps to give the driver a what-for or a lesson in courtesy, one. Instead, he shut off his mower and walked the length of his yard to see about the pup.

He found him in the ditch, still alive. Smiling, his buddy down at the domino parlor would say. Old Roland said a dog with that kind of face was smiling, and Horace would tell him no, the dog was breathing way too hard to have a smile on his face. That particular discussion between he and Old Roland could last an hour, maybe more. But Roland weren't around and Horace didn't reckon the dog had an hour to sort things out. Horace spit sideways to the ground and called to it.

"You reckon to come out of that hole, pooch?"

It said nothing. Rather, it sat on its haunches and looked up out of the hole, waiting for rescue or the punch line to what had to be a shit joke, but a joke it was and, much to its dismay, it appeared to be played on him. To the dog, nothing appeared to be the matter. It was a normal day there, along the meanest stretch of road Lufkin had to offer.

Standing there, Horace wondered what in shit he was supposed to do.

As if to offer a suggestion, along came a screeching mess of wheels and machinery and Horace figured it was to happen all over again, perhaps he would be joining the dog down in the hole. He looked up in time to see a car that, were it not for the tires and carrying-on by the driver, he'd have never heard coming. It was a car designed to save the earth, and had the poor puppy been hit by it instead of the four-door, he'd probably walk himself out of the ditch, had he ever landed there to begin with.

This car jerked to a stop in the middle of the two-lane and the door burst open and out came a spindly fellow, waving his arms and moaning for all the world to come or end, one. Horace took a step back and readied himself, should he have to fight his way out of this, whatever *this* was.

"Oh dear, oh dear," said the man. He howled as if it had been he hit by the car. He ran from his vehicle to the ditch, arms like a windmill. He minded not Horace but instead dropped to his knees at the ditch and let fly a horrendous wail. "This poor animal! This poor, poor creature! What are we to do?"

"This your dog?" asked Horace.

"I've never seen him before in my life!" The man gripped the sides of his head and could very well have pulled out his hair in tufts. "Oh, why? Why? Why is this happening?"

Another mess of screeching wheels and horns a-honking and Horace looked up to see other motorists stopping just in time to keep from hitting the parked car. They backed up behind it and waved fingers and fists at Horace, as if he had a damn thing to do with anything.

"You might want to move your car out of the street," said Horace.

"But the dog!"

"I'm not sure, but I reckon he'll wait for ye."

"I've no time to bother with it. We have to rescue this dog!"

One car aimed to make his way round the do-gooder's abandoned vehicle, but another coming from the opposite direction whipped by so fast there weren't nothing but a passing horn and a series of profanities to mark the moment. The next did the same and finally that driver figured he'd do better to offer dirty gestures toward Horace and his newfound friend.

Corn Hill Road was a cruel mistress.

"You weren't the one hit this dog, was ye?"

The man looked as if he might cry. "Heavens, no," said he. "I would never. That's absurd." He held out his hand. "My name's Bob. I'm a professor at the university."

Horace said he was pleased to meet him. He may have made

some apology for the circumstances, as he was prone to do. He looked down to the dog and wished he'd something to tend after. The dog moved nary an inch. Horace reckoned it to be his back legs hurt, more than likely broken. Still, he'd kept his head together and for that, Horace thought him quite valiant and worthy of more than Bob's sobbing and carrying on. "You got your phone on you?"

"Yes, yes, I do. Whom should we call?"

The line of cars backed up behind Bob's little car honked and beeped. More than a few of them shouted from their rolled-down windows.

"Why don't you call the sheriff and I'll get your car out of the road?" Horace held out his hand. "Pass me your keys."

"They're in the car. It's still running."

It didn't sound to be running but Horace reckoned he was far from knowing the full extent of the situation. He jogged across the single lane and climbed into Bob's car. Inside, it could have been a spaceship. He reckoned the steering wheel and gear shifter and gas pedal couldn't be too far different from something he recognized and he maneuvered the car to the roadside opposite his house with little incident. He slipped her into park.

By now, Bob was waving his arms and hopping up and down. He seemed to be trying to get Horace's attention. Horace figured the drivers to be steamed enough about being kept waiting, and let them pass before trying to cross Corn Hill Road. He'd learned his lesson via the dog, sure enough. All the while, Bob carried on as if being chased by a swarm of hornets. Soon as everyone'd gotten through, Horace made his way across the street.

"We can't call the police," said Bob.

"Someone's got to see to that pup," said Horace.

"I understand," said Bob, "but what will they do to him?"

Horace shrugged his shoulders.

"My point exactly," reasoned Bob. "The barbarians will likely euthanize him, and I won't stand for it. No, the only hope this dog has is with us and I refuse to let him down."

Bob started down into the hole. The dog continued smiling, or what looked like smiling, as Bob stepped nearer.

"What do you aim to do down that hole?"

"We must help him," said Bob. "After all, it's not his fault. It's the cursed system. It's the world we live in. It's the status quo of our society that stands unchallenged. Something so innocuous as a dog crossing the street results in a tragic loss of life. There should be stop signs. The speed limit should be lowered. The monster driving the vehicle should be made to stop. They didn't stop. What do you think they were doing? Texting? Applying makeup? This has to end."

"It's human nature," said Horace, who felt he had little to say any longer.

"Human nature is a misnomer," said Bob. "It's actually human *condition*. To say any human has a *nature* is to deny him free will. To lump him in with the rest of the animal kingdom."

"We should call the sheriff," said Horace.

Bob shook his head and stepped further into the hole. "Don't be ridiculous. The sheriff is part of the whole system. The sheriff will have a series of rules and regulations that will only result in the destruction of this poor animal and—"

Bob had reached out to grab the puppy by the collar. The puppy didn't approve one bit. His nature or his condition, one, kicked in and, in a flash of teeth and fur, he reacted. Horace had heard the phrase "pull back a nub" and, in fact, had used it a time or two, mostly in an instance where he felt he must defend a plate of chicken fried steak or french fries from some curious interloper. But to say *pull back a nub* in this situation would infer some immediacy or even elegance, and there along the ditch on Corn Mill Road with Bob and the poor maligned pooch, he felt it horribly misused.

The dog held on tight as Bob yowled and screamed. Bob did what he could, tugging and pulling and nearly yanking the dog—bum legs and all—out of the hole and nearly up the side of the ditch. There was a ferocity that, frankly, Horace felt hadn't been there previous, neither to the dog nor Bob, but there were both of them, growling and whimpering and wishing they had never met the other, and suddenly Horace heard what sounded like leather ripping and Bob was up out of the hole and relieved of the weight of two of his digits.

Now Bob didn't care so much for dogs. He hated their barking, he hated them in restaurants, he hated the SPCA for keeping them alive when the world was already overpopulated with them and all their various breeds and colors. Bob couldn't stand for them at all and now fancied himself a *cat man*, and told Horace so in eloquent detail at multiple levels of volumes. Nowhere near the front of Bob's brain was his injury, not until he could adequately voice his new stance on current issues, most of which involved the dog in the hole.

"I reckon I should now call the sheriff," said Horace. He flipped open Bob's phone and dialed 911. Phyllis at the switchboard answered and Horace gave her the quick version of events.

"Why did he go down the hole?" she asked him. "You're supposed to leave a hurt dog alone. It's in their nature to defend themselves."

Horace made to tell her it was actually their *condition*, but thought better of it and instead repeated that he should talk to the sheriff. He looked over at Bob who kept his bloody hand by his side as if it were a source of shame.

"Tell Kent he better send a paramedic too," he said, and hung up the phone.

Around about this time, Horace noticed a little station wagon driving slow. A little boy in the passenger seat, about eight to ten years old, looking out the window with eyes peeled. Fingers against the glass. Come to think of it, hadn't he seen that same car only a minute or two ago? Horace removed his hat and swatted something imaginary upon his thigh.

"Oh, hell," he muttered. He lifted his hand in a half-wave and the car stopped. Out came the mother from the driver side. She was harried as all get-out and shuffled across the lawn and Horace made tracks to meet her far as possible from the ditch.

"Have you seen an old blue dog?" she called. She wore a robe, slippers. Hair up in curlers. She'd been doing her thing when the boy came crying about his dog being gone, Horace reckoned. She spoke with her arms, much like Bob. She spoke like folks who'd lived here a spell, much like Horace.

"Ma'am, I don't want to have to be the one to tell you this, but—"

Horace didn't get much more out of his mouth, because along came Bob, bloody stumps and all, waving his hands and calling folks obscene names. With his bad hand, he pointed this way and that and raised all sorts of hell on account of his day was good and ruined for no other reason than his being some sort of Samaritan. He swore up and down one side of the yard then the other and promised hell-fire, retribution, and damnation, but the second he mentioned his lawyer, Horace thought he'd taken it far enough and told him to hush up.

"Someone has to pay," sniffled poor Bob.

About this time, the boy jumps out of the car and across two lanes of perilous traffic, rushed to the hole where he saw his dog, and erupted into tears. Horace raced after him, screaming to steer clear of it, but couldn't get there near close enough and down went the boy, holding the dog by its neck and hugging him for dear life. The boy collapsed into sobbing fits and stroked the pup this way and that. The dog, in the meantime, panted on. Things carried on about as such until the sheriff showed up and, after him, the ambulance.

"Dog looks fine," said the sheriff. "You sure it got hit?"

"Oh, I'm sure," said Horace. "Saw it myself. Wish I could unsee it, to be honest."

"Looks to be just fine," repeated the sheriff.

"It's like he's smiling, ain't it?" asked Horace.

"Dogs can't smile, you idiot," said Bob. "You're projecting. They can't smile, since they don't have a soul."

"I'll run you in you keep up that kind of talk," said the sheriff. "You want to spend the night in jail?"

Bob muttered something or another under his breath, most of it about how no, he didn't want to spend the night in jail, and Sheriff chalked it all up to shock or something like it. He ordered the boys from the hospital to take Bob over to the wagon to clean up his wound. Everyone else stood around, wondering how they were going to get the dog and the boy out of the hole.

"Why'd that man go down into the hole?" asked the sheriff. "Didn't he know better?"

"Why'd you let your dog out?" the mother called down into the hole after the little boy. "Couldn't you have kept better eyes on him?"

"Why didn't that car stop?" asked one of the boys from the hospital. He asked it of anyone and no one in particular. "What kind of animal does that?"

Horace looked at his side yard and remarked to himself that he didn't figure it would mow itself and wondered how long it would be before he could tend after it again. From the ambulance, he could hear Bob carrying on with all levels of hate and pity. Horace wondered if he'd resign from his teaching job, as no amount of human condition could probably restore his faith in humanity.

Sheriff had just finished telling the others about a buddy of his who operated a crane being used over at the construction of the new supermarket. About how maybe they could get him over to help get the boy and his dog out of the hole. Then out came the boy, holding the dog nearly twice his size with its legs hanging useless, paws dragging a scar through the Johnson grass.

"Can we please take my dog to the hospital?" asked the boy.

The sheriff tousled the boy's head and said yes, yes, they could, and led them both to his patrol car. Mother closed her robe and gathered herself best she could and followed after them. No one seemed to concern themselves with Horace or his yard any longer, seemed fine to shuffle away and leave him be all over again.

No sooner had everyone climbed into a vehicle than did the boy step out of the sheriff's Crown Vic and run to the ambulance. Bob was out of the ambulance by now, miserable and forlorn. The boy held out his hand.

"Here you go," he said. In his little hand was Bob's own two fingers. "Thank you for saving my dog."

And the boy was off, bounding back to the squad car, where they hit the sirens and sped away down Corn Hill Road.

Bob looked to Horace.

"What do you intend to do about all this?" demanded Bob.

Horace shrugged. "It ain't in my condition to do much," he said.

"Nature," said Bob. "It isn't in your *nature.*"

"I reckon you and me see things different," said Horace.

"Maybe."

Horace shook his head and reckoned he didn't care much for all that *unto others* bullshit. He didn't care for it and figured it nothing but a crock and he was dead tired of hearing and thinking about it. No, in the long run, condition or nature, his stomach could ever only settle after he'd done what he could and, standing there in his own front yard, he could do very little. So he of ten fingers waved goodbye to Bob and the boys from the hospital and climbed into his own truck, for Lufkin ain't that big a town and he reckoned he could find a gold four-door parked outside of somewhere or another and then and only then would he see what hand God had in any of it.

SIXTEENTHS

You always loved her arms.

Slices of ivory wrapping themselves around you. Sharp, jagged shoulders around which you would run your tongue as you made love. Skin untouched by time or elements, save for one pocked indentation from a TB shot she'd received when but a child. The other with a tattoo of a small heart and dagger, a lonesome scar of youthful indiscretions.

You'd recognize her arms anywhere.

You recognize one of them now, in the bottom of the box, wrapped in butcher's paper. The only damage: brief spots of freezer burn, like the others. Severed neatly just below the shoulder and above the wrist. Scant traces and spatter of blood inside the box, as if prepared by someone skilled. Someone with experience. Someone who had done this several times before.

After all, it is the sixteenth.

Your calendar on the wall has the same date circled each month. Flip through from April, flip back from it. Pick up the discarded calendar from last year. All the same. The center of the month— whether it be a Thursday or a Monday or a Saturday—all circled in red, so not to let you forget. So not to catch you unawares.

And every month, on the sixteenth, a new package arrives.

You carefully lift out the arm, still swaddled in butcher paper. These guys were good. It had mostly thawed, but you still feel a coolness to the skin, especially at the center. She couldn't have been in the box longer than a day. You carry that piece of her across the threshold, through to the kitchen, and out the back to the garage.

To the cooler you bought nearly eleven months ago today.

That was when you finally forced yourself to sell her car. Oh, you held on to it as long as you could. First, keeping it gassed and oiled and wiped free of any smudge on the off-chance she may return. Then, still out of habit or routine, well after you realized she never would. After the fourth sixteenth had passed.

The month before you realized the freezer in the kitchen just wasn't going to cut it.

So you sold her car and made room for this one, the one in the garage. Longer than you are tall, deep enough to hold ten of her. And every time you lift open the door, frozen vapor exhales a heavy sigh and you stand there a moment and count. Count.

Why not call the police and tell them? Why, indeed. That first time you called them, they sat there in your own living room and couldn't be more smug. You spent most the time with your head in your hands, but could still feel them smiling. You could feel them laughing. You could hear them say I told you so, even if they didn't say it.

"This isn't proof that she is dead, sir," said the one who sounded like he was from around here. He pointed with the little plastic evidence baggie, before he realized he was doing it. "Does your wife have any reason to want to leave you?"

You opened your mouth to respond, but nothing flew forth.

The other one said, "We can file the report, sir. But she needs to be gone at least forty-eight hours before we can classify her as a missing person. That would make it the, uh—" He inspected his notepad, then his wristwatch.

"Eighteenth," said the other one.

They came again the second month. This time, they found you more upset.

"Now do you believe me?" You jumped up and down. For the past thirty days, you'd only spoken to them in irrational tones. "You know who's doing this. You know exactly who."

The local one shook his head. "We've questioned Mr. Ilitch," he said. "We've searched every property he owns. We've searched them twice. Nothing ever turns up."

"He told us he would do this," you told them, over and over. "He warned us and still…" You lifted your head and looked up at the two officers. "I should never have listened to you two."

And neither should you have when the officers stood to leave, the one not from around here stuffing that baggie into the pocket of his suit coat. You leapt between them and the door.

"Where are you taking her?"

The cops looked at each other, then the local one said, "This is evidence, sir. We'll be taking it back to the station."

"Can't you let me keep her here?" you asked. "I promise…I

promise, I'll take care of her."

The other officer used his arm to clear enough room for the two of them to pass. He assured you they would take plenty good care of her. He assured you they would do their best.

And along came the next month and with it the sixteenth, and that morning, another box on your front stoop.

That time, you didn't bother with the police. Never would you again.

You run your hand along all the packages, each tightly wrapped in butcher paper, then cellophane. Each positioned just so. For that arm went here, between these five smaller packages and that larger one. And on the opposite end of the freezer, you leave room for another of similar length.

For there would certainly be another.

You close your eyes and the freezer door at the same time. You rest your head atop it for a bit before remembering where you are, then quickly stand and check your watch. You push yourself away from the deep freezer and walk to the kitchen to wait by the phone.

The kitchen.

You still feel her here. As if she still stands before the stove, boiling water or baking cakes or whatever she finds necessary to make their dinner. Can smell the flour in the air from her homemade pastas or the fresh eggs she'd crack to make something chocolate. Something chokes up in your throat, and it isn't those aromas.

You hear things too. Arguments mostly. You hear them throughout the day. Things you used to think so important then that weren't, as well as things that were.

"I'm not going to throw that away, honey. I need to keep it."

Or, "I'm not drinking two-percent milk, I don't like the taste of it."

Or even, "There's a reason you're supposed to change your oil every three thousand miles and it's absolutely irresponsible for you to ignore it."

Or even still, "Honey, it's none of our business. I think we should stay out of it."

"I think we should just tell the police you didn't see anything."

Sometimes you hear her answer back. Out of nowhere, you're doing the laundry or running the treadmill or anything at all around the house and suddenly hear her. As if standing somewhere in the room, where she'd been the entire time.

"There are too many holes in that shirt. You should throw it away."

Or, "I'm only doing this because I want us to be together a long, long time."

Or even, "We're not making enough money right now and that's an expense we should cut out of our budget."

Or even still, "Someone has to stand up to these people. Think about if it was us and how we would want somebody to speak up."

Sometimes, you get so angry. You shout until your chest threatens to burst and rear back a fist to punch a wall, you get so heated up. Then you stop and remember weren't nobody there to begin with. It's just you.

You and a bunch of voices.

Much like that moment here, you sitting in the kitchen and waiting. Waiting. You check your watch and that second hand ticks up top and like clockwork, the phone rings.

It rings again.

It rings a third time and you pick it up.

And just like every other sixteenth at six thirty sharp, no one speaks into the phone. You hold the phone closer to your ear, but still nothing. Only silence.

You realize you'd forgotten to breathe.

In the past, you'd shouted into the phone. You'd screamed and pleaded and bargained. You'd offered nearly everything you had and then some if they'd just put her on the phone. If they'd only give you some sign that she was okay or if she'd already gone to Glory or anything, just say anything at all, but no response ever, save silence. Maybe a stuttered breath somewhere.

You'd resigned yourself to it.

Now you answer and meet the silence with silence. You are long past wondering if she still lived. You are long past wondering anything anymore. Anything except what you'd find in that box when next arrived the sixteenth. You lean back your head, meeting the kitchen wall. The one she'd painted yellow the summer before. Before...

When suddenly they speak.

"You no longer call the police," says a voice. Man's voice. Older man with a foreigner's lilt. Voice that tickles your ear like hairs from a moustache. "You have learned your lesson."

Something in your throat prevents you from speaking.

"Too bad it took you so long to learn it."

The hot sting in your eyes embarrasses you. Once, you thought only of murder. Of vengeance. Your every thought started and ended with you lighting a match and setting fire to the entire world and hoping you managed to burn this bastard down. But two months ago you received her right thigh in the mail and all the hate in the world drained straight out of you.

They had no name for what replaced it.

"How much longer?" you whisper.

"By my calculation," says the man on the phone, "we're looking at another eight months."

And then the line disconnects.

You sit fast in your chair for an eternity. Two eternities. Hold that phone just inches from your mouth, your ear. Can't put it down. Can't put it away just yet. Hang onto it.

Listen as if the man may again speak. Listen hard.

Hear jays shouting back at forth at each other out in the yard. Hear the neighbor coming home from work and his pickup shuddering quiet. Hear a stillness which opens up a canyon inside you, your home, and everything you've ever known to be true.

Then hear her voice.

"Why do you do this? Why do you tolerate it?"

The hand holding the phone falls limp at your side. Your shoulders slump. Every last breath quits your body and he feel yourself a shell of anyone she'd recognize. A wrong number.

"Why don't you move? Leave this behind?"

You stare at the linoleum. The place where she spilled frying oil that birthday you'd insisted on chicken. The spot on the wall where she'd thrown a wine glass at you, but missed. The brown spot on the ceiling that neither of you could ever explain, yet often made stories about from where it came. All those things in the kitchen that remind you of her and every day when you see them, your heart breaks all over again.

You look at all of those things and more before answering:

"I'm not leaving here without you."

And you turn the calendar to the next page.

THE DEPLORABLES

You're tired.

Beat and tired and ready for that no-count husband of yours to get off the toilet so you can use it. Or for that kid of yours to wake and dress himself for school and do it quick, because if he misses the bus and you got to drive him, there'll be hell to pay. Hell to pay for him and for you, if you're late to work again.

You didn't get to bed until damn near three thirty last night because your husband, Trigger, was in another of his moods. The kind he gets from time to time and the only light at the end of that tunnel is a bottle of corn liquor, and before it will knock him cold to the floor, you have to put up with two hours of his hooting and hollering, but it sure beats the alternative.

So you finish your cigarette and stub it to the ashtray, slather butter on a couple of stale biscuits and scrape the last of the scrambled eggs to the plate, then call upstairs again for the boy. Warn him he's got five minutes or you're coming up after him. You'd fix yourself another cup of coffee, but Trigger drained the last of it before stepping upstairs to monopolize the shitter. Instead, you fall into a chair at the kitchen table and spend the next four and a half minutes staring at your own toes.

Then down the stairs comes Trigger, still wearing what he had on last night, right down to the mirrored sunglasses and cowboy shirt. He drops into a chair and eyeballs the plate you've set aside for your son. You scoot it a couple inches further from him.

"You'd steal food from a boy with Asperger's?"

"For the last time, he ain't got Asperger's." He reaches across the table with his fork and spears a chunk of yellowed egg. "That's some shit you say when you get sad. Back in my day, they called it being an asshole, not Asperger's."

You say: "I swear, Trigger Raywood, if you say that shit one more time, I'm liable to take that fork from you and poke out both your eyeballs." You mean it too. There is a short list of things your husband can do to get you riled up and he knows each and every one of them. "You and me read the same articles on the internet. You know good and well what kind of breaks they get in school when it's time to apply for colleges, don't you?"

"What's got you all worked up?" he asks.

"The fact that you don't know speaks volumes, Trigger."

You leave him to work it out for himself while you call up for the boy one last time. Behind you: the scraping of a fork against plate. This weight sinking your shoulders feels like a load of hot, wet towels. You turn to give him the business, but nearly trip over a cleat in the middle of the floor and you stop, wondering for the life of you to whom it belongs.

"Trigger," you say, with a calmness that surprises even you, "I need you to do me a favor today."

"Not today," he says, mouth full of toast. "I got to run out to Diboll and pick up that solvent I was telling you about."

"What solvent?"

His voice raises an exasperated octave. "The one I was telling you about. Didn't you hear a word I was saying last night?"

You honestly can't remember a thing y'all talked about last night. He'd come home rubbing his nose this way and that, swearing he ain't touched any blow, but you know better. You know better by the way he's sniffing and chewing his lower lip. By how he's sucked air through his nose and it rattles all the way back to the bottom of his throat like a mud flap. He don't talk that fast when he ain't doing blow. You get revenge by sneaking off to the bathroom and touching a little of your own. Lie right back to him.

But the joke is on you this morning.

"What on earth are you talking about, Trigger?"

"For the carpet cleaner," he says. "Floor mats. The stuff that goes in the XB-100." The question mark on your face must have spoken volumes because he throws up his hands again and says, "The carpet cleaner Raymond said he'd lend me."

"For floor mats?"

"Jesus Christ, Becca." He drops his fork to the table, where it clatters off the side and hits the floor. He doesn't move to pick it up. "What's the point of staying up all night to tell you my hopes and dreams if you ain't going to remember none of it the next morning?"

"If your dreaming didn't come with a half-gallon of brown liquor and god knows what all else—"

But you don't get to finish because in comes the boy. He's still half asleep, but dressed and ready. He shuffles to the fridge to take a look inside, but you have no idea why because it's got just as much or as little shit as it did the night before, when last he looked. He shuts the door, then shuffles to the sink to fish out a glass clean enough to drink from.

"You better not miss your bus," you tell him. You tell him again, because he doesn't seem to hear you the first time. Then, because he's got difficulties, you tell him once more.

"I know," grunts the boy before stomping out of the kitchen to gather his things and wait by the door. You wish you were still in bed. Covers over your head. You wish for once Trigger would fuss with the boy in the mornings because, if you could do it all over again, you'd insist he wear a rubber.

No. Don't say that. You don't mean it.

"Trigger...without raising your voice...could you please tell me what this TB-600 whatever is used for? Why you got to go all the way to Diboll this afternoon of all afternoons?"

Trigger uses the butter knife to free mud from the tread of his work boots. It drops to the floor and explodes into tiny clodlets of dirt, each one fine and dandy to stay there until kingdom come. He doesn't bother to look up as he speaks.

"You got to ask yourself one question, Becca," he says. "Do you want to live like this the rest of your life, or do you want things to get better?"

You don't dare open your mouth for fear of the fury that may spring forth. In fact, you burrow deep those upper teeth of yours into your lower lip until you find something new to get your goat. Down the street, you hear the telltale whistle of the brakes on the school bus and you see the boy has yet to move from the doorway. You shout at him louder than necessary and ask him why in the hell he ain't run down to the bus stop yet.

"I hate you!" he screams. "I hate both of you and one day I'm going to make you both sorry you were such assholes!"

You don't know what you'd do if you caught him. He's too fast and you're too tired and there's too much clutter. He's out the door and down the sidewalk. You stare after him from the doorway, happy for now that he's boarded the bus and on the way to school where he can do no harm.

"Like you said," says Trigger. "Asperger's."

You sigh. You turn to face your husband and you want to scream, scream loud and long with every inclination to shatter all the windows in the house, but then where would you be? You have no idea when this happened. It could have been yesterday, if it hadn't felt like forever. But it wasn't forever, because you can remember it. You can almost taste it. Trips to the beach. Sitting at the Whataburger with the girls. Hoping Trigger would come around because tonight might be the night you let him...

You find your hand inside the whatnot drawer. What in the hell are you fishing out of there? A screwdriver? What would you do with that? You hate the way coke does your head the morning after. You don't think clear. Not like the level-headed member of the family is supposed to think. If it weren't for the coke, you're certain you wouldn't have your hand in the whatnot drawer, holding tight to a screwdriver and—

Then you see it, that fucking pen.

How you haven't wanted to be reminded of that pen or what you did to get it, so you tucked it away in the whatnot drawer with the screwdriver and used dishrags and little packets of soy sauce from the chink joint up the road. You stare at it longer than necessary and become acutely aware of how fast or slow your reaction time really is.

"Trigger," you say, picking up the pen, "you ain't going to Diboll today. You're going to come with me on an errand and you ain't giving me no sass either."

Folks around these parts have known for years that when it comes to getting something, you need go no further than that dude named Kind. They got stores up and down the highways stretching from Longview to Houston, but there are plenty things can't be found in stores. Plenty things folks want and maybe even need, but won't be nowhere near any shelves or found on sale. No, that's where a dude named Kind factors into everyday life.

But even Kind has to get his shit from somewhere, and there weren't no telling what folks might come offering or even what folks might reckon he'll need. Usually, it's drugs. As far as the dude named Kind knows, marijuana grows on trees. Coke too. Every couple of years or so, heroin will come around again, but mostly these days, it's legal drugs. Legal if you have a prescription, at least. And with all the colleges in the area, he runs a pretty decent trade in things requiring a prescription.

You don't like the look on his face when he opens the door. His eyes go to yours, then head elsewhere. Eventually, they make their way over to your husband, but then go right back to where they'd been stationed previous.

"Kind," you say. "How are you doing?"

"Better now," he says. He opens the door wider. "Y'all come on in."

You do, Trigger close behind. Kind's apartment is in much better shape than your own place, and right away you want to give Trigger a piece of your mind. Sure, Kind is half full of stepped-on East Texas crystal, but often times so is Trigger, so why can't he clean the place up? Pick up his socks at least? You come on inside and stand near the couch, wait to be told to sit.

You notice Kind has yet to take his eyes, rimmed-red, off the hem of your shorts. The ones cut to right about the middle of a thigh that bulges more than it used to. Kind's gotten lost in it and his mouth hangs a touch slack.

"Kind?"

"I sure would like to bite that," says Kind.

Against your better judgement, you ask, "You sure would like to bite what?"

"That." He points to your thigh, swelling just beneath your shorts.

"Why on earth would you want to bite it?"

He smiles. "Because it looks delicious."

Finally, up steps Trigger. He raises his hand like maybe he'll hail a cab.

"Dude," he says, "that's my wife."

"Then you know what I'm talking about," says Kind. He considers the matter settled. He unpauses the video game on the giant flat screen against the wall and resumes playing. Over his shoulder, he says, "You want to spit it out, or would you rather I dive in after it?"

You waste no time. You reach into your pocket and fish out a handkerchief. You hold it high.

"What we got is this here pen," you say. To confirm that Kind's hearing had, in fact, not gone shitty, you carefully unwrap the handkerchief—gingerly, so as not to smudge or break it—and unfurl a gilded click pen, about as thick as two of your fingers. You turn it around and around in your hand. "Do you want to hold it?"

"What the fuck does it matter if I want to hold it?" asks Kind. "I don't care anything about no pen."

"This ain't just any pen," you say. "Me and Trigger stole this pen out of William Faulkner's house. You know who William Faulkner is, don't you?"

Kind looks at you both rather suspiciously. "How the hell did you get into William Faulkner's house?"

"It's a museum," Trigger says. "Anybody can get into it."

"We took one of those tours and when weren't anybody looking, we stole the pen." You can't force the smile from your face as Kind pauses the video game again and drops the controller to his feet. He turns to face you both. "And now we brought it to you."

"I ain't got no use for a pen," he says. He turns back to the flat screen, but doesn't pick up the controller.

"But it's the pen William Faulkner used when he wrote his greatest classics," you say. "Trigger, tell Kind some of the books he wrote with this pen."

"*Of Mice and Men* and *The Sun Also Rises*," Trigger says.

"I'm pretty sure he used a typewriter," says Kind. "And besides, what the hell would I do with a pen used by some writer? It probably doesn't even work anymore."

"Oh, it works," says Trigger. "It works real good. Trust me, I used it."

Kind eyeballs the pen. "What did you do with it?"

"I wrote a story," says Trigger. "At least, I wrote the beginning of one. Hell, I wrote the beginning of seven of them."

"But you didn't finish none of them?"

Quick as the lash, you say, "He may not have finished one, but he sure as fire started them and, let me tell you, when they finally do get finished…boy howdy."

Trigger takes a seat on the couch, though didn't nobody ask him to. You stay right where you are. That look in Kind's eye says he ain't decided yet if he's going for it. A good piece of you wishes Trigger would shut the hell up. A good piece of you reckons if you hadn't brought him along, you'd have already sold the damn pen by now.

To confirm your suspicions, Trigger says, "No, I didn't finish them, but it don't matter because I ain't never started seven stories before I got this here pen. That's how I know it works."

"So what do you say?" you ask. "Two hundred bucks?"

"Two hundred bucks for a pen?" Kind kicks the video game controller across the floor and narrows the distance between you and he. You get every notion he probably would have slapped some sense into you and came about a hair short of doing so. But he seems to gather his wits about him. He looks you up and down, and this time you're fine with it because it appears to calm him some and you really want him calmed.

Kind says: "You know, I entertained you this far because you and me got history, Becca, but I have to say, Al McGuire warned me about getting mixed up with this one here."

Trigger looks like he might go buck-wild at the mere mention of Al McGuire. If there's one thing he's still touchy about, it's that mess with Al McGuire, and six feet of dirt on top of that bastard won't cool him none over it. So Trigger's up and shouting, and this gets Kind all indignant because he won't be talked to like that in his own house and he starts spouting this and that, and you have no doubt in a contest over who can make who angrier, Kind is liable to say some things you'd rather Trigger not know about. And you know for a fact that Kind has a forty-four tucked somewhere in his bedroom along with god knows what all else.

"Maybe a long time ago, I would have paid a girl like you two hundred bucks for a pen," says Kind, "but them days are long past, and I blame this bastard right here." He points a crooked finger toward Trigger. "He done ruined what fruit once tasted sweet and good, and for what? Tell me that, Becca. For what?"

And you sigh.

You sigh because you don't know if he's right or wrong. You sigh because you've had it up to here with all of them. You sigh because every which way you look, whether you take the high road or the low one, either way your clothes end up just as sullied, so you pick up that big, overflowing crystal ashtray and brain the fucker, which drops him straight to the floor.

Kind, that is.

Trigger, on the other hand, ain't quite clear what to say. Both of you look down at the floor and see Kind, he ain't moving. He ain't moving an inch other than the steady stream of purple blood running out the back of his head and a phantom twitch at that bony, grey finger of his, still pointing at your husband.

"What the hell, honey?"

"Oh sure," you say. "Go ahead and put this one on me, will you."

Trigger scratches fast at his head. He opens and closes his mouth. He does this a good while until finally he spits it out.

"Babe," he says, "how's he supposed to fetch us the money for the pen if you done hauled off and killed him?"

Bless his heart, that husband of yours. It ain't his fault, entirely.

91

You blame his parents. His upbringing. They went without for so long, they wouldn't and couldn't know a way out if it looked them dead in the eye.

You? You're different.

And your children will be different.

You'll make sure of it because, as you look around Kind's apartment at the cash, the weed, the coke, the pills—hell, the two M-16s on yonder kitchen table—you and yours may never again know want, if you play it proper. With money like that, you could set yourself up nice and solid.

With money like that, you think, as you drum your fingers across your pregnant belly, you just might not have a single reason to get rid of it after all.

TOWNIES

The story could take place in any town, anywhere in the United States, but it does not. Instead, it takes place in East Texas, where the pine trees grow taller than some skyscrapers, and brief moments of civilization are punctuated by long chapters of dense thicket. Among this was a small town which was bordered by forest on three sides and the waters of a thick, winding river on the other. Down by that river, just off the highway, was a townie bar named Chigger's.

Darcy took the job there for several reasons, none of which she was too proud of. For one, it was a world away from where she came from, and no one would ever think twice to look for her there. Second, she needed the money, because she'd gone through more cash than she'd planned after lighting out on that no-count husband of hers three months previous. Also, she knew her way around bars and had plenty of management experience from a previous life. But most of all, she took the job at Chigger's because it was the kind of place that didn't require Darcy to use her real name.

The woman who hired her was named LeAnne Banks and she owned the joint. LeAnne was a severe woman. To stave away her age, she kept her hair blonde. She had work done on her face. She had work done on her chest. She had work done nearly every place imaginable and drove a car more common for a man in a mid-life crisis than a woman nudging fifty. She wore her skirts too tight and walked the red-rocked parking lot in two-inch stiletto heels.

"This can be a very easy job," LeAnne told her. "We're only open on the weekends now—Thursday through Saturday night—and there are three staff members. Joey and Quinn work the bar and we have a waitress named Melly. They've been with us for years and we think of them like family."

"Yes, ma'am," Darcy said. She took notes. She followed LeAnne across the lot toward the sign on the highway. She'd parked her dusty Hyundai next to LeAnne's sports car. There were no other cars in the lot.

"We also thought of Kurt like family..." LeAnne let the words hang between them like a horse thief. She turned her gaze to the marquee where, beneath the splashy *Chigger's* logo, the block letters spelled out *We Will Miss You Kurt*. "He'd managed this place for us since the first day we were open."

"I heard...it was an overdose? Drugs?"

LeAnne turned chilly. "It was a tragedy," she said. "Nothing more."

An eighteen-wheeler hauling empty chicken cages rattled past them. A tow truck. A four-door filled with Mexicans.

"While it was unfortunate," LeAnne said, "it gives us an

opportunity to turn the page. Once upon a time, Chigger's was a very popular place. My husband was a musician—well, he *is*, anyhow and I bought him this bar six years ago so he could have a venue to play with his band. The idea of it was to give him an opportunity at revenue, but let's be honest: the only thing Hanson knows about money is how to spend it. This is why we need a manager."

"Yes, ma'am," said Darcy.

"My husband—*Hanson*, rather—used to play on Saturday nights. He used his connections to bring other bands to town for Thursdays and Fridays. It was a great arrangement for the longest time. For a while, this place was a rather hot ticket."

Darcy didn't doubt it, but wondered how long ago that was. The bar had great bones, but could use a fresh coat of paint. Scrub brush poked through the red-rocked parking lot. Birds had built and abandoned nests throughout the lettering of the *Chigger's* sign above the front door.

"Lately," LeAnne continued, "the place has run a bit stale. It could use a breath of fresh air. Frankly, I think a woman's touch is exactly what it needs. While we all will miss Kurt, he had a habit of letting things slide. I don't want things to be let to slide."

"Yes, ma'am."

At the base of the marquee was a cardboard box filled with the black block letters. LeAnne stood in front of it and crossed both her arms below her bosom.

"You're older than he likes them," she said, "so I don't believe I'll have to worry about that."

"I beg your pardon?"

LeAnne reached out and wiped something from Darcy's cheek— an eyelash, maybe—with her thumb. She looked her over with a critical eye.

"My husband is a very good man," she said. "But if he has a kryptonite, it would be twenty-one-year-old pussy."

Two buzzards circled overhead. Another called from atop a chalky-barked sycamore by yonder riverbank. Letter by letter, LeAnne dismantled *We Will Miss You Kurt*. She dropped the tiles into the cardboard box with the rest of them.

"I won't be embarrassed," LeAnne said into that box. "I will ask that you keep this in mind while you manage my husband's honky tonk."

"Yes, ma'am," Darcy said.

"If you keep that in mind," LeAnne said, "this will be a very easy job. My husband likes to say, 'If we could properly train monkeys…'" LeAnne tried, and failed, to smile. "At any rate, your first order of business is to change this sign."

LeAnne scribbled something onto a piece of paper. She looked it over a moment, then handed it to Darcy.

"Always spell correctly when you change the sign," said LeAnne. "It's very important that we don't look like idiots."

Darcy agreed and glanced at the paper. By the time she looked up from it, LeAnne had quit the roadside, hobbling across the red-rocked parking lot on her stiletto heels.

Wondering what she may have backed herself into, Darcy got right to work.

Under New Management.

If LeAnne's description of the Chigger's staff as *family* was accurate, then Darcy was given the role of stepmother. None of the three of them—the two bartenders and the waitress—seemed to want her to be there. Whether it was out of respect to her predecessor, or something deeper, Darcy had yet to reckon. Nevertheless, she did her best to get to know them.

Upon Kurt's death, Quinn became the most senior employee. She'd manned the end of the bar closest to the front doors—the *Point*, as it was called—for over five years. She knew nearly every single customer who walked into the bar and what they drank. They knew not to piss her off.

Quinn liked to "tell it like it is." She started sentences with, "If I'm being honest…" She didn't feel comfortable around other women, least of all Darcy. She would carry absurdly long grudges with customers who didn't tip. She was quick with a drink, but even quicker with a comeback. She was resentful—especially toward Darcy—because LeAnne and Hanson had not asked her to manage the bar after Kurt died. But if there was one person upon whom she festooned her rage, it was the waitress, Melly.

Melly seemed forever on the verge of being fed up. A slight, mousy girl, she'd grown up on the other side of the river and had recently turned twenty-one. She had previously been unaccustomed to the attentions of men—drunk, or otherwise—which meant she spent a majority of her shifts in constant bewilderment. *Befuddlement*, would be more appropriate, Darcy often thought. She believed Melly might enjoy this new experience, were it not for those barbed rejoinders from Quinn.

If Melly enjoyed an advance from a man, Quinn would call her a slut. She would detail the sexual history of the man in question. She would ridicule her suitor, then dress her down in some public manner. On the flip side, if Melly spurned the attentions, Quinn took the opportunity to add another knock to that ever growing list:

This is why you'll never find love.

This is why your father killed himself.

This is why your mother drinks so much.

This is why you're such a whore.

Melly cried a lot during her shift. She didn't look people in the eye. She covered her mouth when she smiled. She wore her hair in her face. She didn't like to talk to Darcy while Quinn was in the room.

And she had a ridiculous crush on the other bartender, Joey.

At first, Darcy could not blame the girl. Joey was a handsome man. The splashes of grey in the hair surrounding his temples dignified his boyish good looks. The lines that creased the corners of his eyes when he smiled added a refined quality to his charm. He worked the service bar—pulling tabs and pouring drinks for Melly to serve—and entertained those who didn't want to wait in line for a drink from Quinn.

If Joey had an Achilles' heel, however, it would be when he opened his mouth. Darcy engaged conversation with him only a handful of occasions, but each time his response had been oversexed innuendo, usually pertaining to the body part of a female customer, and delivered with one hell of an East Texas accent. He liked blondes. He liked yoga pants. He liked shirts that showed off a woman's stomach. Darcy preferred to preserve the illusion by keeping their interactions to a minimum.

Darcy thought she might win them over by showing them how invested she could be. By action, rather than words. She wanted to show them she could roll up her shirt sleeves and try to make an impact. She came in during the afternoons—when the bar was closed—and made renovations. A fresh coat of paint. A new finish on the dance floor. A shine to all the brass and the chrome and the dust off the neon.

Darcy didn't mind the extra work. In fact, she preferred it. She was happy to be distracted from her own situation. However, as she settled into a task—freshening up the walls, steam cleaning the couches, removing outdated artwork and hanging new ones—she would inevitably find reminders of her old life. How she'd watched so many home renovations shows on television and wanted to do a project, but Allan wouldn't let her. She wanted to try something new, take a class up at the community college, but Allan refused. Allan didn't believe she should need a single thing outside of their house and grew to be very suspicious of her efforts to leave. *Why do you take so long at the grocery store? What were you talking about with the mailman today? Where are you going?* All the things she could have done and would have done, if only she had left sooner. All the things she could still do— like run a bar, save some money, maybe get a place of her own—if she could just concentrate, and leave all that old business behind.

However, none of these efforts made the slightest impression on the other members of the staff. When Thursday rolled around and they each reported for duty, their reactions to the changes could not have been more different.

Quinn sighed and said, "So apparently, the front door is red now," as if there was nothing more to notice. Joey inspected the walls of the women's room where Darcy had painstakingly painted over each and every bit of graffiti, even the bits which mentioned him by name. And Melly would not dare say a word about the changes, but Darcy found her smiling at the service station, which had been reorganized, and the brand new check presenters which had been replaced for the first time during Melly's employment.

Whether they acknowledged them or not, Darcy believed the staff appreciated these efforts, and, in turn, would grow to accept her.

The clientele was a different matter altogether. To listen to folks who drank at Chigger's, its heyday had passed. Gone were the nights of long lines to get in the doors, of live music jamming from the stage and speakers, of a crowded dance floor. Business had slowed to a trickle. Everybody missed the way things used to be. Everybody wondered if their favorite bar would ever return.

Darcy heard it all and from every customer because she'd taken it upon herself to check IDs at the door. It was the position her predecessor had held since a door guy had quit months before Kurt's death, so the duty fell to her. While she couldn't wait for business to pick up so she could hire someone to man the door, she took the opportunity to get to know Chigger's dwindling clientele and what were their concerns.

"I don't care much for deejay music."

"Drink prices have gotten too high for their own good."

"I guess Hanson and LeAnne don't darken these doors no more..."

"Place cleaned up real nice, though."

And many more opinions which increased in number as the hours grew later. The men adapted to the new management easier than did their wives or girlfriends, but Darcy mostly kept to herself during business hours and did little to encourage interaction beyond managerial interests.

More important to her were the opinions of the staff. During her third weekend at Chigger's, Darcy took advantage of down time during setup or breakdown of the shifts to individually approach the three staff members and get their assessment on Chigger's flagging fortunes.

"You're not Kurt," Quinn told her after that Thursday night's shift, one where sales had been remarkably bleak. "He's been walking these floors since the first day Chigger's was open and people came to know him. When they see you instead of him, it makes them sad."

Joey's impression had been far less negative, yet still of little use.

"One way to get more people in here," he reasoned before Friday's shift, "is to abandon the strict *twenty-one and up* policy. At least, just for the women."

"State law forbids us from selling alcohol to people younger than twenty-one," Darcy told him.

"We don't have to sell them alcohol," Joey had countered. "All we have to do is attract these young women into the bar so that the older men have something to look at." He finished cutting limes and lemons, then added, "Have you ever thought about holding wet t-shirt contests?"

Of the three of them, Melly offered the best feedback. Careful to deliver it while Quinn was on her cigarette break out back, she caught Darcy in the women's room.

"Back when Chigger's was real popular," Melly said in a low whisper, "Hanson and his band played every Saturday night."

"I heard," said Darcy. This was an understatement. If Darcy had a nickel for every time she heard about the good old days...

"The place seems real nice now," Melly said. "Everything is cleaned up and painted fresh. It's almost like a whole new bar, only nobody knows how good it looks."

"Thank you." Darcy's cheeks flushed hot. "That's very sweet."

"I bet if we talked LeAnne into letting him play one Saturday, that would bring everybody out. Once they see how nice it is now, maybe they'll forget all that old drama and come back out."

Darcy had to admit, it sounded like a pretty good plan. After all, hadn't LeAnne wanted "a breath of fresh air"? Maybe Melly was right, and one big night could showcase the new direction they wanted to go. However, one thought nagged at her.

"What *old drama* are you talking about, Melly?"

Melly's eyes widened. Her cheeks drew inward and her mouth formed a tight little O. She dropped her gaze to the ground, and a limp lock of hair hung over half her face.

"Just…" Melly fussed with her pens and papers. "Just…it's only a suggestion, that's all."

With that, Melly quit the women's room and returned to her shift.

Darcy thought it a good enough idea to approach LeAnne. So confident was she of this plan, she could little expect push back. However, she found her employer's reaction to be somewhat of a surprise.

"I've asked my husband to give up his delusion of being a country rock star," LeAnne said.

Darcy insisted upon the meeting, and LeAnne accommodated her at a Tex-Mex joint off the highway. LeAnne kept her skepticisms to herself until after the meal, when Darcy had fully presented her case.

"It's taken Hanson a long while to accept the fact those dreams of success have passed him by," she said. "It's time for him to find a more meaningful way to contribute to our household."

"You wouldn't agree that this could kill both those birds with a single stone?" Darcy countered. "You yourself admitted that we've classed Chigger's up over the past month. What better way to show the regulars how far we've come than to have Hanson and his band draw them back in."

LeAnne plucked her napkin from her lap and folded it into a tight, neat rectangle. She laid it into the center of the plate. She appeared to measure her every thought.

"People used to come from all over East Texas to hear them play." LeAnne's voice sounded twenty years younger. "He used to really draw a crowd."

"That kind of crowd is exactly what we need right now," said Darcy. "We need one opportunity to show everyone that Chigger's ain't like it used to be…it's *better*."

LeAnne nodded, skeptical, but warming. "It would have to be a one-time thing," she said. She placed her credit card at the end of the table and watched it until the waitress collected it. "I don't want Hanson getting notions. It's taken him a while to get used to staying home on Saturday nights, where he gets in far less trouble. I don't want him to forget how old he is, or to whom he is married."

"Of course not," said Darcy. "A one-night engagement. A special appearance with Hanson Banks and the Pine Curtain Boys."

The waitress returned the bill with LeAnne's credit card. LeAnne looked Darcy over a good while.

"I like you," she said. "I not only want you to clean that place up, but I want it to stay clean."

"Yes, ma'am," said Darcy. "You have my word."

Hanson Banks came as advertised. He suaved back a shaggy dark mane, down to about his shoulders. He was a man who appeared to use plenty of moisturizer. He fought his mid-forties, and appeared to be winning.

He arrived early and was fussing with the wiring on the stage when Darcy unlocked the bar for business. He joked comfortably with Quinn and Joey while they set up the bar. He tinkered with the lights. He walked with a swagger, but one that wilted after LeAnne caught Darcy watching him.

"Women always tell me how handsome he is," LeAnne said. "Sometimes, I picture him without the hair and the attitude. Do you know what would be left? Imagine how that nose would look if he were bald, or how beady his eyes would be."

Darcy opened her mouth, but could think of nothing to say.

"In bed: he's average, at best." LeAnne looked for gum on the bottom of her shoe. "Just so you know."

Said Darcy, "I was thinking of running a special on longnecks tonight."

LeAnne spent the early part of the evening flitting from the back office to the Point. There, she would talk in hushed whispers with Quinn. Occasionally, she would ask Darcy where something had been moved, or where was some file or another. She carried with her a frenetic energy, as if nothing in this world could soothe her.

After seven, more and more people arrived at the bar. Where folks usually came dressed casual, on that particular Saturday there were nice, pressed sport jackets. Crisp collars on starched shirts. Barely worn ten-gallon hats. There was the thick smell of aftershave and hairspray in the air. The room was loud with voices.

LeAnne took a position at the foot of the stage, where she received each visitor. This long-time friend, or that customer of many years. All of them came to congratulate her on how good the bar looked, or how nice it is that she spruced it up, or how sorry they were to hear about Kurt.

"I'm sure going to miss him."

"He was always quick with a joke."

"Shame nobody saw it coming."

"He didn't look the type."

"The bathrooms look so much cleaner now."

LeAnne would allow no man to hug her. Most men already knew this. Those who didn't would be braced by her handshake, firm enough to keep them at a comfortable distance. Just as resolute was her appreciation of women in proximity to Hanson. Those, she warned off with a steely glare. On the rare occasion that message was not received, she would interrupt them with a voice that could chill magma.

"Please excuse my husband," she would tell them. "He's only got a half hour before his first set and he has yet to check the sound."

Once they started playing, folks forgot all their cares. They kicked up their heels and strutted from one end to the other. They didn't think once about Kurt, or new paint, or how things used to be. All they cared about what the music and the good times and how maybe they were back, this time to stay.

LeAnne, however, took exception to two women in particular. Not so much that they wore skimpy outfits which showed off their gym memberships. Not that one of them was tattooed and blonde and the other was a black girl with hair extensions. Not that for all their years—they were in their early thirties—their arms were carved from tighter sinew, their legs from finer coil. Not that they danced with an energy which suggested they could be lovers. LeAnne's exception was that they'd positioned their carrying-on directly in front of her husband.

Tensions whirled in their periphery. One woman cussed at her man who she'd caught staring at the white girl's ass. Two dudes in close proximity became aggravated at one another. The two women ate it up and doubled down on their antics before LeAnne decided enough was enough.

"Okay, ladies," she said as she took them both by the arm. "You've had your fun. I think it's time for you both to leave."

"Excuse me?" The black woman whipped her hair behind her shoulder. "What seems to be the problem?"

"I think you know what the problem is," she said. "Let's go."

Neither woman budged. The blonde crossed her arms, tattooed with lightning bolts, tattooed with a mermaid on fire. The black woman arched her finely toned back and squared her solid shoulders.

Behind them, Hanson and the band kept tempo. *Nothing to see here...*

"Everybody else is here to have a good time," LeAnne said to them. "Nobody here is in the mood for any trouble."

Said the blonde woman, "Maybe you have no control over that."

"Do I know you?" LeAnne cocked her head sideways. "You look familiar."

The blonde smiled. Her friend did not.

LeAnne raised a hand to Darcy, who watched from the front door. She snapped her fingers. Darcy came.

"Darcy," she called over the music. "Please see these two ladies to the parking lot."

Both women stood their ground.

"Ladies," said Darcy. "Please."

Darcy was relieved when neither woman put up further struggle. She wondered the entire trip off the dance floor and through the crowded bar what might happen when they reached the parking lot. How would she react if one of them threw a punch, or wanted to prolong their embarrassment? However, once they'd quit the building, they appeared resigned to it.

"This place is a shit hole," said the black woman.

"Then you won't mind leaving," answered Darcy.

"This place is going down," said the blonde. Her legs, tattoos of rattlesnakes, tattoos of pills spilled from a bottle. "Don't be surprised if it takes you down with it."

Darcy looked to the highway behind them. Headlights. Taillights. No lights. She wished these women would hurry along it.

The blonde thought to add more, but stopped shy of speaking. Instead, she looked into Darcy's eyes, like maybe she saw something of note inside them. Whatever it was drew a grim smile to her face.

"See you around," said the blonde. They cackled across the red-rocked lot until they reached a dusty green Mustang, then climbed inside it.

Darcy waited until the women themselves were taillights before quitting the parking lot with a shudder, and stepping back inside the bar.

If there was a book on how to please a crowd, Hanson Banks and the Pine Curtain Boys could have written it. Everyone expected the first encore, and there'd been occasions in the distant past at Chigger's where a relentless audience had requested a second encore. Once, Bad Company had slummed it through town and given into demands for a third encore. But four encores—*four encores*—had never been called for in those parts, never once in history.

Darcy wondered if there might have been a fifth, were it not for last call. The collective groan when she'd brought up the house lights could have knocked over a garbage truck. One by one, the merry men and women wiped sweat from their foreheads, paid their tabs, then filed out into the night.

"What a wonderful evening!" Darcy called to a room filled with plastic cups, beer bottles, the detritus of a damned good time. "I never knew there were so many people in this town! And all of them came here."

"I'm going to make my rent with tonight's tips," Melly said as she wiped a spill.

"It's nowhere near as busy as it used to be," said Quinn.

"Oh, come off it, Quinn," said Joey. "We were busy enough."

Darcy's heart warmed toward Joey, thinking he might not be so bad aft—

"Did you see those jeans Lara Wilson was wearing?" he asked. "They were so tight, I could see what she ate for lunch."

Hanson stepped behind her carrying a guitar case in one hand, the other one at his wife's shoulder.

"What a night, huh?" said Hanson. "Did you like the music?"

"Like it?" Darcy blushed. "I loved it. You guys were wonderful."

"Thank you for putting this together," said Hanson. "It felt just like the old days."

"I wish y'all could play here every night."

LeAnne's eyes nearly rolled out of her head. She slipped out from her husband's arm.

"And yet here we are, at nearly two in the morning," LeAnne sighed. Hanson took the hint, and the husband and wife excused themselves.

Darcy, however, shook it off. She shook all of it off, because for the first time in a long time, she felt like she'd accomplished something. She felt like she was a whole new person. That she had identified a problem and set out on her own to solve it.

No, she reminded herself, not on her own—as part of a *team*.

Her stomach, her chest, the all of her buzzed warm in that thought, and with it, she set to running a broom and mop along the floor. She helped Quinn with the trash cans. She counted the till with Joey. She pitched in with the rest of the staff and helped get the joint spic and span, just like new, in under an hour.

"We work well together," she said aloud, once they'd locked up for the night. Outside, the highway was dark. Darcy could hear the river below them. Could hear a crisp hum from the starry universes above them. "I think we can really make a go of this."

Quinn cocked her head. "Have you had anything to drink?"

"No." Darcy sighed. "I'm just happy, is all." She turned her back to take the keys from the door, and as she returned to face them, found they had already started for their cars.

"Good night," she called after them.

Joey waved. Quinn and Melly didn't seem to hear as they continued towards Quinn's car. Darcy needed no reminders that she was alone in this world, but that never stopped them from coming. She stood and watched the sky and looked for what her daddy once told her was Orion and had been doing so for nearly two minutes when she found herself awash in headlights.

It was Quinn's car. Melly, from the passenger seat: "Hey," she called, "we're going to go to Whataburger. Do you want to come with us?"

Although she would never call herself a vegetarian, it had been a long time since Darcy had eaten meat. It had also been a long time since Darcy found herself out after three in the morning on a Saturday night. Worst of all, she could not remember the last time she had communed in the company of other women.

When Allan started to change, he'd first been leery of other men. While it hadn't been terribly common for Darcy to meet alone with another man, it had also not been out of line. An old friend from college, the occasional drink after work with a co-worker. Darcy loved only Allan and had never entertained the slightest fantasies otherwise.

So when Allan first expressed his reservations, she'd respected them. She would apologize and make some excuse, then politely decline the invitation.

However, when he began to disagree with her meeting other *women* alone—without him—she pushed back.

"What are you girls doing that's such a secret?" he would ask.

"There's no secret," she'd told him. "We're just having a chat."

"Then you'll find no problem if I join you."

It wasn't long before they stopped meeting with other people altogether.

The drive-thru line at the Whataburger spilled out onto North Street, as it was the only game in town after midnight. However,

Darcy didn't mind in the slightest. She was having such a good time, she reckoned she could sit in Quinn's backseat until sunrise, enjoying someone's company besides her own.

They told stories. They listened to music. They passed a small bottle of citrus vodka that Quinn kept in her glove compartment. All the while, inching ever closer in line to place their order at the speaker box.

"What was the problem with those women tonight?" asked Melly.

"What women?"

"Those two on the dance floor," Melly said. "The tattooed girl and the black girl."

"Oh," Quinn said. "Those."

"They were causing problems," said Darcy. "So LeAnne told me to ask them to leave. No big deal."

"Problems?" Quinn's smile rarely put Darcy at ease. "What kind of problems were they causing?"

Darcy thought about it and realized, for the first time, that she never understood why exactly LeAnne had ordered the two women banned. It hadn't occurred to her to ask.

"LeAnne…" Darcy couldn't find the words. "She said…"

But she'd said nothing, hadn't she?

"Those ladies weren't causing any problems," Melly said. "LeAnne kicked them out because they were hot."

"Shut up," said Quinn.

Melly did not. "She probably saw Hanson checking them out and got pissed."

"That's not true," said Darcy, though she had no way of knowing for sure. "I'm sure she had good reason to—"

"Tell her, Quinn."

Quinn side-eyed her co-worker. She addressed Darcy via the rearview mirror. "LeAnne doesn't like competition."

"Quinn and LeAnne used to be good friends," Melly said, quick so LeAnne couldn't tell her:

"Shut up, Melly."

"It's true. Back when Chigger's first opened, they ran thick as thieves. They would go out and party—"

"Melly…"

"Then, LeAnne started making a little money and it all went to her head."

Quinn took the bottle of citrus vodka and kicked back another belt of it. She said nothing as she passed the bottle to the backseat.

"It doesn't matter," said Darcy. "LeAnne has everything. There's no way Hanson would look twice at women like that."

Quinn nearly spit vodka out her nose. She rested her head on the steering wheel and belly laughed. She made as big a deal as possible to show Darcy how silly she sounded.

"I could tell you stories," she said when finally she composed herself. "I wouldn't…but I *could*."

Then, to stop Melly from giggling, Quinn added, "And so could Melly."

Darcy reckoned there to be some magic formula which might suss those stories from Quinn. For all she knew, the next pull from the vodka bottle might do the trick. However, she'd decided she didn't want to hear them. So far as she was concerned, she didn't care to ever hear a cross word about her employer, the woman who had delivered this happiness upon her, this ability to stand on her own two feet, to commune and break bread with her fellow woman. Darcy wanted all the world to feel like that exact moment, but for certain, not the moment after, for that was when Melly erupted into conniption.

Later, the two rednecked boys who saved their lives would argue the proper nomenclature. The one in the red ball cap told them all it was a timber rattler, while the skinny boy who'd shot it called it a canebrake. Either way, they both regarded it as dangerous, and Melly to be damned lucky not to have been bit.

How did a rattlesnake get under the passenger seat? Nobody could divine. Everyone had their own theories. One of the boys swore recent rains drove them to town from the riverbanks. Melly blamed Quinn's habit of leaving open her car doors. Quinn worried less about how it got in, but more about how long it had been there.

Darcy's concern: *Were there more?*

But something else bothered Darcy. It yanked at the corner of her mind like a beggar at her coattails, but she couldn't quite separate it from the million other things swirling at her. After all, the evening had been nothing, if not eventful.

Melly had felt the snake stretch across her ankles, then coil at her feet in the dark. She'd known immediately what happened and didn't need the interior bulb to show her its black diamond pattern, its thick yellow bands. Its angry thorn of a rattle, the color of sooty ash. She'd jerked her legs into the floorboard. She'd thrown herself out the car door.

Up from the shadowed floorboard screamed the rattle, spat the hiss. Melly's hullaballoo out beneath the streetlights in the drive-thru line, her screaming, her shouting over and over the word—*that word*—and Darcy, Quinn, both out of the car, shortly behind.

The two men had come from separate pickup trucks, but each carried with them a rifle. They competed for the honor—paper covers rock, two out of three, rock beats scissors—and one rustled the rattlesnake from Quinn's car while the other shot it, there in the

Whataburger parking lot.

"She's a beauty," said one as they stood over their kill. "Six feet long?"

"Five and a half," said the other.

"Pretty long for a canebrake."

"Timber rattler."

"Either way..."

The shock of it had all but dissolved for Melly. "He's kind of cute," she said of the one in the ballcap. She spoke in a hush, so Quinn could not hear.

However, for once, Quinn had become too preoccupied to fuss with Melly. She'd yanked her phone from her pants to call for a ride—"I'm never setting foot in that car again."—when she'd found a text from LeAnne.

"What the—"

Quinn thumbed buttons on her screen, then stepped aside for a conversation which she carried on with a frenzied shush.

"I can pull your car out of line," offered one of the cowboys.

"And I can drive you ladies home, if you like," said the other.

Melly played coy with their attentions, and Darcy reckoned her in for one hell of a long con. However, it would not last.

"I just talked to LeAnne," said Quinn as she rejoined them. The color had freed from her face. "There's been an accident."

"What?" Darcy braced herself. "What kind of accident? Are they okay?"

"Not with them," said Quinn. "It's Joey."

Melly drew a quick breath. Darcy held her hand.

"What happened?"

"Joey drove his truck into a tree," said Quinn. "Right off the Loop.

He'd just taken an exit and blown through the stop sign."

"What?"

Said Quinn, "Joey's dead,"

Melly collapsed to tears, right there in the Whataburger parking lot. Darcy would have thought to comfort her, if she thought anything at all. Instead, she stood there useless, her arms hanging beside her in idiot fashion.

"He wasn't drunk," whispered Darcy. "He wasn't even drinking. Right?"

Quinn shook her head slowly. She had yet to blink. She took her time culling her words.

"That's the worst part of this whole thing," she said. "He didn't die from wrecking his car."

Later, Darcy remembered knowing what Quinn was going to say, long before she said it. The words she said next were imprinted in her brain, much like the sound she'd heard only moments earlier, the sizzle which came from beneath Quinn's passenger seat.

"Joey was killed by a rattlesnake."

They kept a good six-foot distance from Darcy's Hyundai, still parked outside Chigger's, for the better part of ten minutes before Darcy spoke.

"We should call the police," she said.

"No," said Quinn. "It's a bad idea to ever call the police out here."

"That's ridiculous," said Darcy.

"This is how we do things in the country."

Quinn kept her eyes fixed on the same spot as Darcy and Melly: the handle of the Hyundai's driver side door. The window glass reflected the big silver moon. The paint flecked red with East Texas mud.

They drew sections of straw cut from Melly's Whataburger cup. Darcy drew the short one. She averaged one step per minute. She reckoned the sun would be up before she ever reached alongside that car door.

Darcy told herself she'd be able to handle this. After all, she was a brand new person, miles away from who she had been when she ran out on Allan. She'd uncovered deeper layers to herself. Had they been there all along? Would she have found them on her own? Would she have stood up to him eventually? She'd let things slide with Allan. She'd gone to bed crying—instead of standing up for herself—the first time he'd tried it. After two years of it, she'd hardly come to think twice.

This Darcy, she told herself, would square her shoulders and not back down.

This Darcy, she told herself, would slice his throat while he slept.

This Darcy, however, was shoved aside by an impatient Quinn, who could no longer stand the suspense.

"I'll do it," she said. She moved with a bluster. She jangled the door unlocked, then threw it open before leaping backwards to safety.

From a distance, each of the three women peered into the shadowed floorboards. They kept at the ready. They held their breaths and listened for the telltale rustle among the fast food wrappers, that horrible hiss of the rattle.

Over their shoulders: a hoot owl. That summer's cicada. The ripple of yonder river.

Still, they listened.

"How will we know if it's under there?"

"I don't know."

"What do we do if we don't find one?"

"What do we do if we do?"

"What makes you think we'd find three rattlesnakes in one night?"

"What made you think we'd find two?"

For the second time that night, something nagged mighty at Darcy. It tickled her ear like a whispered warning, but she could make nothing of it. Not while she awaited the answer to a question which had yet to be asked.

"I'll get a broom," she said.

She returned from the bar with a pushbroom. While more awkward to hold than the regular broom, the stick was longer and offered more distance from its end. She much rather preferred to hand it off to Quinn. More than that, she preferred to call the police, but for the third time that evening, Quinn talked her off it.

"You don't to call the police out here," said Quinn. "Not for this."

At any rate, Darcy felt responsible. She managed this bar. These employees were her charges. If she planned to ever earn their respect, she would have to take the lead.

She jabbed the end of the broomstick—slowly at first—beneath the driver's seat. She shushed along the floorboards, from one side until it slapped against the other. She did it a second time, then a third.

"Now try the backseat," Melly whispered.

Darcy did. The front floorboard, the back…

Nothing.

"Can you reach the passenger seat?" Quinn asked. "Or do we need to open the other door?"

"I can get it," Darcy said.

"We're going to look like such idiots," Quinn said. "We're going to laugh at ourselves later."

Darcy wondered if they would ever laugh again, considering what had happened to Joey. She wondered why they weren't waiting for police, or why they'd yet to call LeAnne and Hanson. She wondered a lot of things as she stabbed that stick beneath her car seats, but all she said was,

"I hope so."

"This is ridiculous."

"Shhhh."

Front seat and back, Darcy tried over and over. Her confidence grew with each pass along the floorboard. She began to feel disappointed, as if she'd been robbed a dragon to slay. It took time to satisfy her, but eventually, she'd forced herself to reckon with it: there was no snake in her car.

That left Melly's.

Melly's station wagon was a hand-me-down, all she had left from a father she'd barely known. It cost her more in upkeep than it was worth, but she'd never once thought about getting another car, until that moment in the approaching twilight.

"I could just leave it here," said Melly. "I've been meaning to look for something new."

"We have to check," said Quinn.

"We don't have to do anything," Melly said. "I'm fine with taking taxis. I'm fine with bumming rides."

"We have to know."

This time, Quinn took the broom. As she repeated the process with Melly's station wagon—first the driver side, then the passenger—Darcy felt something again nag at her. This time, more insistent. This time, the whispers gave way to murmurs.

Quinn gently opened the backseat of the station wagon. She stuck the broom's tip into the driver side. She leaned over for the opposite seat. She punched it once beneath the seat, then a second time. It was upon the third time that the stick leapt free from her hands and Quinn scrambled from the car.

"Oh!"

The broomstick leaned out from beneath the backseat. It worked and jerked. It danced electric. It shot bolts incandescent. Then, up came that rattle. Mean and terrible, and full of hate, a fuse burning its way to a firecracker or a fission bomb, and no stranger to the three of them, for its earlier echoes had yet to subside.

"Well," panted Quinn, "that answers your question."

Darcy stomped red clay toward Chigger's front door.

"Where are you going?" called Quinn.

"I don't care what you say," Darcy replied over her shoulder, "I'm calling the cops."

"I wouldn't do that if I were you," said Quinn.

"You're not." Darcy reached the door. She stuck her keys in the lock.

Quinn cut the distance between them. She held closed the door with a flat palm.

"I really think this is something we should try to handle ourselves," she said.

Darcy shook her head. "I disagree. This is hardly a coincidence and you know it. One snake, maybe. But Joey? This? I'm no fan of police either, but four rattlesnakes in one night warrants the opinion of a professional."

Quinn cocked her head. "You mean three," she said. "We didn't find one in your car."

Along came Melly, her face white as a bedsheet. Darcy noted the fear in her eyes.

"Darcy's right," said Melly. "There were four."

Quinn squinted. "Where? Where was the other one that I missed?"

"Tattooed to that blonde lady's leg."

Darcy removed Quinn's hand from the door before she opened it, then stepped inside to call the sheriff.

D arcy could have screamed, would it have done a lick of good. They were too far out in the country. The morning, workday traffic would have drowned all noise. If anyone had the opportunity to hear or the notion to care, the sheriff or one of his many deputies would have simply flashed their badge and sent that Samaritan along their way.

She sat on the opposite end of the bar from Quinn and Melly while the lawmen trashed the building. They smashed glassware with nightsticks. They threw tables into the walls. They scuffed the shine off the dance floor with their steel-toed boots, then—when they were finished—the sheriff himself stepped face-to-face with Quinn.

"I know she's new here," he said with a drawl thick as treacle, "but you, dear lady, got no excuse."

Quinn met his glare. "I tried to tell her."

"You didn't try hard enough."

The sheriff walked easy. The heels of his boots crunched broken glass. He chewed chaw like cud. He mozied alongside Darcy, then leaned at the bar like he might offer to buy her a drink.

"You're not from around here."

Darcy shook her head. "No, sir."

"I wasn't asking you," said the sheriff. "I was reminding you."

Behind him, one of the deputies grab-assed another. One of them snickered. Another one checked his phone.

"I'm going to speak real slow," he said, "to make sure you understand what I'm telling you."

Darcy dropped her gaze to the floor.

"No, ma'am," he said. "Be sure to look at me when I'm talking to you."

She obeyed.

"Now, I'm real sorry about what happened to Joey. I never had anything against him. I thought he was a good ol' boy."

Sheriff tipped his hat toward Quinn and Melly. He returned to Darcy with no such courtesy.

"And I hate that you three ladies had such an ordeal this evening," he said. "If I were you, I'd make sure you don't leave your doors open, because maybe next time you might not be so lucky."

"Lucky?" Darcy choked. "There were rattlesnakes in our cars. Our co-worker is dead. How can you possibly call that lucky?"

Sheriff said, "Lucky didn't none of the three of you get bit. I'd call that pretty damn lucky."

"There was no luck about it," Darcy said. "Or coincidence, either. Somebody was trying to kill us. I know who it was. It was—"

"A blonde lady with tattoos and an African American woman with extensions." The sheriff turned his head and spit a brown squirt of juice onto the back of a busted chair. "Driving a green Mustang. You kicked them out of the bar, so they've infected your motor vehicles with serpents. Is that the story you're sticking to?"

Darcy nodded.

Sheriff looked to Quinn and Melly. Both of them lowered their heads.

Sheriff turned to his deputies. "You hear that, boys? She's sticking to her story."

One of the deputies smashed the mirror on the far wall with his baton. Another pulled down the stuffed stag's head which hung over the jukebox. From the men's room, Darcy heard glass shatter.

To Darcy, the sheriff asked, "What's your story now, hon?"

Sheriff was kind enough to ask his deputies to shoot the snake in Melly's car. They rifled through Quinn's floorboards, to make sure another hadn't found its way inside. They saw the two women down the highway, while the sheriff stood with Darcy beneath the purpled sky of morning.

"Your employers and I, we have an understanding," Sheriff said in a low grumble. He cocked his head toward Chigger's. "If I have to come out here...well, they're not going to want me to come out here."

Darcy thought of all the work she'd done inside that bar. She thought of all the work she'd have now to do.

He continued, "If it were up to me, this place would be gone. I'd have it razed to the ground, then plant trees—tall Texas pines—so nobody would ever think twice about the land they was driving past. I'd erase it from all memory."

Darcy kept her eyes on him, because he'd told her to. She didn't want him to ever tell her anything. Not ever again. She wanted him to quit talking. She wanted all the world to quit talking and never again speak another word. If she had her way, she'd crawl beneath the covers of the bed in her shitty apartment and never crawl out. She'd stop for wine or whiskey on the way home and drink herself to oblivion.

But not until this sheriff stopped talking.

"You seem like a real nice girl," he said. "But you're in over your head. I'm not the kind of man who carries on about karma. It's not a word I'm able to fit my mouth around. I'm more liable to say something like, *If you lie down with dogs, you're going to get fleas...*" He nodded toward the dead rattlesnake stretched along where Melly's car had been parked.

"Or something along those lines."

Darcy said nothing, for fear that she could little speak it without screaming.

The sheriff stared at something far, far up in the sky through a leathered squint. He passed his chunk of chaw from one side of his tongue to the other. He brought down his head and turned that squint toward the sign over the door, which read *Chigger's*.

"I reckon time has a way of working things out," he said. He removed his hat for the first time to climb into his cruiser.

"Give my regards to LeAnne."

A ll things considered, LeAnne took those regards in stride.
Darcy would never have returned to Chigger's had LeAnne not asked her to meet that following Monday. Darcy let herself inside the front door of the bar with the key she had every intention of returning. She found LeAnne inside, standing in the dark atop the back counter in her stiletto heels. She reached behind the top shelf stocked with fancy bourbons, where she fitted a plain, ornamental box.

"These are Joey's mortal remains," she whispered with a reverence.

"Bourbon was his favorite drink. He took it with a handful of ice and called it a Kentucky Sno-Cone."

Darcy fingered the door key from her own ring of keys. She set it down flat on the bar top. If LeAnne noticed, she didn't let on. She kept her sights on that box filled with Joey.

"We were his only family," LeAnne said. "He came here—much like you did—with no friends, no one to look after him. Using a different name…"

Darcy opened her mouth. LeAnne held up her hand.

"Please, dear," she said. "Help me down."

Darcy did. Once returned to earth, LeAnne brushed invisible dust from her skirt with both hands.

"Joey was more than an employee," LeAnne said. "He was like family. Everyone here is like family to Hanson and me."

LeAnne stepped back to admire her handiwork. Darcy noticed for the first time another handcrafted box—its identical twin—on the shelf next to it, behind the vodka bottles.

Kurt?

Darcy's shoulders shuddered. She turned her back to the cremains and faced instead the wreckage across yonder dance floor.

"We have to talk," she said to LeAnne.

"Quinn has told me about your little *theories*," LeAnne said.

"There's more to them than just *theories*," said Darcy. "Don't you remember those two women? Saturday night, the ones who—"

"Theories," LeAnne said, "that really should be put to bed." LeAnne walked to the center of the room and picked up the remnants of a shattered chair. She turned it upright and set it alongside a splintered table leaning on three busted legs.

She continued, "I'd argue that there are more important things to think about. For instance: if we want this bar up and running by Thursday, we're going to need to get started immediately."

Again, LeAnne waved off Darcy's attempt to speak. She reached into her glittered purse and rummaged free a credit card.

"Go to Home Depot," she said. "Fetch you a few Mexicans. I don't care how you handle it, just make sure you handle it."

"But...but, the sheriff..."

LeAnne's eyes narrowed to slits. "We can't back down to the sheriffs of this world," she said. "I'd expect you, of all people, to understand."

Darcy fought the urge to lower her head. She held LeAnne's stare until she thought her stomach might burst.

"We don't give in because these men demand it from us," said LeAnne. "We don't allow them to roll us over. No, we stand up to them. We stand up for ourselves. More important, we stand up for *each other*. How dare they defy *us*?"

LeAnne stopped mid-harangue to again consider the urn behind the fancy bourbons. She took a half-breath, then held it.

"Joey wasn't so innocent..." she said. If there were more to that thought, she kept it to herself. Instead, she took up Darcy's key from the bar counter. She pressed it to the credit card and extended them both toward Darcy.

Darcy accepted neither. "I was thinking," she said, "what if we let Chigger's stay closed a little while? A week, maybe two? Give folks a little time to separate these tragedies from the good times we want them to have? Maybe—I was thinking—we could do a little rebranding. I read a website where—"

"Change our name and run away?" LeAnne frowned. "You were lucky to get this job. I don't imagine there's much market in this part of the world for someone with your…*background*."

Darcy opened her mouth. She closed it.

"Or lack of a background, is more like it." LeAnne dropped all pretense of civility. She folded both of Darcy's hands around the credit card and key. "Other folks in town might not be so understanding of a single woman with no social security number or credit cards. Other folks in town might ask questions that I didn't ask. That's because they don't understand what it's like to have to make a hard decision because a man backed them against the wall."

"But he's the law," said Darcy. "What good is fighting the law?"

"I'm not talking about the sheriff," said LeAnne. "I'm talking about all of them."

The old Darcy would have tucked tail and ran. She would have put East Texas—hell, the *whole* of Texas—in her rearview. That Darcy had been replaced by the current one, who threw her shoulders into the work in front of her. With every table she fixed, every wall she mended, every little destruction wrought upon Chigger's by that horrible sheriff, Darcy felt herself grow stronger. She was no longer the woman who suffered at the whim of Allan, or any other man.

As she worked, she wondered what she might look like in a pair of two-inch stiletto heels. She considered, for the first time, a boob job. She thought about highlights for her hair.

All of that—and every other thought—came crashing to a halt that Wednesday afternoon when she pulled into the Chigger's lot and found the building awash in fire.

Upon sight of this inferno, all the fight sapped from her. Darcy realized, for the first time, how small had been her universe, and how infinitesimally tiny she had been within it.

The firefighters, to and fro. The flames, ever upward. Darcy stepped out of her Hyundai to admire the calamity of it all.

On opposite end of the red-rocked parking lot, the sheriff stood with his arms crossed. He shuffled chaw from one cheek to the other. He wore sunshades bright by the light of the flame. He stood flanked by two deputies with schoolboy eyes. He motioned with two twitched, crooking fingers for Darcy to join them.

"Your natural inclination," he said, "would be to think I had a hand in this."

He stared further to the flame. "You'd be incorrect."

"Then who?" asked Darcy. "You have to believe me now that someone is behind this. If you don't think it was those two women, fine. Who, then?"

Sheriff turned his head upward, as if the answer lie in the stars above. He brought his gaze down to earth, as if it didn't.

"There's been a whole lot of mess since you've come to town," he said. "I don't gamble much, but I know how to read the odds."

Thick fingers of flame licked the night purple. A rafter imploded, sending a fountain of ember from the center of the building. The neon popped in the *Chigger's* sign, hanging on a single hinge.

One of the firefighters whistled. Sheriff turned their way and nodded.

"Shut her down, boys!" called a fireman.

"Shut her down!" called the rest of them.

The hoses lessened. The fire sighed.

"You're just going to…" She'd answered her own question before it'd been asked.

"I could drain yonder river and still lack the water we'd need to put that baby out," he said. "She's going pretty good."

The *Chigger's* sign fell from the door. The plastic bubbled. The wood crackled. Darcy did not step back from the heat. She welcomed it.

"Is there any point in telling you I had nothing to do with this?" Darcy asked.

"Nope." Sheriff chewed his cud. "Not that I don't believe you…"

The firefighters took off their hats. They popped open soda cans and drank from them by the light of the conflagration.

"There are forces at work here," said the sheriff. "Ones that are bigger than you and me. I'm inclined to step out of the way and let them pass."

He lowered his sunshades so Darcy could better see his eyes.

"But they need to hurry up and pass."

Darcy understood. She counted the miles and minutes between her and the apartment. She weighed them against the distance to the state line. How far she could drive on the current tank of gas.

One of the deputies took a phone call. He tapped Sheriff's shoulder and spoke into his ear. Darcy took the opportunity to take leave, and had halfway reached her car when the sheriff called to her. She turned and found him holding his hat at his side.

"She didn't make it," he said.

"Beg pardon?" asked Darcy.

"Your friend," he said. "She died in the ambulance on the way to the hospital. Smoke inhalation is what they're saying now. How long they keep saying that…that's anybody's guess."

"My…friend?" Darcy could barely say the word.

The fire twinkled in Sheriff's sunshades. He took them off and squinted her way. She'd passed the test.

"Quinn," he said.

"She was inside when the place went up."

Darcy measured her every belonging back at her apartment against how bad she'd need it. She'd stashed six hundred bucks in the refrigerator. She kept an emergency credit card inside her dog-eared copy of *Eat, Pray, Love*. A second one inside the pocket of a winter coat. She could leave it—all of it—behind if absolutely necessary.

However, one thing kept her from making time for the county line:

She needed to see Melly.

Melly lived in an apartment building just outside the Loop. Darcy found the front door unlocked. She wanted anything else in the world, save taking one step inside. However, she told herself she would do so because it was the kind of thing a strong woman would do. Darcy was a strong woman now, she told herself. She said it over and over while she crossed the threshold. No matter what she might find, she was a strong woman.

Into Melly's apartment: Nothing on the walls. The furniture, plain and tattered. Newspapers, pizza boxes. Ashtrays and scattered cigarette butts.

Melly sat at a small dining table jammed into the back half of the kitchen. A single, bare bulb hung overhead. Its light twinkled bright in Melly's glassed, black eyes.

"Melly?"

In front of her was a half-drunk bottle of red wine. A glass stained purple at the lip.

"Melly…?"

Also, an empty pill bottle.

"What did you do?"

Darcy slapped up the pill bottle. No label. She threw it to the floor. She grabbed Melly's cheeks. They'd turned chilly. Darcy waited until she felt the girl breathe.

Dammit.

"What did you take?" Darcy asked, slapping her. "How many?"

Dammit.

Darcy jerked her phone from her pocket and flipped it open. She dialed 9-

"Wait."

-1—

"Please…don't."

Melly choked. She fought something down. She closed her eyes, then opened them.

Darcy kept her thumb at the ready. She hung the phone in her arm at her side.

"Who are they?" Darcy asked. "Why are they doing this?"

Said Melly, "It was supposed to be somebody else's turn to suffer."

"What?"

"I did my time." Melly closed her eyes again. "It was somebody else's turn."

"Melly, baby," said Darcy, "you need to let me call for help. Someone is—"

"Angie." It took everything she had, but Melly licked her lips. "Angela."

"No, it's me: Darcy. Baby, I'm going—"

"Angela Dossett," she said. "Angie."

"You're not making any sense." Darcy again dialed. 9-1—

"We killed her."

Darcy's thumb froze.

"What did you say?"

Melly coughed again. She sighed. With muscles like molasses, she poured herself another glass of wine.

"We killed Angela Dossett."

Darcy folded shut her phone. "Tell me," she said.

"She was the new girl," Melly said. "Kurt said he hired her because we were getting too busy for just one cocktail waitress, but I know why he hired her. She went to school up the road, which was funny, considering she was way dumber than the rest of us. You never saw one of us sleep with Hanson Banks, did you?"

Darcy pulled up a chair to the table. She sat in it.

"Hanson Banks had sex with the new girl?" she asked.

Melly nodded. "It was going on for a while," she said. "Maybe three weekends before LeAnne found out. She got mad at all of us for covering for him. She hated us because we knew it happened and never said anything to her. She said it embarrassed her."

Darcy opened her mouth. She closed it.

"We got it bad, but Angie got it worst of all," said Melly. "LeAnne wouldn't let her quit. She gave her the guilt trip. You've seen her do it. She manipulated her into believing she could never leave or she would be ruined. And every night, LeAnne made it worse on her to stay. Joey did. You can believe Quinn did. In some ways, Quinn was the worst. That girl kept putting up with it, thinking it would end one day, but it wouldn't."

"And you?" Darcy asked.

"My turn was over." Melly shrugged. "It was supposed to be somebody else's turn to suffer."

Melly faded out for a brief moment. Darcy waited for her to come to. Melly took a drink from her wine glass.

"They found her in the river," Melly said. "She'd been in it for two days, they believe. That's all they know. Did she jump in? Was she pushed? Did she kill herself on purpose or was it an accident?" Melly shrugged again. "The first thing I'll do when I see her will be to ask her. But she and I will both know I had a hand in it, whatever it was."

Melly's breathing shallowed. Darcy picked her phone up from the table.

"And LeAnne?" Darcy asked.

Melly whispered, "We're not just employees. We're family."

Darcy stood from the table. She returned her cellphone to her pocket. She watched the color quitting Melly's cheeks. Lips.

"Angie was the lucky one," Melly said. "She had someone to settle her debts for her. She was somebody's daughter... somebody's sister..."

Darcy stood over top of Melly and watched the young girl die. When those lights had been properly extinguished, Darcy set upon every surface she'd touched inside that apartment and wiped it clean. She let herself out of the room by holding the doorknob with her shirt sleeve.

The world outside looked different to her. The sky a different shade of blue, the birds overhead with a different song to sing. Darcy realized nothing would ever again be the same for her.

This time, there'd be fewer regrets.

One last stop.

The Banks' home off the golf course was abandoned. A neighbor told Darcy that Hanson and LeAnne kept a deer lease about a half hour outside the Loop. It didn't take long for Darcy to figure out the address and find her way out there.

Asphalt gave way to gravel which gave way to brick orange clay. Pine needles. Thick brush and overgrowth and way out back, Darcy found the cabin. It was nicer than most. The wood had a rich finish. The yard around it was freshly landscaped and, much to Darcy's chagrin, festooned with more than a dozen rattlesnakes.

Seven, eight of them in the front yard, coiled loose like thrown rope. A pair of canebrakes, sunning themselves in the driveway. One glided its way behind a fallen log.

Darcy watched it all from the safety of the Hyundai. Her instinct had been to lock her doors, but she fought it. Also fought the urge to run. She unfastened her seatbelt. She measured her breathing.

She climbed out of the Hyundai and stepped across the yard like it was a minefield. Careful to keep plenty of distance between her and the snake on her left, licking and kissing the air. The snake on her right, drawing its triangle of a head into its coil. She watched for any signs of warning. She felt for any change in the atmosphere. She counted the steps from her to the porch and plotted a new course with each footfall. She made sure not to—

A gunshot cracked open the sky. Darcy's periphery crackled. In it, every snake drew back. All around her, rattles cranked up a spit. Her stomach filled with ice cubes.

Ahead of her, LeAnne held a skinny rifle to her shoulder. Behind her, a rattlesnake was missing its head. Five feet of it stopped sudden at a tiny crater filled with pulp and gore. Darcy's ice melted.

"I had even money it would be the one six feet ahead of you and to your left." LeAnne kept her eye through the rifle sights. Darcy could not tell where she aimed. "I was wrong."

"You know why this is happening, don't you?"

LeAnne looked over top of the gun sight. "You know, they have a behavior pattern. Each of them operate the same way. If they feel threatened, they will attack. They tense, they strike, then they use the rattle. Often times, if you hear the rattle, it's too late."

"I know about Angela Dossett," called Darcy.

"They don't rattle to warn you off the first strike," said LeAnne. "It's to warn you off the second."

Darcy watched the rattler—the one beneath the log—twitch.

"I need to know," she said, "did you kill that girl?"

LeAnne fired again. This time, one of the snakes in the driveway; its head exploded. The remaining serpents vibrated at a higher frequency.

"We're all supposed to be in this together," LeAnne called. "We're supposed to look out for one another."

"LeAnne…"

"It's one thing for Hanson to sleep with another woman. I get it. He's a musician. It comes with the territory. You don't marry one and not expect a bit of that. But one of my employees? In front of everyone?"

LeAnne next shot missed by an inch. She followed with a second shot that cut a snake into two pieces.

"Kurt…Joey…" LeAnne took a deep breath. "Quinn and that little bitch Melly…all of them…they all knew."

One snake slithered into the flowerbed and out of sight. Another Darcy had yet to see slipped from behind a clay garden gnome.

"Did you push that little girl into the river?" Darcy asked. "Did you kill her?"

LeAnne twisted her face into a tight scowl. Darcy realized that would be her only answer.

"Go home, Darcy." LeAnne's shoulders slumped. She lowered the barrel. "There's two kinds of woman in this world. You aren't the kind you think you are. It's time for you to run back home to him."

A thought struck Darcy. She asked, "Where's Hanson, LeAnne?"

"Who?"

"Your husband. Where is he?"

LeAnne sighed. "He's inside."

"Maybe you should send him out."

LeAnne considered at first one snake, then another. She took in the whole of the yard, then sighed again. Her fight had ended.

"LeAnne…can I talk to him?"

LeAnne raised the rifle to again snipe another snake, but seemed to think better of it. She lowered the barrel, then lay the firearm onto the top step of her porch.

"We're supposed to be in this together," she said, resigned. Unarmed, she opened her front door.

Darcy took a careful step backward.

"Goodbye, Darcy," said LeAnne before slipping silent back into her house.

"Go home."

F orget the six hundred bucks in the freezer. Forget the emergency credit cards. Forget the clothes, the books, the magazine subscription. None of that mattered anymore. Darcy had done this before.

Forget Darcy.

She did not stop until the gas needle tickled E, and even then she considered keeping on keeping on, climbing out the Hyundai door and legging the rest on foot, not to stop until there were no more roads left to run, no more winds left to carry her.

Instead, she landed twenty miles shy of the state line at a gas station grateful for the business. She collected coins from her cup holder, pennies from beneath her floormats.

She stood, wondering which way to go, when along came that green Mustang, covered in the same color mud as the Hyundai. Out spilled those two women. One of them black, with colored extensions. The other blonde, with tattoos. Tattoos of a spilled bottle of pills on one leg. Rattlesnakes on the other. A mermaid on her elbow, dancing in flames.

The black woman unscrewed the Mustang's gas cap. The blonde unhooked the nozzle. When she turned to fill her up, Darcy noticed a different tattoo etched across her finely tuned back—a tombstone which read only the word: *Angie*.

They filled their tanks in silence.

Finally, Darcy said, "I'm leaving town."

The black woman nodded. "So are we."

"Our work back there is done," said the blonde.

Darcy swallowed thick. "If I had known…"

"We know."

The only stoplight in that entire town turned from green to red, with nobody in sight to run it.

"Where you going?" asked the blonde.

"I don't know." Darcy shrugged. "How about you?"

The black woman said the name of a little town about two hours down the road. She said it through her teeth.

"Ever heard of it?" she asked.

Darcy nodded her head. "That's where the cops shot that little black boy. What was he, fifteen years old?"

"Fourteen." The black woman turned to face the horizon yonder. "He was fourteen."

"Oh."

"He was unarmed. Minding his own business. Playing in his front yard."

Darcy couldn't believe the earth spun at the same speed all the time. She swore it sped up sometimes, while it slowed down at others.

"Anyway," said the blonde, "that's where we're going next."

"You should ride with us," said the black woman.

Darcy shrugged. "There's a big difference between you and me," she said.

The black woman shook her head. "Not really."

"LeAnne said there's two kinds of women in this world," said Darcy.

"She's wrong," answered the blonde. "It's more than that."

The gas quit pumping. The blonde returned the nozzle to its handle. She leaned against the Mustang, alongside her friend. They watched Darcy for what felt like an hour.

All the while, Darcy thought of Melly and those moments she'd allowed herself to smile. She thought of Quinn and all the ways she'd devised to keep Melly from doing it. She thought of Joey. Of Kurt. Of Hanson, and all the Hansons of the world, as well as all the Joeys and Kurts. She thought of LeAnne and how many of them were there, and how Darcy could work from now to Judgment Day and never come close to weeding the world of them.

All of them, she thought of once—there in that parking lot—then thought never of them again. As she measured the driver's seat of that Hyundai against the backseat of that Mustang, there was only one face she saw in her mind.

Only one name.

"I'd love to ride with you," she said. "On one condition."

The black woman licked her lips. A twinkle struck the blonde in the eye.

"Name it."

"After we're finished with your business down the road," said Darcy, "I get to choose our next stop."

The smile across them was infectious.

The three of them became taillights.

PART TWO

LAKE CASTOR

BEDTIME STORY

There's but a sliver of light in the hallway and you frown, because she was long ago told to shut off the light. But that frown melts quickly away because you love her and everything that makes her what she is and, more likely, what she will be. So softly you open the door and mind the little creak in the hinge, the one that makes her look up, see you, and smile.

"Mommy," she says.

"Honey," you say, "you are supposed to be asleep. Why is your light still on?"

"I can't sleep," she says. "I'm scared."

"There's nothing to be afraid of," you tell her.

"I'm afraid of Big Jack Caro." She whispers the name, as if there were more than the two of you in the house.

You only take half a breath. "What—How do you know about

Jack Caro, honey?"

"I hear you and Daddy talking," she says. "They talk about him everywhere. At school. Is it true Big Jack Caro killed Suzy Egan's daddy?"

You hold onto that half-breath for dear life. Children will talk. Hide what you will, they will find it. For years, you have secreted Christmas presents about the house, always in a new spot, and hasn't she ferreted them out each and every time? How can this be different?

"Mr. Caro is a sick man, sweetie." You say it as you bring the covers up tighter around the bottom of her chin. As if the blanket were made of chain mail or chicken soup. "He's not well."

"They say he's mad because his little boy died. Is that right, Mommy?"

"He's very upset," you say, "but that doesn't make it right, what he's doing."

No matter what they say on the news, you want to tell her. You want to tell her that all those people protesting outside the courthouse and the state capitol and the job sites popping up around the county…all those people are just as sick as Mr. Jack Caro and, no matter how bad a hand he'd been dealt, there still existed the Ten Commandments and a Bill of Rights and a Golden Rule, all of whom still heralded to the heavens *Thou Shalt Not Kill*.

That Mr. Jack Caro was a nut. An environmental wingnut. The type of guy the two of you would have laughed at on the news or a one-hour drama on TV when he tied himself to a tree about to get cut down or a bulldozer about to raze a copse of withered pines. The kind of guy who made more than enough noise when he didn't have a job, but Mr. Caro had a job. He worked at the school until he got fired for bringing his politics into the building, then lost it after his little boy—

"Why are you crying, Mommy?"

You can still see Mr. Caro holding the signs. That look of mad desperation on his face. The pictures of his boy, missing teeth. Missing hair. The pictures of flames shooting from the taps and faucets and wells around the county. The vitriol and vengeance he spouted as his boy grew sicker and sicker. As if he spent less time pointing fingers and more time tending to his own family. But you can't blame him. The horror he must have endured watching his boy die slowly in front of him. You can't imagine, but it is no excuse.

Bill Egan—Suzy's father—found in the office trailer up at the job site off Highway 42. It, being the first murder, had a spin of mystery about it, but everyone knew who'd done it. Jack Caro, less cryptic about the next one: the lawyer found shot to death in his car at the parking garage downtown. Or the representative sent down by the energy company, the man who helped all those families negotiate the mineral rights, helped them get the most money for their land. They were still looking for his head.

These are the things you can't tell your daughter. Instead, you focus on the things you can tell her.

"Mr. Caro won't be coming here, sweetie."

"Is that why we put in all those alarms?"

You brush away a lock of golden hair from her forehead. You pick away a strand from her cheek.

"We put those in to keep you safe."

"From Mr. Caro?"

"From everything."

Lance had them installed not after the three lawyers that were found dead near the hydraulic equipment, but after the pair that weren't. Those two sent down from the corporate offices that were last known to have checked into the hotel downtown, but then mysteriously vanished from the face of the planet. How every law enforcement agency from here to Washington had sent resources, yet still nothing. You'd never seen him so rattled.

"He's not so stupid to come after a senator," your husband had told you over and over again. Still, the next day he had bars fitted into the windows and bought each of them a gun.

With your daughter, you have more room to negotiate.

"How about I leave open the door," you reason, "just a little?"

"And leave on the light?"

"And leave on the light."

She smiles sweetly and closes her eyes. She makes likes she's sleeping, but you know better. You wrap the blanket around her even tighter, then kiss her forehead.

You kiss it again for good measure.

And once outside her bedroom door, you reach into the pocket of your robe and hold fast to the tiny revolver, feeling warmer knowing it is there. You doublecheck the alarms, then check them yet again. You inspect each lock one more time.

You take vigil on your ottoman, the one facing the door. The third night in a row. Fresh pot of coffee. Eight rounds ready to go.

For you are not like Mr. Jack Caro. You will stop at nothing to protect your child.

THE JOE FLACCO DEFENSE

The blood puddled beneath her husband, then slithered between the kitchen floor tiles she had only last week re-grouted. Another reason to hate him, although she'd long lost count. Had she bothered to handle things wearing something other than her best ass-jeans, she'd jam the knife into him three or four more times. Plus, she remarked, if so much as a drop of his insides landed on her mahogany cabinetry, there'd be no pulling her off him.

Furthermore, the phone began to ring.

She let it go to voicemail. She considered her hands full. But what to do first? Close his eyes, surely. He still wore that indignant expression, and she'd never get anything done if she believed him still to be thinking, "I don't see what's the big idea, Kate...you're overreacting." She reached out, thumbs to eyelids. Still, the phone rang.

She snatched several sheets of Quicker-Picker-Upper from the roll on the counter and stuffed them furiously around the spreading muck—forming a sick sort of Hoover Dam or moat—hoping to staunch the flow and, again, the phone rang. This brought sweat to her brow, a new urgency. She could have lost her mind, had not the machine picked up after the fourth ring, then:

"Hal, this is Keith," said the voice on the recorder. "Is everything okay? I'm worried about you."

Her stomach flew headlong into fits. Her mouth dropped open and she found herself unable to move. *How in the...?*

"Ha-ha, just kidding. I figured something was up because it's been fifteen minutes and you ain't responded to my trade request. That's a record. Anyway, call me and let me know everything's—"

Her entire body became a muscle tightened. She could shit a pearl, for want of a grain of sand. Her hand squeezed the saturated napkin and blood wretched from it and she stopped herself just shy of a scream.

Fantasy fucking football. That son of a bitch. Hadn't this been what it was all about? Couldn't take out the trash because he had to update his team. Couldn't be bothered with the dishes because SportsCenter was on. Couldn't take her to dinner because the Ravens and the Colts were on TV, and God forbid he offer to—

And even as he lie bleeding out, still with the fantasy football. She closed her eyes and took first one breath and then another and resolved that no, if she were going down for this, she wasn't going down for fantasy football. No, her husband was getting chopped up and scattered about her backyard gardens and no one would be the wiser.

She just needed to buy some time.

She raced to the computer. Logged on. Tapped out his password—

theismannsknee01—and clicked here and there, searching the screen like mad. That night oh so long ago—three seasons, to be exact—when he'd excitedly shown her what fantasy football was all about, shown her his team and how well he'd drafted and what he'd done to win the big matchup the night before and the difference between rotisserie and head-to-head leagues. All the while, his voice trailing away in some parts, the baptism of a chasm cleaving between them and her not ready to recognize it. Not yet.

Click, tap, tap, click and there it was: the trade from RGIII-PO—Keith, a rabid fan of both *Star Wars* and the Redskins. She tapped *approve* and hoped to high heaven she'd bought enough time to remove the hands and feet from her dearly departed when there was a knock at the door.

Open just far enough to stick her face through, she greeted the neighbor.

"Hey, Kate," said he, "is Keith around?"

"No...he, uh..."

The neighbor scratched his head. "Is he okay?"

"Why wouldn't he be okay?" She checked herself for errant blood spatter. "He's fine."

"You want to tell me what gives?" He didn't wait for an answer. "Look, he talked me into joining this league and I know it's my first season and all, but this is starting to smell a lot like collusion."

Behind her, the phone rang. "Collusion?" she asked.

"Exactly. That trade he accepted, what kind of asshole does he think I am?"

She shook her head, hoping it would suffice. She promised to relay the message and assured him that he would never collude and blah, blah, blah. He gave her the stink-eye, as if she might be lying and said:

"I hope not. He told me himself how important integrity is in fantasy football."

On the phone, Keith again. "Is Hal...*okay?*"

Ruined a perfectly good blade from my Michael Kors collection, she wanted to say, but didn't.

"First, he takes all day to acknowledge a trade, then approves one he would never accept in a million years. Normally, he'd counter-offer and—"

Sweat, dripping like icicles. She would vomit, were she not standing on her carpet, so she took a seat and put the back of her hand to her forehead.

"Hal's fine," she said. "He can't come to the phone. He cut himself and he's—"

"Sure, tell him he's a chump. He could have held out for Celek and the Pittsburgh defense, but whatever."

Her brother beeped in on the call waiting. She took the phone off the ringer. A text buzzed on her husband's cell phone. An IM popped up on his Facebook account. She could turn everything off, she reckoned, but knew she'd get the body no closer to her rose garden before they'd all be in her front yard, pounding on the door and unable to direct elsewhere until they saw his face—the one that had already begun to turn purple—and she knew she needed to act fast.

She leapt into his office chair. Clicked here and there. First, ESPN. Then Yahoo! and a couple sports blogs he'd bookmarked. She studied old transactions and interactions recorded on his fantasy hosting site. She had a head for numbers and took them on with a fervor, focused. After a fevered forty-five minute cram session, she clicked the button marked SMACKTALK and typed:

"Laugh now, but the Chiefs will be pwn3d by Cam Newton and expect even crazier moves from me this season, noobs! #FutureLeagueChamp #Moneyball."

She had no idea what those words meant, but something had taken hold of her. Sitting in his chair, maybe. His soul, infused into the monitor or maybe the keyboard. She had no idea, but worse, no time to think about it. She watched first one *like* appear below her post, then another *like*, and soon everyone in the league had seen it and approved and began to SMACKTALK below it, and she wondered how much time could pass between banter before the jig would be up.

The first nice thought regarding her husband in years: he was an excellent note-taker. Meticulous, even. She ran through notes on yellow pads, Post-its and even the digital files he kept on the fantasy site. Immersion. When she saw Roy Helu picked up off the waiver wire, she fired a quick shot at the team named Norv Turner's Revenge, who she could only imagine was their butcher.

"No way Helu gets carries this year with a mobile QB under center. 2B RB behind Morris. Boo-yah!" She'd never used the word *boo-yah* in her life and held her breath until the first two *likes* trickled in, for she had indeed used it properly.

Still, it wasn't good enough. The games were only three days away.

Damn Thursday game, she silently cursed. She knew she needed coffee and raced into the kitchen—stepping gingerly over Hal's carcass—to brew it.

If she could only go back in time... As the coffee brewed, her snap-decision haunted her. That instant reflex, that sudden response which, at the time, seemed so normal and now could only serve to ruin her in the long run. Why oh why did she do it? Looking back, accepting that Cam Newton trade was a blunder, despite his quick feet and a shoddy Kansas City defense, but there can only be one Steve Smith, and the Panthers inability to commit to the run left their quarterback vulnerable. But in life, there were no take-backs. She'd need to make lemons from lemonade. She'd need to *tinker*.

And come Thursday, she found solace. She battled Show Me Your TDs valiantly, with only C.J. Spiller and the Tennessee defense playing, she had the fortune of going against a guy who'd drafted Chris Johnson ridiculously high. *Hadn't they learned by now?* She reveled in the victory perhaps a little too much for the next three days, but took comfort that Hal loved to gloat. She let down her hair.

Speaking of Hal, he got a touch rank by Sunday. She went so far as to open several packages of pine-scented car fresheners and had every intention of hanging them in the kitchen, but things got a little nuts with a trade between one of Hal's co-workers and the bartender where he hung out, so she needed to weigh in. Besides, with the games on the horizon…

They Call Me The Brees, otherwise known as Hal's boss, posted angry messages about Hal's absence from work, and she even fielded an email or two when she had time, but found herself grateful when HR called and told him not to bother coming in. They Call Me The Brees took more issue with his starting wide receiver leaving the game in the first quarter, hence his loss to jims_team, from whom no one expected much.

No one saw her next move: stealing Antonio Gates from the waiver wire. They thought his best days were behind him, but she knew he put up great numbers against Seattle. Hal's refusal to draft him in the ninth round proved what she'd never liked much about him in the first place: sentimentality. Refusal to see the nose in front of his face due to some misplaced notion that should have been cast aside at the first sign of trouble. Was that not written all over his expression the first time she jammed the knife between his third and fourth rib? The surprise? Well, Hal, had you read the leaves in the bottom of your teacup, and by teacup, she meant the fury mounting within her when she'd seen he'd again neglected to tend to the dishes, well…then it'd be him and not she going into Monday night with the matchup on the line, wouldn't it?

The phone calls, the texts, the IMs. All of them wondering what had come over him. How he'd become so focused, so dominant. How his vision had expanded well beyond 20/20 and he, for the first time in his life, could see the big picture, that which entered it long before it approached the frame. Her, with SMACKTALK screaming, "Welcome to the new me!"

They began to get suspicious.

And still, the smell. It only got worse. She closed herself off from the rest of the house, coming out only to eat and eliminate, and rarely so at that. She'd catch wind of him and wonder what she'd seen in him in the first place. Remind herself that he'd let Gates sit on the waiver wire and get angry all over again.

She moved throughout the league. She prepared to kick the snot out of Chris Cooley's Screenshot the next week. She traded for a receiver and freed up room to improve her flex slot. Didn't fall for Robbie Gould. She clawed her way to the top of the waiver wire. Her passion unmatched. And she cared not for the smell growing stronger from the kitchen. She cared not once for the stack of bills piling up below the mail slot.

And she cared not once for the police who came knocking at her door, her with Monday night still to go.

MISCELLANY

There's a filling station just south of Durham, North Carolina that raised a ruckus a while back because the owner refused to take down a Confederate flag he'd hoisted above the building. Imagine how folks from miles around flocked to see what would happen when the National Guard came out to tell him to take it down. How for years and years after, old timers would bend your ear with the details of the Klan, the protests. The cheers and jeers.

Not since that day way back when had anyone paid any mind to Gerry Tompkins's place or what he said or did. The old timers still hung out around there, but for the most part, people got their gas and goods a little closer into town. Tobacco dried up around there long ago and there weren't much travel on those roads any longer. Just folks lost on their way out of town. Neighbors that came day after day for years and years until one day they didn't. Until one day they were gone.

But when those two came into Huck's Country Express and robbed Gerry Tompkins blind, they got folks started. Breathed new life into them, you could say. Now they had something to talk about again. Something besides how hot it was this year or what Duke or North Carolina did during the off-season or what may or may not be the reason why so-and-so's barbecue don't taste like it used to.

You had to go no further than Tompkins himself to hear how dramatic things were or weren't. For more than a year after, folks would get held up in line while trying to buy eggs or Lotto tickets or what have you while he told one guy or another the same damn story he'd been telling since it happened. How the kid acted suspicious when he first walked in. How he wasn't much to think about, but something seemed odd about him, all the same. How Tompkins had looked away, went back to stocking cigarettes.

"I mean, he wasn't black or nothing," Tomkins would say for years, as if the surprise were still fresh. "Here he come, looking at this or that, picking stuff up and setting it down. He's looking in this corner and along the doors and every which way, when finally he gets him a bottle of coke and tries to pay me with a fifty dollar bill."

"That's how they scope you out," Grit Beecher would often add. Grit, on that day and many, many afterward, would sit in one of the lunch booths and read a paper, smoke on a cigar, and jaw with damn near anyone who gave him a minute or two. Grit and Huck's Country Express went hand-in-hand. "They give you a big bill so they can see what's in the register. That's what the kid did. I saw him peek over the counter and look in the register while Gerry made change and I thought something was a little fishy."

"But like I said, he wasn't black," Tomkins would always explain.

There weren't many places like his left. Most of them got bought up by developers or fellas in cahoots with big oil companies. Used to, there was a Jimmy's Mini-Mart, a Ronny's Highway Shop, and even a Ronny's Too on the other side of town. But soon the sign saying *"Jimmy's"* got smaller and smaller until one day it was gone, replaced by a bulky neon *Exxon* or *Mobil*.

Tompkins usually offered that as a reason why he didn't have drop safes or video cameras. Actually, he had video cameras. They just didn't record anything. He quit buying tapes for it years ago, and when it went on the fritz, he never bothered to replace it. Don't ask him why, but he fixed damn near everything in that gas station when it broke. Never bothered one minute with the video camera.

So the kid takes his change, then goes and stands by the door a bit. He looks out the window and nobody can ever agree if it was a little wave or a big wave or what, but most everybody believes it was a signal. Then he stops at the magazine rack and picks out one of those Hollywood magazines and starts reading.

Another thing most folks never agree on is what the man looked like that came in next. Tomkins said he had salt-and-pepper hair, put him at about five-ten. Grit said he was taller, had brown hair. Sandy Hightower, who'd been in the back aisle choosing between potato chips, agreed that he had brown hair, but for some reason gave him a beard, which didn't anyone else bother to do. Hell, they couldn't even agree on what kind of gun the man pulled or whether it came out of his pocket or the front or back waistband of his pants.

But they all agreed there was a gun. And they all agreed the man put it in Tomkins's face and shouted, "Give me all the money." He saw the others and moved the gun from each of their faces. Then back to Tomkins. He said didn't need nobody to be a hero. He said nobody has to get hurt.

Didn't any of them think about the kid at that moment, but he stayed over by the magazine rack. He flipped through the pages. Grit always thought it plenty strange when the boy called over to Tomkins and asked him if this was the most recent issue of the Hollywood magazine they had. Said it was at least a month old and has he got the new one in yet.

"I told him I didn't and he didn't say no more about it," Tomkins would always say. "He set the issue back on the magazine rack where he got it then turned his attention to the stack of newspapers down at his feet."

The man with the gun, on the other hand, was all business. He motioned with the barrel, steered Tomkins to hurry, slow down, take it easy. Pointed it toward a carton of filtered cigarettes and told him to throw those in with the cash too. Tomkins did what he was told. He hunched his shoulders as he rifled through the drawer, unable to get the money out of the till and into the sack fast enough.

What happened next, everybody agrees on.

"In comes Officer Sherrill," as Sandy Hightower would tell it. "And it ain't just him, but this is a day that he's hosting one of the Explorer Scouts. The ride-along program brought kids up from the high school and taught them what it was like to work as a policeman. That particular Sunday, Mr. Sherrill had the Kessler boy with him."

The Kessler boy was Jimmy Kessler, a sophomore who had no shot of ever working with a police department, on account of his weight. Jimmy Kessler never met a candy bar he didn't like and when he walked into the Huck's Country Express that Sunday afternoon, his Explorer uniform stretched at the buttons. In fact, Grit Beecher seemed to remember him with a Snickers in his mouth.

"First thing I heard was the bell I keep over the door," Tomkins would say. "It rang just like it had any other time somebody walked in. So I looked up at the door, just like I would any other time. And first thing I thought was, *I'm so glad the police have come.* I thought that for about a split second, then didn't think it no more."

"I remember Sherry saying something about how hot it was and then it all got started," Grit would say. "I remember wanting to jump up and down and tell him to look out, the guy's got a gun, but things happened too damn fast. Before you know it, they was shooting."

One of the bullets hit the doorframe. They dug out the bullet later, but Tomkins never had the frame fixed. He'll take anyone and everyone over to the door and point it out. Show them where the first bullet went.

"Missed Sherrill's head by yay-much," he would always say, holding his hands about a foot apart. "Sherry had just as much time to get a good look at him before that man squeezed off a shot. Didn't even have time to get his gun. He grabbed the fat kid he brung with him and dove into the whatnot aisle."

The "whatnot aisle" was the aisle closest to the door. This is where Garrett Tomkins kept automotive supplies and other things he'd found folks needed over the years. Sometimes folks needed cat food. He kept it in the whatnot aisle. Maybe you needed to grab a toy on your way to visit with a youngster. Those were also kept on the whatnot aisle.

"If it ain't food or drink, more than likely it ends up in the whatnot aisle," Tomkins often said.

The whatnot aisle is where Officer Sherrill and fat little Jimmy Kessler landed, Sherrill shielding the kid with his body while trying to fetch out his own sidearm. Tomkins went down behind the counter,

Grit and Sandy Hightower hit the floor. But that didn't mean they couldn't see everything that unfolded.

"Gerry had one of those bent mirrors up in the corner," Grit said, "so that he could catch kids trying to take shit off the candy aisle. You can see the whole store off those mirrors, and the fella with the gun, he's right in front of me and Sandy Hightower, but Sherry, he's a few rows back. I look up at the mirror and you can see him crawl on his belly toward the end of the aisle, gun in hand. He was looking to get a shot at that fella with the gun."

"I liked to shit my britches," Tomkins would say. "I ain't afraid to say it. I've had a colored boy in a time or two who talked rough but ain't never been gunfire in the store. The fella already shot once, and I saw him inching down the aisle, I saw Sherry inching down the aisle... Like I said, ain't nobody ever fired a gun in my shop, and it looked like there was about to be somebody killed there. And if the fella got the drop on Sherry, more than likely he'd have to kill us all so there wouldn't be no witnesses."

This has always been a great spot to pause for dramatic effect. If Grit told the story in a bar somewhere, he found it advisable to suddenly empty his beer, knowing folks would buy him another so he would stick about and tell what happens next. Tomkins would take the opportunity to ring up another customer or two, let folks get antsy. Sandy Hightower, on the other hand, never had a problem launching into it.

"That kid...we'd all forgotten about that kid," was how she'd tell it. Sandy Hightower talked with her hands a lot. Right here, she'd get a workout. "That kid, he must have been watching the whole thing on the shoplifter's mirror and maybe he was worried that Officer Sherrill would shoot his buddy. Anyway, the kid isn't going to take it. He's up and running and next thing you know, he's got a gun in the back of Sherrill's neck."

Tomkins always shakes his head. He'll walk around the counter and take folks by the arm to the whatnot aisle and point to a spot on the shelf that's empty. He'll wait until you look at the spot before saying, "This is where I used to keep them. I don't keep them there no more. Not since that day. No, sir."

Them are the plastic toy cap guns he'd sold on the whatnot aisle since the eighties, back when toy guns were more socially acceptable. Back in the old days, toy guns looked like real guns. But a few black kids got shot by well-intentioned policemen and, come to find out, the gun was fake the whole time, just some toy. People—mostly Northerners—picketed and petitioned and all of a sudden, fake guns needed to look more fake. The company that made the gun Tomkins sold on his whatnot aisle compromised by sticking a red tip at the end of the barrel. Problem solved.

"But that little red tip don't do nothing for you when it's buried in the back of your neck, I don't reckon." Grit slapped his palms against each other, like dusting chalk off erasers. "That kid, he jams that gun into Sherry's head and tells him he'll blow it off if he so much as moves another inch."

"Don't Sherry or the fat boy he brung—don't *nobody*—move another inch."

About this time, if you're hearing about it at Huck's, Tomkins will take you around the end of the whatnot aisle and show you just where Officer Sherrill lay. He'll point up along the row of ice-cold coolers and draw his finger up alongside where you both stand.

"Around comes the older fella," Tomkins will say. "He ain't none too pleased with Sherry at this point. I reckon he'd have put a couple rounds in both him and that little fat fella if it weren't for the kid standing there with the little cap gun saying don't worry, I got it under control."

Sandy Hightower will shake her head and furrow her brow. "He didn't have to kick him. Officer Sherrill was just doing his job."

"He kicked him once, good in the ribs," Grit tells it. "Fella wore size eleven Ariat boots and he put the tip of one right into Sherry's side, then told him to get up. Told us all to get up."

Officer Sherrill has never liked to talk about it. Rarely will he. However, there are occasions—usually regarding alcohol—where his side of the story is readily available.

"The suspect ordered myself and the other patrons of the store to line up by the cooler door," Sherrill said one night at a wedding reception. His cousin Bob had just got married to a little girl from Greensboro and he felt a bit festive. There wasn't a single person in attendance who hadn't heard the story at least a dozen times already, but none of them had ever heard it from Sherrill.

That night, he said: "The older suspect had already relieved me of my sidearm, or else I probably would have opened fire the second he told us to line up. They called Gerry around from behind the counter and told him to join up with us, asked him if the beer cooler could be locked from the outside. At this point, I felt the most important thing was to keep everyone calm, since we were outgunned."

Someone made a joke about the kid's cap gun and Sherrill stopped talking. A few beers later, he had to be restrained and taken home after he fired three rounds into the wedding cake. Folks figured it best not to talk to Sherrill about it after that.

The kid is the one who thought to remember to ask after their phones. While the older man held the gun on them, he came around with one of the station's go-bags and had each person drop in their phone. He pulled out Sandy Hightower's phone and thumbed around at the screen, asked Tomkins if they had wi-fi. Tomkins told him no, he didn't have wi-fi, and then the older man got a bit fussy.

"He told the kid to quit jacking with the phone and the kid answers he was just checking the news." Tomkins shook his head. "They put that sack of phones over on the counter, well out of our reach, and shoved us on inside the beer cooler."

"This is getting to be old hat for us," the kid told the older man.

Grit will tell you they were all in that cooler, freezing off their asses, for the better part of an hour. Finally, in walked a couple black kids and, once they heard everybody hooting and hollering inside the cooler, they offered to let them out.

"It's the first time I seen ole Gerry happy to have colored kids in his store," Grit said. "Let me tell you."

Around about this time, most folks will ask Gerry Tomkins has he bothered to fix up that old camera system yet. He's got two answers, depending on how well he knows you. If he don't know you well, he'll laugh and say hell yes, he's fixed those cameras. What do you think he is, stupid?

But if he does…if he knows you pretty well, he'll look first this way and then the other, then lean in real close and tell you, "Hell no. There's just something not right about me sitting under a camera all day. I don't care what year it is." Then he'll take you by the hand and lead you all the way to the back of the store, then open up the cooler and point his finger inside. Follow his finger and he'll show you the brand new coat rack hanging on the wall above the twelve-packs. He's got four fur-lined coats hanging off it.

"But that don't mean I didn't learn nothing."

I'M THE ONLY HELL MY MOMMA EVER RAISED

The woman caught Donnie Ray off guard. She never so much as said her name, nor offered her hand to shake. No sooner had she laid eyes on him than she stomped across the asphalt in front of his momma's house and threw wild a finger to his face.

"You can't park there." She pointed to his eighteen-wheeler. It took the length of the yard where the Stringers used to live. Where she lived now. "If you park in front of my mailbox, then my mail won't get delivered."

"Ma'am..." Donnie Ray didn't like how his voice creaked out of his throat. He couldn't remember the last time he'd spoken to someone else. "Something tells me I'm not going to be long, so..."

Rather than finish what he was saying, he cut her a look from beneath the brim of his Stetson. Normally, that shut folks up. This woman, however, would not be deterred by something so simple as a pair of cold, road-weary eyes.

"That's what the man said who drove that pickup right there." She pointed to his uncle Ollie's rusty red Chevy, which had been parked beneath the willow tree in Momma's yard. "And the man driving that blue car, and the family in that station wagon."

He knew some of the cars parked in the front yard, some he didn't.

"And I don't know for certain," she said, "but I'm pretty sure you can't drive that thing down a residential street. Maybe I ought to call somebody and find out."

Donnie Ray pulled his Stetson off his head and held it at the waist. He'd stopped to change after taking his brother's call. He was many things, sure, but a man who would stand at his momma's deathbed wearing dirty work clothes was not one of them.

"Ma'am, maybe you heard my momma's sick in there." He felt his back teeth grind. "Has been for a while."

"I hate to hear it, but—"

"I can't tell you much except I'm told she's not long." Donnie Ray could see Darrell, his brother, watching them from the front screen door. He looked older... "They wouldn't have called me if she weren't pretty far gone."

The woman had more to say, but something told her to keep it to herself. It sure wasn't Donnie Ray, which didn't make a lick of sense to him. Out there—in the real world—folks gave him a wide berth. Or, most did. The ones that didn't cut him one had good cause not to, whether given or taken, which gave him good pause when dealing with the little housewife.

"Ma'am, if you don't mind..."

"I'm real sorry to hear about your mom. Mine passed, oh, about eight, nine years now. Cancer. It was real horrible, especially at the end."

Donnie Ray squinted.

"When finally she went, it was almost a relief," said the woman. "Now, I don't mean to sound like an ogre, but she was in so much pain. We'd done all we could do, so it was all over but the shouting. And there was plenty shouting, with all of her affairs to look after. Nearly drove our family apart, it got so bad."

Donnie Ray promised he'd punch himself if he offered her the slightest of condolences.

She did not need them: "I hate to see that happen to a family." She leaned forward about an inch. "You all have discussed her affairs, haven't you?"

He knew she imagined the place with a fresh sod and green grass. Without Momma's flowers she grew out of coffee cans or clawfoots or TV sets…out of an old toilet or old barbecue grill or old what-have-you. Maybe a fresh coat of paint and a few new boards across the house or, hell, maybe with the place burned to the ground.

"She's got people handling that," Donnie Ray said. His fingernails dug into the brim of that Stetson. "Me, I'm just here to see my momma off. So, if you will kindly excuse me…"

He shouldered past her.

"You got an hour," the woman called after him. "Then I call the city about that truck."

The screen door slapped shut behind Darrell as he stepped onto the porch to greet his brother. Darrell was a big old boy and his good clothes liked to tug open at the seams. He drank from a can of beer and sucked on a plug of chaw. He side-eyed the neighbor woman, then spit tobacco into the brown grass between two of Momma's coffee-can marigolds.

"That woman ain't nothing but mean," Darrell said. "I can't believe some of the things she gets away with saying to Momma."

Donnie Ray looked his brother up and down, from his tennis shoes to the fish hook in the bill of his seed store hat.

"Me neither," was all he could say.

M omma wanted to know who else was out there, standing in her living room.

"Oh everybody, I reckon." Donnie Ray held his Stetson at his belt. He kept a tidy distance between he and his momma.

"Is Tommy out there?"

Donnie Ray lowered his head. "Tommy died three years back, Momma."

His momma laughing is what got him to look up. She'd lost nearly everything to her except for that grin. She laughed so hard, she fell to a fit of coughing.

"I know he's dead," she said with a wink. "I'm just funning with you."

Donnie Ray did his best to smile. "They're all out there, Momma. Uncle Dave, Barbara…Uncle Branch…"

"Those kids?"

"They're out there."

Momma rolled her eyes.

"You don't like Branch's kids?"

She spoke slow all her life, so folks wouldn't miss anything. She spoke slower now. "Let me put it this way," she said. "If those ones are the future of this family, it's a good thing I'm headed for the door. I couldn't stand to watch it."

The skin tightened around Donnie Ray's lips.

"It's the morphine, son."

Donnie Ray nodded.

"I've never took so much as a drink my whole life," she said. "The only wine I ever drank was at church and I always felt like I'd need help back to my pew after. This morphine has me wishing I could go back and do things different."

"Oh? Like what?"

"For one thing, I wouldn't have waited to now to take morphine."

It was Donnie Ray's turn to laugh.

"I wouldn't have wasted so much time trying to get your sister into a college." His momma looked to the wall. "A lot of good that did me."

"Her husband takes good care of her."

"I reckon so."

Donnie Ray took a knee alongside the bed. He felt thirteen years old again. It was the same bed she'd shared with his daddy. He could remember standing in that very spot on Christmas mornings, begging them both to wake up so he could open presents. He could remember hiding beneath it when he played games with his big brother and sister. Or how his head had caught the edge of the frame one day when he and Darrell were rough-housing, and needed six stitches. The bed seemed smaller now, as did his mother inside of it.

"Want to know what else I would do different?"

He did. More than anything.

She licked her lips with a pale, purple tongue.

"Do you remember the night your daddy died?" she asked him.

"I never forgot it," said Donnie Ray. Were he the kind of guy to expound on things, he'd have told her he spent more than his fair share of time remembering it. How if he had three wishes, he'd go back to that sticky summer to wait behind the feed store where his daddy worked. He'd wait to catch those bastards that stuck him and left him to bleed out. He'd make them pay.

"I tried so hard to be a good woman," said Momma. "The way I was raised…they'd look down on us, much like I reckon they do now. Your grandfather was a rough-and-tumble sort and my mother, she…I worked so hard to make sure we didn't turn out like that. That's what everybody expected."

It took all he had for Donnie Ray to reach under that blanket and take his mother's bony wrist. There was very little warmth to her.

"But when I saw your father that night…"

Again, she fell to coughing. She'd worked herself up something fierce and Donnie Ray wondered if this was it.

"Momma, settle down. I'll run fetch Aunt—"

"You'll do no such thing," she said. "You'll sit right there and let me finish my story."

Donnie Ray returned to his knees. "Yes, ma'am."

"I'd had my suspicions." She looked to the ceiling. "I'd seen the way he smiled at her in church. I'd catch him whispering into the telephone late at night. Or taking the dog for extra long walks."

"Momma—"

"And I knew when all of a sudden he was coming home an hour later from work…"

Donnie Ray thought his chest would explode. His jaw hung on a loose hinge.

"When I pulled into the parking lot," said his momma, "I found them parked in his pickup truck. She had her face in his lap and I don't reckon I could stand the look on his face. His stupid, stupid face."

His momma opened her mouth wide and made a face like a fish on the riverbank, sucking air. It took more than a moment for Donnie Ray to realize she was mocking his father's orgasm.

"I didn't realize I was holding a steak knife until I'd already stuck him with it."

She let that sit a bit before she started up again.

"I got him a couple more times for good measure. That woman didn't know what was going on, she kept working his crank. Maybe she thought he bucked and hollered because she was that good, I don't know. I guess she got to wondering why all this blood was washing down over her, because she looked up to see me sticking him with the dinner knife and she wasted no time climbing out of that pickup."

Donnie's grip tightened around his mother's wrist. For years, he'd imagined the faces of the men who had killed his father. He'd seen them every time he'd gotten into a bar fight, or needed to defend himself from another inmate in the Yard. One night, he'd taken so many pills, he'd seen them in a girl he'd picked up at a truck stop and taken down an old service road.

Now, all he could think of was the sad look on his momma's face.

"Why are you telling me this, Momma?"

"I told you there was things I would have done different."

"You don't need to worry about that now, " he said. "None of that matters."

"But it does, son."

Donnie Ray waited for her to catch her breath.

"I ain't sorry I killed him," she said.

"Yes, ma'am."

"I'm more sorry I didn't kill her."

Donnie Ray looked into his mother's eyes. The lights were on, sure, but not for much longer. She drew herself upright.

"For months, I sat by that window in the living room. You know what they'd say about me?"

"That you were waiting for Daddy."

She nodded. "They said I'd lost my mind."

Donnie Ray remembered. She'd sit by the window, rub her fretting cloth between thumb and forefinger, and study the horizon. Once a kid in school said something about it and they'd had to peel Donnie Ray off him. Kid ate through a straw, but didn't talk shit about his momma anymore.

"I wasn't waiting for your daddy," she said. "I was waiting for the police. I thought any day that woman would break down and tell her husband what happened and soon they'd come to fetch me."

Donnie Ray dropped his head into his hands. He'd withstood some torture in his time, but nothing like his mother's deathbed.

"But that woman never broke down. She never told her husband, and they never came to arrest me. After a while, I started to wonder what kind of woman couldn't be bothered by what happened, and what your father saw in her."

She shuddered and fell quiet. Donnie Ray held his breath. He would have held it longer, had she not started up again.

"It got to where it was all I thought about, and here I lay." She looked her boy dead in the eye. "I want not to think about it ever again."

"There, there." He pat her wrist. "It's okay, Momma."

"It's not okay," she said. "Not in the slightest. I can't lay here dying knowing she still draws air. It will eat at me all the way to heaven."

"For all you know, she's long gone, Momma. How do you even

know she is still alive?"

His momma pulled a scrap of paper from beneath her blanket. It had been written with a shaky hand.

"This is her name and where she lives," said his momma. "And where you'll find her tonight."

Her arm felt warmer, and Donnie Ray had no idea if it was because his own blood had run cold.

"I can't ask your brother," she said. "He's a big old boy, sure, but he's sweet and simple."

"No...Momma—"

"Him and your sister. But you...you've carried with you a darkness I ain't seen in my other ones."

Donnie Ray wiped his face with a flat, sweaty palm.

"More than Darrell, more than Barbara..." It took all she had to manage the rest of her words. "You can see me to the door in peace."

He exhaled, and felt no further cause to stand.

When finally Donnie Ray's momma passed, it took nearly a week. One by one, the cars disappeared from the front lawn. They relocated across town to Bynum's, where the old man running the place agreed to set her into the ground next to their daddy.

They did it on a sunny day.

She'd asked for a simple box, but her family thought different. Barbara got her husband to throw in some extra money to send her out real fine. She wanted no fuss, but they reckoned her in no position to negotiate.

There, by the graveside, Donnie Ray knelt at the box for longer than he should have. He said his goodbyes, and not for the first time that week. When he rose to his feet, he found his brother Darrell and their Uncle Branch waiting for him.

Said Donnie Ray, "Boys…"

"We got a couple matters to discuss," said Uncle Branch.

Donnie Ray wore a brand new pair of slacks. He stuffed his fists into them.

"Momma left us the house," said Darrell. "All her things."

"Way that neighborhood's going," said Uncle Branch, "that ought to net a pretty penny."

"I don't want none of it," said Donnie Ray. "I've done fine on my own thus far."

"Now, Donnie Ray…" If Darrell had more to say, he kept it to himself. Instead, he turned to Uncle Branch for the words.

"It's probably best if you sat down with us and took a look at a few things."

Donnie Ray looked back at his momma's coffin. Over the hill waited two Mexican boys with shovels. They smoked cigarettes and waited for their day to end.

Uncle Branch said, "Last thing we need is for you to get down the road and change your mind."

"I won't."

"Because getting you on down the road is real important to us." Uncle Branch, feeling his oats. " Last thing we want to do is get in your way of it."

"I'm on my way."

On the way out, Donnie Ray touched the box they'd put her in. He thought back to when he was a kid. The last time his daddy signed him up for Little League. How he'd struck out to end the game and every kid made sport of him. How it was the only time he'd seen his daddy cry. And he thought back as well to the look on his momma's face after Donnie Ray'd shown the other fellas exactly what he could do with a baseball bat.

He'd thought about that look on her face his entire life.

He thought about it then at that fine box his brother and sister put her into, and reckoned they'd have plenty far to go in order to catch up to him.

Donnie Ray wasn't halfway back to his big rig when up came Darrell. He'd finally mustered the gumption, but kept a distance of ten, fifteen yards.

"Donnie Ray..." he called. "It ain't like you was there for her anyway."

Donnie Ray chewed on it some.

"Maybe," he said. He decided he'd stop by that neighbor lady's on the way out of town. It wouldn't take him longer than ten minutes. "But I'm here for her now."

A LOT PRETTIER (WHEN YOU SMILE)

Mistress commands me to kneel, so I kneel.

She demands I crawl across the floor on all fours, and I obey.

Mistress requires tribute, so I whip out my credit card. I pay. I use a separate bank account which Mistress ordered me to keep secret from my wife. This is how she prefers we transact, and I am happy to oblige.

Mistress rewards my tributes with downloads and expects me to watch them twice per day. Once upon waking, and again before I retire for the night. All day, I think about sneaking another peek, but I don't dare. Not without permission. That would make me a bad boy. Or, so says Mistress.

When Mistress says pay, I pay. She tells me when to get hard. She commands when I go down, down deeper, down deeper still. She tells me when to wake up. Three, two, one. Mistress snaps her finger and I am no more. Long gone. Out of breath and cleaning up the mess.

Mistress tells me to board a plane. She says take the red eye. Get in early, she says. Book a room, get cleaned up, then await further instructions.

I'm not a bad boy. Honest, I'm not. I'm just a squirrel, trying to find a nut. Or, at least, I was. Now, none of it matters a hill of beans because no matter where I am or what I'm doing—no matter if I'm singing hymns at church or having a catch with my son or fucking my wife—no matter anything at all, Mistress pops into my mind. She takes over. Her voice eases into my ear as if she's standing next to me, where she's never been, as Mistress and I have yet to meet in person.

Until tonight.

The room is lovely and I hope it pleases Mistress. She likes fine things. She enjoys her little tributes. Champagne. Caviar. Roses. I replaced the hotel linens with silky sheets I bought from a fancy online department store, ones that won't irritate Mistress' perfect skin. Once everything is just so, I take a seat in the high-backed chair and wait.

It isn't until hours later that my telephone rings. Her voice tickles the hairs of my ear, its timbre pokes into my scalp like tiny fingernails. Soon, she is inside me. Inside and outside, everywhere at once, holding me in the palm of her hand like a baby sparrow.

"What is your room number?"

"Four-oh-five."

And she squeezes tight her hand, which causes baby sparrow to wiggle, too dumb to buck or break, instead, left to squirm and squeal as that careful dying of the light narrows to pins, bright, tiny pins, getting smaller, smaller, smaller still until Mistress so kindly releases her fist and the bird, eyes yet to open, takes flight in fresh air.

The knock at the door.

Mistress wears up her hair. Mistress removes her jacket, then drops it to the floor. She does not wait for me to offer the champagne before she helps herself to a glass, knocks it back, then pours herself another. And why should she not help herself to as much as she wants? After all, doesn't it belong to her now?

Doesn't everything belong to Mistress?

"Do you want me to be happy?" she asks.

"Of course, Mistress."

"Do you promise me?"

"I swear to you, Mistress."

Still, this delivers me no satisfaction, for Mistress has yet to smile. Have I not pleased her? Are none of my efforts up to snuff? Would that I could burn down this entire hotel should Mistress find a solitary flaw, and I await her command to do so.

I tell her of the restaurants in the area, careful to remember the details of them all. Mistress' every fancy will be catered. Thai. French. Italian. Her wish is my command and I tell her so, but am still taken aback when she says,

"I'd prefer to stay in tonight. Wouldn't you?"

My only possible answer is, "Of course, Mistress. Then we shall stay in."

Still, the only smile she offers is faraway and fleeting. An afterthought. She takes a seat on the bed and unzips her black boots which climb all the way up to her lovely little knees. She removes her gloves. She unbuttons and unbuckles and soon she reclines on the bed in her brassiere and stockings and her cold, steel eyes and says to me:

"I'm so tired."

"Yes, Mistress."

"I'm so very, very tired and the only thing I want is rest."

"Yes, Mistress."

"And you want me to rest, don't you?"

I nod my head.

"I didn't hear you."

"Yes, Mistress," I say, quick as the lash. "I want you to rest."

She nods her head and turns her eyes elsewhere. Mistress is sad and I don't know how to please her. I am worthless. I am pitiful. I fight the urge to throw myself at her stocking feet and beg, plead, beseech her for instruction on how better to placate her, but she has yet to command me to speak, so I remain silent.

"You'll do as I say, won't you?"

"Of course, Mistress."

"Good." She licks her lips. "Then I want you to place both your hands around my throat."

I stand fast. I blink my eyes. I blink them again.

"Did you hear me?"

"Yes…of course, Mistress. It's just that—"

"You are falling deeper," she says. "Deeper and deeper still. Three, two, one—" she snaps her fingers "—and you are mine."

The air quits my lungs, but what good is it to breathe? My feet no longer touch the floor, because nothing is more inconsequential than the laws of the universe. I belong to Mistress. Nothing more bears any claim. She is my sun, my moon, my stars, and my sky. Mistress. Mis-Tress.

"You will do whatever I say, won't you?"

"Yes, Mistress."

"Because your mind belongs to me, your body belongs to me, and you belong to me."

"Yes, Mistress."

"And when I tell you to do something, you will do it. Correct?"

"Yes, Mistress."

"Good." She tilts her head further back, arching her chin to the ceiling. "Now I want you to put your hands around my throat."

My fingers touch behind her small, delicate neck. Her skin, oh so warm. Her throat tightens as she swallows once. For a moment, something flickers behind her eyes, but she is quick to blink it away.

"Mistress…" I can't do it. "Mistress, I…"

"Now I want you to squeeze me tight." She licks her lips. "And no matter what, you are not to stop. Not until I say so."

"Mistress…" My fingers contract. My palms press flat. My thumbs dig deeper into her sweet flesh. "Mistress, please…"

"I'm so tired," she says. "And my children…they don't…they can't…"

Mistress can no longer manage the air from her lungs. Her trachea convulses. Beneath me, her beautiful torso twists, her hips buck against me. Her precious mouth opens, but offers her so little respite. Her eyes remain fast upon my own. Meanwhile, I'm screaming at her, shouting, pleading at the top of my lungs to *release me pull the trigger say the goddamn safe word*, but no sound comes from my mouth as my hands wring tighter the life from her. All the while, her eyes… her eyes…

Mistress is frightened, Mistress is sad, Mistress is angry. Mistress is fading. Mistress is no longer struggling. My hands squeeze tighter and tighter still but nothing, no one, not even Mistress can stop the tears streaming from my cheeks. Mistress turns blue. Mistress lies still. Mistress breathes no more.

Mistress is gone.

It would take ages for me alone to pry my fingers from Mistress' throat, but, fortunately, I don't have to. However long it takes…there is a maid screaming and shouting, then the hotel manager. He slaps at my back and yanks at my shoulders. Soon, the police. Paramedics. All of them struggle like mad to free her from my grip like a vise and yes, soon enough, they manage. Soon enough they rip her from me and pin me to the ground and restrain me with handcuffs, and when they stand me upright and face me to her, still lying on the bed, over and over they ask me how, how can I do that, how in all that is good and holy could I live with myself and what do I see lying on the bed before me? Not the forgotten corpse of my Mistress who stands proxy for all I could ever love or long for in this world. Not her perfect skin turned pale or her throat rubbed raw. All I see lying on the bed before me, curled in lips long gone purple, is her smile.

Her smile.

And that baby bird, soaring high in the updrafts, never again to touch feet to ground because Mistress is smiling, Mistress is pleased, Mistress has finally found happiness.

And so then have I.

LET'S BE AWFUL

1

Vagina.

Pussy.

Twat.

Gash.

There are many names for what I have between my legs.

Many more than what can be counted here. It's like the word snow to an Eskimo, I reckon.

Except ain't nobody gone to war over snow. It's no one thing, either. At times, it's very warm down yonder. Other times, there's no colder place on the planet. Sometimes it's soft, still other times it can be awful hard. I've worn it both bald and bushy. There are days when no earthly rose smells sweeter. Then, there are the other days...

I'm what most dudes would call hot, at a brief distance or a quick glance. Step closer and you'll find a crook at the tip of my nose from a car accident many, many years ago. Or a scar from a long ago cat scratch. Or freckles, if that matters. Step even closer and you might catch some of my points of view, which have been known to rankle.

For these reasons, and more, I've found it best to keep folks at arm's length. Every so often, I let someone in. And every time, I've come to regret it.

This past April was no exception.

2

The guy's name is John. I know him from work. He'll do damn near anything I ask him, especially if I ask it while I'm leaned over the beer cooler. I give this guy a peek of my pooper, then ask him to do my sidework. He'll fold a hundred napkins if I wear that one shirt which shrunk some in the wash. I ain't filled a sugar caddy since last summer.

But we're not at the restaurant and I'm not asking him to marry ketchup bottles. I'm asking him to break my ex-boyfriend's nose. He finally got the job done with a baseball bat, after realizing his fists weren't cutting the mustard.

The ex, all the while, choking on tears and screaming to high heaven. He's got a lot to say, I'd imagine, but who can make it out with the bubbles blowing out the crack in his nose. The busted front teeth. The split lip. I get some of it—

bitch whore shit fuck cunt

—but it don't matter, not a bit, unless he tells me the password to his PornHub account. The one hosting that goddamn video of me and this piece of shit going at it over on yonder bed beneath yonder

Star Wars poster.

"I don't want to have to ask you again," I tell him. "I'd rather have John ask you."

John hitches the bat and old dude nearly falls out of the chair we've duct taped him to. He squiggles and squirms, still having at it—

slut fuck shit piss fire

—and I tell John he ought to maybe fire one across his kneecaps.

3

I only seen my daddy cry twice in my life. Once when they put my momma in the ground, and the other when I came home to do some laundry and found him hunched over his desk, in front of his computer.

Guess what was on the screen?

Guess what I was doing to stupid peckerwood here.

I should have my head examined, letting him take a video. *But you're so sexy. You got no idea what you do to me. I want to think about you all the time, even when you ain't around.* I don't even ask what that's supposed to mean. He's got nice hair. He's usually pretty quiet, which gave me plenty to wonder about. Sometimes that's all it takes. Don't judge. It gets him hot and that gets me hot and so he positions his cellphone on the bedside table against the lamp, props a Bible so it don't topple, then promises three more times *won't nobody ever see it, trust me,* and shit, I better trust him because we only used a rubber that first time, so fast forward four shitty months and there's my daddy, sobbing at his PC, my legs on the screen in front of him, hiked high around this shitbird's shoulders.

I take the bat out of John's hands.

I'm going to get that password.

4

Leviathan.

The A is made with the little at-symbol we use for emails.

Clever.

He quit wailing a while back. That don't mean he ain't got plenty to say.

"Lemme guess…" He's eyeballing John now. "You two are just friends, right?"

"Shut your mouth," John tells him.

"No, no, no. I get it. I was there." Fucktard spits blood and one of his teeth skitters across the floor. "She pushes together her tits with her elbows when she talks to dudes. Why do you think she gets better tips than everybody else? Why do you think everybody asks to sit in her section?"

John looks over, as if to ask permission for another go with the Louisville Slugger. I'm too busy to answer, logging on, tapping out the password, scrolling, scrolling, scrolling. This piece of shit…little dicked motherfucker… Did I tell you about that first time? No, I didn't, because I'm not some miserable, fucked up shit running my mouth all the time, but there we are, having at it on the couch after he finally got drunk enough to make a move and I practically have to *rape him* to wrest him from his britches, and I'm thinking wow, this guy can't be all bad because he heads immediately south, doing due diligence, and it's running through my head…

…maybe he's the one…

…no, he's down there, stalling for time while he tugs at it, trying to wake it up, but it won't wake up, he's gotten himself too drunk. I may have plenty awful to say about him, but he's committed, I'll give him that. He's got a little blue pill tucked away in his wallet for just the occasion—not a rubber, mind you, but a little blue pill, this ratbastard piece of...—but he says swallowing it will take too long so he crunches it up, chops a line and snorts it up his nose, then asks if I'd like another drink while we wait. But I deal with this because for some reason I feel I deserve it for some sin real or imagined and—

There it is. The fucking video. Click the menu box next to the title. The title. *Big Stud Drills Horny Teen.* Teen. I'm twenty-fucking-eight, you pervert dirtbag. Scroll down to the bottom. Delete. Click that shit.

Permanently delete your video? This cannot be undone.

You bet your ass it can't.

5

"She wasn't the prettiest thing in the world, but she was paying."

We're almost out the door when it hits us. His mouth. If we leave him duct taped to the chair, he'll hoot and holler the rest of the night until some well-meaning neighbor kicks in the door and sets him free. No, better he cool his heels a bit before loosing himself sometime in the morning.

I grab the roll of duct tape and kneel to his head. I grab both cheeks with my hand to turn him upward.

"One day," he says, "your ankles will thicken."

"Beg pardon?"

"You were born white trash, and you'll forever be white trash."

I smile down at him, because honestly I'm running short on

options.

I remind myself that, at one time or another, he'd been mighty sweet. I keep that at the forefront of all thought as I yank a sturdy strip of tape from the silver roll.

"You won't never make nothing of yourself," he growls. "The best chance you ever had of being someone…honey, you just deleted it."

I slap the tape across his lips before he can say anything else, because I got Zen. I got peace on earth running out my ears and plenty to share and under no circumstance am I going to let this guy do any more damage to my chi. He's a cancer upon my spirit and, from this day forth, I will give him no more power, just so long as he shuts his fucking mouth first, so I yank another strip and another. Then another. Fuck it, I stretch the roll round and round his head and, it's muffled, but he's still hollering behind seven layers of tape, eight, nine…fuck this guy, ten. Still going so he gets a punch to the throat then I'm slapping his head, making fists, punching, I stand and put my toe into his ribs two, three times, then I'm kicking high in the air because John's got me in a bear hug, pulling me off this piece of shit, but I'm calm, dammit, I'm calm…I'm chill.

"Put me down."

"Are you going to quit kicking him?"

"Put me down, John."

He gives a minute but he puts my feet back to earth. It's then we notice old boy here…peckerwood on the floor…

He's no longer breathing.

6

John's got it all figured out.

"He must have choked on the duct tape," he says. He's finally given up trying to peel it off old boy's face. He's closed his eyes with his thumb and forefinger. He's sat down next to him, head in his hands.

"We're so screwed."

I pull my cell phone from my pocket. I run my fingers along its protective case.

"When the cops find him…man, we're so screwed."

I thumb open my menu screen. Camera app. Click it alive.

"Cops ain't going to find him," I tell John.

"What do you mean they ain't going to find him? Somebody's going to come looking for him. And even if he's a piece of shit like you say and don't have any friends, the neighbors will smell him after a day or two and somebody's bound to—Hey, what are you doing?"

Click. Click. Click.

"You're going to help me one more time," I tell him.

"Help you? Hey…quit taking pictures. Help you with what?"

"We're going to bury him."

"The hell we're not. I ain't going nowhere near—Hey…I'm serious…quit taking pictures."

I thumb shut the screen. I pocket the cell phone. I take two steps backwards.

"Yes, you are, John. You're going to do exactly what I tell you. You will, or you will be in a whole mess of trouble, and I don't think you want that, do you?"

7

I'll never again be daddy's little girl.

I've accepted that. Moving on…

He didn't need to say that last bit. About being white trash...I didn't grow up with much, sure, and just because I happen to be from the South and talk like I do...there's no need for all that kind of chatter.

No need at all.

Like I said, I may not have much, but I make use of what was given me, because I know there'll come a time when I'm given nothing ever again.

Like John.

I'll make use of him, so long as he keeps doing what I ask him.

Know what else I'll make use of?

Brains.

Smarts.

Moxy.

Know-how.

They got a lot of words for what I have between my ears. And trust me, if you had a lick of sense, you'd steer clear of a woman like me, one who knows how to use them.

IT'S MORNING AGAIN IN LAKE CASTOR

They pulled Jessi Spangler's body out of Blood Holler on a dark, grey morning in September of 1985. She'd been half buried just deep enough to discourage the coyotes and buzzards, and the Lake Castor police might never have found her had they not received an anonymous tip in a phone call the night previous. The girl was seventeen years old, beautiful, and very popular in high school.

She'd been in that hole for two weeks.

I know because I helped put her there.

I didn't kill Jessi Spangler, but I know who did. Hell, half of Lake Castor knew who did it. You could step into Grady's Barbecue on Broad Street or Charlie Fetter's barber shop downtown—or anywhere else, for that matter—and be hard pressed not to hear folks whispering behind cupped palms about *That Dix Boy* or *Those Brothers* or *That Family Out There*. Conspiracy theories ran wild and the police ran

186

up one tree and down another, but at the end of the day, nobody doubted Randy Dix had been the one to choke the life out of that girl.

What they didn't know was what to do about it. Randy and his brother Billy didn't have much by the way of parents. Their momma took off a couple years back with some guy in a Jeep Scrambler and never looked back. Their daddy fell simple after a bad batch of shine. The boys and their sister did all right for themselves thanks to a lack of God and a connection with some black boys up in Baltimore. For years, folks blamed the steady uptick in production at yonder mill because of what they smoked, snorted, or shot, coming from their little trailer on the edge of town.

The police could do little about it either. Time and again they'd sent an officer to roust them, but the Dix boys were cagey. They had hideaways all over town where they kept their stashes, and usually enjoyed a good twenty minutes head start on the cops, because they always knew they were coming. They hauled both brothers to the station several times after they dug Jessi Spangler out of the hollow, but never found anything they could pin on them. Both boys stuck to their story and neither showed signs of cracking. To keep folks at ease, they'd roll down to the Back Back where the blacks lived and bust a few heads, say they were running down a few new clues. Nothing ever turned up.

Alvin Spangler went on a tirade and swore before God and everyone that he would not rest until he found justice for his little girl. Night after night, he'd go on a toot then stand before everyone at the 809 or Dixie's and blame folks for turning their backs on his baby girl. He'd point his finger toward the other side of town and say he had half a mind to go down there and seek justice on his own. After a while, even he grew tired of it, and went back to work at the mill like everybody else.

Eventually, things settled down and folks quit talking about it. They knew the Dix boys sold drugs and they knew there was little they could do about it. They knew—more than likely—Randy Dix killed the Spangler girl. And they knew he'd never be punished.

What they also didn't know was *why*.

"It was a sex thing." Noah Spencer, eighteen years old in 1985. Dropped out of Lake Castor High his sophomore year. He drove a Z/28, held the Galaga high score in the arcade at 7-Eleven, and was best friends with Billy Dix.

He also had been there the night Jessi Spangler died.

"That girl… Folks think she was one of the good ones, but that's far from the truth. She took up with Dave Albany and he was what… twenty-two, twenty-three? What do you think they did together, go to church? If you ask me, that girl was a freak."

Noah only put to words what everybody was thinking anyway: "If she was such a good girl, then what was she doing over there to begin with?"

"The girl was there to score." Jaron Little, eighteen years old. Black. Once caught four touchdowns in a single game against Whitfill, yet entertained no scholarship offers from area colleges. Instead of carrying the pigskin at UVA, he carried ounces of cocaine from the Dix Brothers to the Back Back. "You could see it in her eyes, man. She'd near-abouts do anything to get it."

"It wasn't for her; it was for me." Dave Albany, twenty-four years old. LCHS Class of '79. Laid pipe at the mill since the day he received his diploma. Parked his Celica across the street every day after school and jammed hair metal while waiting to pick up his girlfriend. "It's all my fault. I work hard, so I play hard, and I wanted some for the weekend. I told her it was real important to me to score. I told her—" He cleared his throat and steadied himself before continuing. "I didn't want to be seen around those boys, and I knew she went to school with a couple of them, so I sent her to fetch it for me. I had no idea it would end up..."

Dave, too, would eventually put it behind him. At Jessi's funeral, he sat with her best girlfriends, on account of her parents would let him nowhere near the rows reserved for loved ones. Allison Wabash particularly took a shine to comforting him, and soon the Celica returned to its 3:30 vigil across the street from school.

Still, he was adamant: "It wasn't a sex thing. She loved me. We loved each other. If she had sex with one of those boys, then she was drugged or raped, one."

"It was contractual...I mean, it was constru—I mean...she was willing," Noah said. "Maybe she didn't want to do it, but when push came to shove, she handled her business like a champ. She got it done."

"She didn't want to do it," Jaron said. "But she did it."

"Fuck yeah, she did it." Billy Dix, twenty-four years old. Second oldest of four children by Wayne and Phyllis Dix. Drove an old Ford pickup and lived in a trailer on the far side of town. Estimated to be the second or third wealthiest citizen in Lawles County. "Randy's a maniac, for real."

As a rule, no one talked about Randy and Jessi in front of Billy Dix. However, from time to time, Billy would get zonked to the max and start bragging on his brother.

"An apple don't fall far from its tree."

Billy himself had a reputation. Folks say he's the reason why the school cafeteria used plastic cutlery, and why James Hampton had that scar down the middle of his hand. They say he beat the Mexican out of Hector Martinez. Word has it if the cops looked long and hard enough, they'd find plenty more bodies up and down Blood Holler, all of them folks who got on the wrong side of Billy or his daddy or their other brother Ricky.

But if Billy's chest puffed over what Randy done to that little girl, then it was more on account of Randy's reputation than his own. You see, Randy wasn't known around Lake Castor for being brutal. Where words like *violent* and *terrible* were often linked to the Dix clan, Randy got good grades. Randy stayed after school to study, not for detention. The youngest Dix boy had a gentle side to him.

Which was why his older brother hated him.

I got there after ten that night. You could count on four hands the places I'd rather be in Lake Castor than the Dix trailer, but none of them sold good snow. By the time the shit made it to the Back Back, it'd been stepped on so many times and, these days, the blacks preferred to smoke it in pipes. I was a long way off from that.

Me? I got the taste for it one night after a Lake Castor Tiger game. Everybody spazzed after a buzzer beater in overtime took down Tucker and we didn't want the night to end. Lucky for us, Mal Henry had a taste he scored off some seniors and we kept the party going all weekend. By Sunday we were coach potatoes, zoning out to MTV, brains melting to puddles on the floor, but what a weekend.

I never looked back.

Sure, I had some issues, but I'm not going to make it an episode of *Donahue*. Me and mom didn't get along, my grades had gone to shit... I could play a little guitar and me and a couple boys liked to jam in the garage from time to time, but only recently had I come to realize it would never be anything serious, and, best case scenario, I could hope for a full-time job at the mill when I wrapped up things at the school. Grass and booze were baby food compared to what sweet release I got from the coke, and where better to get it than the source.

No matter how much it sucked going to the source.

The Dix trailer never had any shortage of drama. If someone was lucky, the only thing they left with was hurt feelings. Mostly, it was a tattoo or something pierced. Billy grew bored rather quick and often needed something to keep entertained. He didn't understand folks wanted convenience from a drug dealer: A quick in-and-out was asking far too much. He had shit stashed all over the woods around his trailer so a quick raid from the police would produce nothing. All he asked was that you wait a minute while someone ran to fetch it.

And while you waited, why not stick around a bit for the show?

The night Jessi Spangler died, all I wanted was a gram. I told myself over and over I didn't have time for Billy Dix's bullshit. If he made a production out of it and things lasted longer than one side of a cassette tape, I was out. With or without the shit. I wasn't in the mood for it.

Man...

"Shhh, shhh."

Noah Spencer answered the door with a finger over the shit-eatingest grin I'd ever seen. He led me by the arm into the trailer and closed the door behind him. Also in the room: Jaron Little, Bryce

Franklin, and big bad Billy Dix. All of them tried their best to keep stifled the laughter as they listened intently to the silence in the room.

"What's going on?" I asked.

"Shhh!"

Billy held up a finger, then tiptoed across the shag to a closed bedroom door. He put his ear to the wood paneling and listened.

"What's going on?" I whispered.

Jaron Little looked none too pleased. He rolled his eyes and shrugged his shoulders. A thin sheen of sweat slicked his forehead and he hitched a thumb toward Noah and Bryce, giggling on the couch.

"These honkies," he said. "It's always something."

"I ain't heard nothing for five minutes," whispered Billy.

"Maybe he's licking her snatch," Noah whispered back.

Billy grabbed a cassette case—*Invasion of Privacy*—and threw it at Noah's head. Missed. Shattered against the coffee table.

"My brother ain't no faggot," he hissed.

"I didn't say—"

This time, Dokken caught him in the ear.

"Say it again and I'll cut off your head."

Billy quit wearing shirts in April. He spent most days lifting barbells under the carport next to his brother's broke down Mustang. He drew on himself with India ink and a safety pin. He'd gotten better with it over the past couple months, but still he wasn't Nagel. He'd pierced himself in nearly every imaginable spot on his body, and then some that weren't.

If Billy said *shut up or I'll cut off your head*, you shut up.

"If tonight proves anything to you barf bags," he growled, "it's that my brother ain't no faggot. You hear anybody at that school say it and I want you to bring me their name."

When he put his ear again to the door, I turned to Jaron and asked what in good hell was going on.

"You know that white girl Jessi from school?" He motioned to his head. "The one with the big hair?"

He could have narrowed it down a little more, but I nodded.

"She rolled past, looking to score a little toot. Only Billy raised the price on her and she didn't have enough. He said she could work it off and she told him to gag her with a spoon. He said he'd gag her with more than that and if she didn't do what he said, he'd make sure she couldn't score nothing else in Lake Castor."

"Lame."

"For sure. He said she had to pick any one person here and spend ten minutes with them in the bedroom, then she could get the coke."

"She got to pick?"

Jaron shook his head. "Man, I can't tell you how scared I was that she was going to pick me. I can't have that shit right now. I got too many problems without some coke-starved white girl."

"Wait. You're telling me she picked Randy?"

"That's what I'm saying."

The math didn't add up. "Really?" I repeated. "She picked *Randy*?"

"Hey, man, maybe she thought it was the one dude in the room who—"

Billy hissed from the door: "Will you two fairies shut your yaps?"

We did.

"For real, Billy," said Bryce, "maybe we ought to open the door and check on them."

A new grin took hold of Billy. Nothing could send a person off their lunch easier than a new smile from Billy Dix.

"Oh, that's bonus," he said. "That's fucking grand."

With Noah and Bryce saddling alongside him, he put his hand to the knob. Again, he held up a finger to shush the room, and with the flourish of a magician, threw open the door.

W hen the cops found her, nobody knew what to make of it. She'd been stripped naked and thrown in the bottom of a shallow hole, then covered with dirt, leaves, and muck.

"By all accounts, she had been a very pretty girl," said Deputy Lorne Axel of the Lawles County Sheriff's Office. "You couldn't have told as such by what we dug out of that holler."

"There was blunt force trauma to the back of her head," said Graham Maloney, the county coroner. "But most likely what killed her was strangulation."

Some of the other police talked about the smell, or what time and the elements do to certain parts of the body after death sets in. Some even talked about how long a hike it had been to get to the grave and how much further it'd be carrying a dead girl. Not Lorne Axel. He'd gone to school with Jessi's daddy Alvin, and when it came up in discussion, he'd look up or down, but never in anyone's eye.

"It's a damn waste," was all he'd add.

W hat the hell did you do?"

Randy was inconsolable. He'd huddled himself like a ball in the corner of his bedroom, knees tucked beneath his chin. His face had run red from bawling, and his shirt had been ripped to tatters. His chest looked like it had been worked by a bobcat.

"She wouldn't shut up," he said through the sobs. "I told her to shut the fuck up and she wouldn't shut up."

He looked to the center of the room.

"Why wouldn't you shut up?"

I remember my first thought was, *Oh, that Jessi.* How I'd thought the whole time it was Jessi Carroll in the room with Randy.

No.

They'd meant the other Jessi.

They meant the one who sprayed maybe three different kinds of hairspray into her hair every morning. The one who kept extra purple cans in her locker to freshen up between classes. The one from my third period history class last year, who sometimes would have at me in the hall, and sometimes wouldn't. The one who dressed preppy and had eyes the color of a summer lawn.

That Jessi.

The one lying on Randy's floor with eyes gone cloudy and neck twisted at an unnatural angle. Her tongue lolled half out of her head and a light froth of foam gathered at the corner of her lips. One of her legs propped against a small beer fridge in the corner. Her hands balled to fists. The skin around her throat had been rubbed purple and she wore a polka-dotted skirt which now bunched around her ankles. I tried—tried real hard—not to look, but my eyes went all the way up her legs to where she'd quit shaving and how—

Jaron made a break for it. He bolted like a rocket and cleared half the living room before Billy Dix shut him down with nothing but his voice.

"Don't move, boy," Billy growled.

Jaron's eyes liked to pop out of his skull. "Look, Billy, man…this shit ain't got nothing to do with me. You don't understand—"

"I understand you're about to run out of a trailer where there's a white girl dead on the floor."

"I got walk-ons next week at State," Jaron pleaded. "I got nothing to do with this shit and you know it, man."

"You got everything to do with this, boy." Billy yanked him back into the room and closed the door behind them. "All of you do."

Jaron never made the team at State. He was faster than anyone else and certainly had the hands. Jaron could light up a room with his smile and couldn't nobody smooth talk the ladies better. Somebody somewhere at that university didn't think he had what it took to hide his grades, and he came back to Lake Castor to run coke for his cousin.

Two months after we dropped Jessi Spangler in that hole, he turned up dead in a creekbed, shot twice through the chest. It was big news, on account of how big a star he'd been for the football team.

"It was all that shit he was driving into the Back Back," said my daddy after reading about it in the paper. "Cocaine is real bad among the blacks."

"It's a shame he couldn't just say no," my mother added.

"I heard it was because somebody wanted his shoes," said a kid in class. "They're always shooting each other for their shoes."

"So long as they keep it on that side of town."

At no time did the cops bust any heads when it came to Jaron Little. Nor did anyone ask questions. One day it was big news, then the next it was forgotten.

"Best to let them sort it out on their own," said an old man at the barber shop where I got my hair cut.

"They say they want to be treated equal," said one person to another in the supermarket checkout. "But you don't see white folks acting like that to one another, do you?"

Two months later, Noah Spencer drove his Z/28 into the concrete wall at Old Man McCarthy's place going about fifty miles per hour. While he lay in a closed casket, I sat in a funeral pew with Bryce Franklin. It was the first time we'd spoken since that night.

"You and me," he said in a low whisper.

"What do you mean?"

"Out of all the people who buried that girl," he said, "you and me are the only ones still alive."

He smiled when he said it, so I shrugged it off.

But one thing bothered me: Billy and Noah had been thick as thieves since grade school and Billy was nowhere to be found at the funeral.

"It's because him and Noah were super-tight," Bryce said, much later. "He didn't want nobody to see him cry."

"I hear it's because the cops put the screws to him over the Spangler girl," said Welch Thompson, another guy we knew.

"He can't take a shit without three deputies wiping his ass," said yet another.

Still…

Me?

I got worse with the coke. However, I didn't want to go around the Dix house for it anymore. Instead, I rolled down to the

Back Back to talk to Anton or G-Cru or Smooth Baby Pop. I went up to the hills to see the Mullins crew, who everybody knew cut that shit with rat poison. I even scored a couple grams off Mr. Canary, the theater teacher, who needed a couple bucks to tide him over before his paycheck.

I did nearly everything in my power to keep from rolling back over to the Dix house, until the day I had to roll back over to the Dix house.

I came up the gravel rock path to the carport on yonder side of the Dix trailer. I found Randy bent beneath the hood of his Mustang, where he'd been for the better part of six months. He'd surrounded himself with posters of Heather Thomas and Kelly LeBrock and Catherine Bach. He'd wiped oil and grease alongside his cheekbones and neck. He'd worked a good spackling of sweat down his back.

"Billy's not here."

I didn't look him in the eye the night we put Jessi Spangler into that hollow. Nor did I that February afternoon beneath his carport.

"He said I could talk to you or your sister, one."

Randy wiped grease from a socket wrench. "You here to score?"

I nodded.

Randy wiped his hands with a sooty towel and led me in through the back door.

The first line leveled me out. It had been a while since I'd had shit that good straight up the nose. The second one got me where I wanted to be. I considered a third, but I needed to save something for when finally I got the fuck out of there.

Randy popped open a beer from his small fridge and offered me one. I sat on the couch in his bedroom and stared at the spot where we'd found Jessi Spangler all those months ago. My leg shook like the dickens and it took both hands for me to calm it.

"I really don't think I should stay—"

"Have one."

I did.

"You don't come around much anymore."

"Well…"

On his wall: posters of Whitesnake. Motley Crue. The poster for *Heavy Metal*. Susan Anton in a red swimsuit. Loni Anderson. The cast of *Charlie's Angels*.

"I don't see you much at school anymore," I told him. "I heard you dropped out."

"You heard?" Randy replaced his wry grin with a furrowed brow. "What good is school going to do anyone in Lake Castor?"

I tried to think of an answer, but instead, I choked up another line off the back of his *Pyromania* cassette case.

"I know what the president said…*It's morning again in America.*" He set his beer down on one of his stereo speakers. He'd hardly drank a drop. "Maybe it's morning in America, but it ain't morning in Lake Castor. The goddamn sun is setting."

"What are you going to do if you don't go to school?"

Randy turned to me. "I'm going to be just like my brother."

I didn't mean to laugh. I'd been running my finger along the back the cassette case and sucking it clean. I stopped myself and apologized, but the damage had been done. Randy looked at me with several shades of *et tu* shrouding his face.

"I didn't mean—"

"You don't think I can be like Billy?" he asked.

"Randy, I—"

"Go ahead, say it." Randy hitched his button-flys at the waist. He squared his shoulders. "You don't think I got what it takes to be a Dix."

"I didn't say that. I—"

"You don't remember what I done to that girl?" Randy paced the floor. "You don't remember how I done that to her with my bare hands?"

I didn't want to hear another word. I wanted to clap both hands over my ears and shut out the noise. I wanted to run free of that trailer and not stop until I'd reached town. I wanted to do a great many things to keep from hearing about that night, but instead I fixed my eyes upon a collection of empty Sundance Sparkler bottles and kept them there.

"It was so simple," Randy shouted. "She didn't want to be in here and neither did I. She could have picked any guy in the room. I did what I was supposed to, so why couldn't she? Instead, she kept talking about me and her were the same. Over and over, she's saying, *We both got secrets, Randy. We both hide who we really are.*"

"Randy...I don"t—"

"I told her to shut up. Just do what we were sent back here to do before my brother—" Randy eyeballed the door to the living room like someone might hear. "Just shut up and do it, but she kept wanting to talk. She kept wanting to say how we're the same. Guess what? We ain't the same. One of us is alive and the other one..."

If I laid out another line—even a tiny one—I'd only be left with two or three skinny rails for later. If I saved it, I'd start a heavy comedown and I'd need more to kickstart me again. But if I did it now, I'd be down in the Back Back at all hours, howling through the streets for more until—

"She didn't know shit."

I shook my head, then nodded it. Then shrugged my shoulders.

Randy watched me shake out a little more dust onto the back of the Def Leppard cassette. I scraped together a line with the edge of my driver's license, then tooted it up my skull with a rolled up two dollar bill. I sat back on the couch and watched his ceiling fan oscillate.

Randy took a seat on the couch next to me. He smelled of sweat and motor oil.

"I'm like my brother, goddammit."

Without looking to him, I said, "I know you are."

"Just like him."

I nodded my head again.

"When my brother wants something," he said, "he reaches out and takes it."

"That's what you should do."

"Really?"

I nodded my head again.

Randy grabbed me by the cheeks and pulled me to his mouth. He tasted of corn chips. His tongue reached me well before his lips and he used it to shove aside my lips and make his way inside. He was half on top of me, swinging a leg over my lap and pinning me to the couch. He panted through his nose, blowing hot air across the stubble of my face.

"Ran—"

I wasn't much, thanks to the drugs. I tried to muscle him off me, but he had me by a few pounds. When did he put on pounds? He held tight to my face and I could feel his stiff cock against my rib cage as he positioned himself atop me and I wondered if this was how it was going to happen, if this was where my life would change, if this was e line of fucking demarcation, and the tears burned hot against my alls.

opened my mouth wide to scream, but that only let him further into me.

When the garage door opened, Randy hopped off me and pulled his pants taut at the front. He raced to the opposite side of the room and pretended to fuss with the cassette deck. Billy Dix wandered in, smoking a Winston and eyeing the two of us.

"What are you homos doing?" he asked.

"Kurt came by for some coke," Randy said, half out of breath.

"Did he get it?"

Randy nodded.

Billy looked to me. "You need anything else?"

I didn't trust my own voice. Instead of saying a word, I nodded my head.

"Then get the fuck out of here."

I did.

Man...did I ever.

Bryce Franklin ran his motorcycle into a telephone pole. He was still alive when they loaded him into the ambulance, but somewhere on the trip to the hospital in Tucker, he died.

"I heard he told the paramedics it was Billy Dix who done it," said Harold Creamer, a kid from school. "I heard he talked the whole way, but ain't none of it good in a court of law, since he had a brain injury."

"I heard they ran his motorcycle into the telephone pole."

"I heard it was because he was about to go to the cops over the Spangler girl."

"I heard…"

Honestly, it didn't matter what anyone else heard. Never did anybody in this town ever get a damn thing right. To them, it's always guessing.

Know what I heard?

I heard a branch break outside my bedroom window. I heard a car start somewhere down the street. Sometimes I hear the *tick, tick, tick* of a time bomb, and I spend the rest of the evening wondering when it's going to go off. I hear silent footsteps behind me, wherever I go.

But I got this sneaking feeling I won't hear it for long.

LOVE THAT DON'T QUIT

One minute, you're at the Dollar Store, inspecting cost-effective cleaning supplies. Next minute, you're sitting rigid in a straight-backed chair at a table finely dressed. Top-dollar cutlery. Unchipped china. The smell of something freshly hunted and roasted from a kitchen on the other side of the wall. Brief flashes of the woman cooking, singing "Goodnight, My Love," perhaps a bit off-key.

Have you been drugged?

You catch flashes of her as she crosses the kitchen, from one side to the other. As she clangs and scrapes and gathers, you check out the rest of the room. Look for a quick egress. Door, just over your shoulder. Door to your right.

But...

She enters the room. Blonde...once. Still holding fast to her figure, which long ago abandoned her. You imagine she frittered away the best of her savings for the makeup job plastered upon her face. Still, you'd find no fault in yourself for fancying her. Not tonight, at least.

As soon as you remember how you got there.

"I couldn't remember if you liked chicken or ham," she says in a sing-song voice. "So I made both."

You blink two or three times. You know her? How much time passed between here and the Dollar Store? Sure, you drink your fair share, but…

Speaking of, she hands you a bourbon. Rocks. Splash of water.

"Just like you like it," she says, as if reading your mind.

You shake off a shiver, then swallow. Say: "Do we know each other?"

Her lips purse, as if she'd just sucked a lemon, but only for a moment. As if changing a song on the radio, her smile returns. Dead, distant smile.

"Who really knows anyone?" she says. She sets the drink in front of you and you sip carefully from it. "Especially after all this time."

"What, did we used to screw?"

Not your best joke, sure. You can tell by the way her fingers squeeze into fists that maybe she doesn't appreciate your sense of humor. She closes her eyes. She counts to ten.

"I'm just kidding with you," you say.

Still, she does not laugh.

You tell her, "It's a joke. An ice breaker. You know, one time I was talking to a girl in a bar, and she asks do I remember her. I ask her did we used to screw. She got all mad, and you know, it turned out we did. Not only we did, but previous to that, she had been a, you know…her inclinations swung towards the ladies."

She lowers her head and shakes it. Your blood runs cold.

"Wait a minute," you say. "That wasn't you, was it?"

"No," she says through her teeth. "That wasn't me."

"Of course not."

"I wish…" She stops herself, before starting again. "I wish…"

Her fingers unclench. She opens her eyes.

Again, she smiles.

"You're being silly," she says. "Of course we know each other."

"From where?"

"We've got plenty of time to catch up over dinner," she says as she kisses the top of your head. She returns to the kitchen, saying over her shoulder, "I'm almost through in here, so enjoy your drink. I'll only be a moment."

Windows along the far wall. Curtained. Just beyond, it's dark outside, which strikes you funny, as it was daylight when last you remember things. Back at the Dollar Store.

"Excuse me?" you call toward the kitchen. "Can you remind me how long you've been cooking?"

She ducks her head around the corner. She laughs at a joke only she understands, then returns to her work.

You've seen that look before. The one in her eyes. That smile. Maybe not on her specifically, but in women. Crazy bitches. That moment a chick goes from something mysterious to something… *other*. When she first realizes that she can't have you, but why not? She gets everything else she wants, so why should you be any different? That look that says everything she does is justified. The trips past your house. The phone calls well into the night. The following you here and there. The key scratches on your car.

You've found yourself in enough fixes over the years and don't aim to end up in yet another, so you quietly push the chair from the table. You stop for just a second, hear her still busying herself in the kitchen, then start again for the door. Better safe than sorry, you tell yourself.

"Where are you going?"

You freeze. You turn and face her. She's thirty-one flavors of hurt.

"I have to be somewhere," you tell her. "I should have—"

"But I spent all afternoon in the kitchen," she tells you. "You don't appreciate all I do for you. You never have."

"Look," you tell her, "maybe you and me ain't such a—"

"I wish you wouldn't leave."

One minute, you're standing upright. Next minute, you're sprawled upon the floor. Arms askew, this way and that, and your legs—

Where are your legs?

You open your mouth.

Where the bloody fuck are your legs?

She's on top of you, arms crooked below yours. Lifting you from the floor and dragging your torso back to the straight-backed chair. Mumbling something about how you should have listened, you should have loved, should have, should have, should have... All you can hear is the screaming from where once were your legs and soon you realize that ain't where the screaming comes from. No, that screaming comes from you.

"You'll feel much better once you finish your drink," she tells you.

Funny, she doesn't look that strong, but she manages you back into the chair. Despite the absence of legs, you are seated upright. Kept there, thanks to bungee cords.

You can't drink the cocktail fast enough.

"Will you please tell me what is happening?" Your cheeks burn with tears. "Will you please tell me how I got here? Tell me what happened to my legs?"

She smiles as she spoons out lumps of mashed potatoes onto each of your plates.

"Three wishes," she says.

"Do what?"

"I was given three wishes." She pours more bourbon into your glass. "You know, like *I Dream of Jeannie* three wishes."

"Wha—"

"I could have wished for anything," she says. "Anything in the whole world."

"You're lying!"

"Funny, I know. I didn't believe it either, but I've always been told if you want something bad enough. If you can picture it in your head…"

"But, why?"

"I've always loved you," she said. "Even though I knew I was just a one-night thing for you."

"This is impossible."

"Eat your dinner. Enjoy."

You fight to remain upright. You are sliding down in your seat.

"This is insanity."

She smiles. "I really wish you would enjoy spending time with me."

One minute, you're miserable and crying. Next minute…

AN AFTERNOON WITH THE PARKINSONS

A car full of jailbait whizzed past like a rocket and beeped its horn until it screamed up and down the neighborhood. Their high-pitched wails could be heard until they were long gone.

"That's my dad," said Peter. He shrugged his shoulders and walked faster than the other boys. The mood to dribble left him, and he put the under-inflated basketball beneath his good arm. Davey had been his best friend since they were six. He glared at the other boys with his cool, blue eyes.

"Laugh and I'll bloody your nose." No one laughed.

Somebody's dog barked.

Peter and Davey hung their heads as they passed me while the other boys studied something far away. I watched them trudge by like battle-weary Joes after a good fight and struggled to find a funny thing to say that would get them rolling, but my crotch started itching and I scratched it. When I finished, they were gone.

Simmons pulled into his circular driveway thirty minutes earlier than normal. I imagined him fired from his job and having to have the grass re-installed over his circular drive since he could no longer work. It was the only one on the street; I remember before it was ever there, back when it was only St. Augustine grasses and weeds. He checked his mail, looked right through me, then went inside to his cozy little lair.

Those girls raced past again with another round of honking and hollering. I figured that meant that Peter and Davey and their friends would be rounding the corner soon with the basketball like before, but they didn't. Instead, somebody called for their dog.

"Sybil! Sybil! Here, girl!" Sharp claps and whistles.

I smiled at the autumn breeze.

"When will your husband be back?" a man asked Molly. He pecked her cheek lightly and lingered for something more. Molly looked up and down the block and smiled, all nerves. I'd always liked that woman's smiles. She had a lot of them. I guessed she smiled at Simmons's being home so early and maybe having to lose his circle drive. I did.

She touched his shoulder and whispered something. I meant to hear it but I got distracted by happy dog owners finding their Sybil.

"That's good," I said aloud. "Real nice."

The man goosed Molly's backside and jogged down the walk past me toward his car. After he sped away, Molly lighted a cigarette and stared at the street. I practiced some conversation in my head that I might strike up with her, but in the end, thought better of it. A minute or so later, she tossed her cigarette behind the shrubs and went inside her house.

Tires screeched somewhere. Later, I even heard a siren. My nose itched for seven full minutes before I scratched at it, and when I finally did, I promised I'd make it all the way to eight next time.

Mrs. Simmons let out their cat. The little tabby sniffed at things along the circle drive then vanished in mid-air. I laughed and figured those things will sometimes happen.

I got worried about the honking girls. They'd been gone for a whole hour. One of them, I recalled, had been very pretty, but jailbait. That's what we called flirty little girls like that when I was younger: jailbait. I bet with myself that they had boyfriends somewhere like pretty girls always do.

Peter went into the house just before dark like I always heard his momma tell him. He was a good kid, even though he never smiled and waved at me anymore. When he was younger, he'd always smile and wave at me. He just walked past me now. I never minded really, but I noticed all the same.

I notice everything.

After it started getting chilly, Molly and Peter stepped out onto their porch. Molly had that rag in her hand again. She looked more tired than she did back when my nose was itching. Peter was angry at something, but I didn't quite know what.

"I want to move, Mom," he told Molly. He said some more but I was listening to Miss Ellerbee's blender going at it from down the street. She lived three houses down, but I still heard her blender from time to time. I had some good hearing. "...can't take it anymore, Mom. *Why?*"

Molly didn't say a word. She lit another cigarette and watched her own smoke for a while. She smoked it all and threw the filter behind the bushes with the others.

A blue pickup drove by real fast. It was one of those newer models and the music was up loud enough for us to hear. I pointed at them as they sped past but they ignored me. It didn't bother me, really.

"Peter," Molly whispered, "it's almost suppertime." She looked at the sky. "Get your father inside so we can eat."

Peter slowly took my hand with his good arm and led me from the lawn chair.

"Peter," I said. Finally, I said it. "Peter."

"C'mon, Dad," he said to me.

We passed Molly on the porch. She wiped at her eye with a finger, and at the same time she dried the wet off my mouth with that rag.

"Peter," I told her. Great. I was going to smile but she kept wiping at me too much with that rag. Instead, I planned to do it tomorrow.

I stopped at the doorway and waited a second while walking a bit in place. Peter tugged at my arm real hard, but I wouldn't go no matter how hard he pulled or whined at me, not just yet. I kept walking in place until finally I heard Miss Ellerbee's blender stop blending, then I let Peter take me inside. He hadn't even heard the blender, and I bet Molly hadn't either, but I sure had. I'd noticed it all right.

I notice everything.

BLOOD HOLLER
(A TRILOGY)

ONE

"*The Murder Ballad of Samuel J. McCarthy*"

Despite weather warnings, Sam McCarthy woke up early, drank a cup of coffee, then started for his morning walk. He carried with him his trusty walking stick, a light jacket, and a hardened resolve that would not be swayed by cold, wet weather, or the threat of snow. Weathermen foretold winter storms to start anytime after noon, but McCarthy planned on returning long before that mess. The town panicked, of course, with news of impending weather and descended upon the grocery stores, stocking up on staples. However, it took more than a few flurries to dissuade Sam McCarthy when he had things to do.

His path took him across his old cow pasture, through his new one, then along the border of his cotton field, three months fallow. From there, he'd turn on a trail that led him through his timber lots before eventually becoming a piece of forgotten property he'd once sold to the state. McCarthy walked this trail every day, determined to stay fit. He'd grown leaner with age; his skin stretched tighter over his face and body, exposing sinew and twisted muscle, his face hawk-like with eyes that saw well beyond what others could see.

As he approached the trailhead, he relied more on his walking stick, a varnished mahogany number topped with a gilded, heavy skull which he had named Hank. Those around town who bothered to speculate on Hank thought it named after the musician, while others conjured tales of an old lover from his pre-war days named Henrietta who may or may not have existed. But McCarthy had named that stick after a younger brother who'd died before they'd grown from boys, died long ago from a snakebite. McCarthy carried Hank everywhere—on walks, to the bank, around town—but rarely leaned on it in public, carrying it like a bandleader with baton rather than a cripple with cane.

McCarthy felt a tickle in his throat and knew he'd be hoarse by the day's end. This weather could do that to a fellow. He preferred to "tough it out" rather than succumb to some idiot doctor and his drugs. He believed most people were unnecessarily frail. This had driven his wife crazy, but she had gone to her Kingdom a few years back and left no one to hassle him about doctors and pills and other whatnot.

This trail was root-strewn and still muddy from the wintry mix the night before. It weaved in and over Ten Mile Creek, which had once been called Awaneeta Creek, until McCarthy had renamed it, since "it runs through Ten Miles of [his] land and [he] wouldn't have any features on this land be named by murderous savages, namely the Cherokee." Once out of town, the creek would return to its rightful name on the official maps, even though locals in every hill and hollow knew it as Ten Mile. Word had it that McCarthy would bequeath every inch of his timber lots and unfarmable land to the state for a park rather than let it fall to his son, who McCarthy considered feeble and effeminate. There was little question when that happened, the state would soon purge Awaneeta Creek from history and memory to honor their fallen benefactor.

Few birds bothered with this weather, and the half-frozen river kept still. All the world was grey, quiet. Only faraway were there sounds—probably miles off, at the freeway—but they were as significant as shushes from a seashell.

If he heard them at all, McCarthy paid them no mind.

Barney Kerns entered the woods from the side opposite the river. He, too, walked deliberately, but was hardly the outdoors type. He knew well of Old Man McCarthy's day-to-day affairs, and that knowledge could have come from anywhere: Pep rallies for the local high school football team that McCarthy boostered. Or down at the Farmer's Grocery off FM 809, where he spent weekend mornings jabbering with other farmers over coffee on the way in to tend their land. Or at the dentist's office, where Barney's mother had been a receptionist.

Had been. She'd not only been fired after a clerical error regarding one of McCarthy's appointments, but the old man had made cruel and unnecessary sport at her expense for some time after. Yukking it up with old-timers outside the Winn-Dixie. Lewd comments after her at the concession booth during the homecoming game. The vitriol could have hinted at something more scandalous, but it was little more than a powerful man swatting a fly with a pickup truck.

But this was not why Barney chose to murder Old Man McCarthy.

Barney crossed the half-frozen creek using the remnants of a long forgotten Eagle Scout conversation project, then quickly picked up his pace. The cold air laid across him like sheets and he'd chosen his jacket for the task rather than for its warmth. A lone hawk soared silently over the tops of the loblollies above him, but even Barney knew they'd find nothing in this weather. However, he knew not all hunters would quit the day without quarry.

Barney had chosen a knife rather than a gun. In this still, frozen landscape, the sound of a gunshot would send folks running. Barney could get close with a knife. He could stick the old man nine, ten times before he knew what happened. Barney could watch the life quit the bastard's eyes. He would remind him of all the people lying up in Nokomis Cemetery that he'd soon be joining.

People like Ollie Churchill and Dean Hergenrader. McCarthy lived on a bend in one of Creechville Road's many curves, and throughout the years, many careless drivers—some drunk, some plain stupid—had gone off the road and onto the old farmer's property, a few times, nearly running into his house. One day, McCarthy'd had enough and erected a six-inch thick concrete barrier at the edge of his land. Kids called it Willard's End, after the first person killed there. Dean and Ollie, two guys Barney had known since fourth grade, were the sixth and seventh. People pleaded with McCarthy to take down the wall, while he in turn demanded they stop planting crosses and leaving flowers on his property.

Or, further back, the young boys shipped home in bags from Vietnam because Mrs. McCarthy—rest her cursed soul—had flunked them in school, which sent them to the jungles rather than college or the tobacco fields. Barney could remember trips made by boys and veterans to get drunk and piss on her gravestone because their daddies or their buddies hadn't come home. In the eleven years since she'd passed, the marker had to be replaced three times. Each time, McCarthy defied those vandals with a new stone, bigger than the last.

Barney reckoned there was little recourse against a man like McCarthy, no matter how many graves he filled. To whom could he complain? McCarthy was the town's treasurer, and had been for thirty-two years. After the town's tide turned and the mill closed, McCarthy had more money and land than the banks in town, so his fortunes were tied to the whole of Lake Castor. No one bothered to oppose him in elections, nor did he need to campaign.

No, thought Barney, there was only one way to handle a man like Samuel J. McCarthy.

McCarthy swung his walking cane with each step like a metronome, ticking, tocking. The trail pitched to a steep incline as it reached out from the valley carved by Ten Mile and became rockier, the ground harder. As it leveled, McCarthy entered the section of the forest named Matchstick Holler by his son, mostly because of how the trees arranged as they fell from the steep, rocky hills. Here rested uprooted trees, rotting logs, splintered stumps, and acres of scrub brush up past the knees. The woods grew dense. Roots scattered beneath their trunks and splayed across the trail like sunning copperheads.

In the distance, McCarthy saw another figure nearing him. It was not uncommon to encounter another hiker along this section of trails. Years previous, after his wife went to Glory, he'd made peace with the inevitable and put his affairs in order. He'd set in motion plans to bequeath the timber acres and creek to the state, as well as the funds to maintain it from vandals, neglect, and kudzu. As time passed, more took to the trails, appreciative of the new access. However, McCarthy still kept open his eyes for ne'er-do-wells.

Which is exactly what he found in the approaching figure: Lucy Kerns's kid. He considered the boy a loser, much like his father before him, much like his mother. Brutish and bullying with others his age, Barney had never amounted to much. He'd kept bad company as a youth and would no doubt continue to do so, as would—most likely—any offspring he managed to infect upon future generations. McCarthy reckoned the boy short of any Biblical authority in his life, which left him with no set moral code. He knew him to fear not Hell, but jail, which alone would never keep Lake Castor safe. He thought the boy deficient of any civic value.

Yet still, ever the consummate Southerner, he waved as they passed on the trail.

That's when it happened. McCarthy had only passed the boy when, behind him, he heard a mad shushing through the wet ground cover. A frenzied rush. Then, he felt it.

In retrospect, he remembered the sequence of the attack: two quick, hard footsteps. A blow from behind. The sensation of sudden, intense heat at his back, as if someone had touched him with a cigarette or a match. McCarthy resisted the urge to cry out. He knew he had been stabbed. He knew he had to act fast before it happened again.

Rather than wait for the next attack, McCarthy swung back his left elbow, catching his attacker at the jaw. They both struggled for balance. Barney swung the bloodied knife wildly with his right hand

and tried to catch the old man a third time. McCarthy raised his walking stick over his head and brought Hank's gilded skull down upon Barney's hand with such force that the bones in his fingers instantly pulverized.

Barney yelped and howled. His middle finger skittered across the rock and into the brush, the opposite direction of his pointer. Two other fingers shattered. The younger man collapsed to the ground, clutching his hand and howling.

McCarthy lost his footing. His arms flailed wildly as he tumbled down the steep embankment. A fallen tree prevented him from falling further into the icy waters of Ten Mile. He took a second—only a second—to catch his breath, to gather his bearings. Blood pooled on the wet layer of leaves and rusty pine needles. He could tell by the pain and flow of blood that the kid had nicked something necessary. He grasped wildly at the wound to try to staunch the flow, but he could barely reach. Up atop the embankment, Barney's moans withered. The old man had to act fast.

On the other side of the creek, up the opposite embankment and up a short way through the woods, he could reach the highway. McCarthy reckoned it a lot of pain to swallow to flag down a motorist if he wanted to survive. He rounded the tree trunk and made for a skinny section of creek where he could ford over the rocks. He staggered some, imbalanced by pain, shock, or even urgency. He didn't care that, as he crossed the creek, his feet sometimes missed the stones and ended up in the half-frozen waters. He moved too fast, had too much on the line. He splashed and thrashed his way across, then began his climb up the embankment.

Once up top, his adrenaline peaked. He'd clawed at dirt and tree root and stone until finally he'd climbed out of the hollow and fell immediately to the ground. This time it took more—more than he seemed to have—to stand. Across the street, he watched Barney search for a spot to cross. The boy had removed his jacket, then wrapped his crushed hand with it. McCarthy put it in gear. He stuck to the trail, knowing that crashing through the woods would spend too much energy. Just on the other side of a stand of trees was an old service road, long forgotten and in disrepair.

The air he breathed seared hot to his lungs, clawed at his throat. He felt his wounds tug themselves wider, opening more with each step. Life drained from him through a hole in his back. He felt drunk. He struggled first to maintain a straight line, then to stay on his feet.

The old service road, just up ahead, just through those trees…

McCarthy went down hard. His cheek slammed frozen earth. Nothing moved, save for his heaving chest. No birds, no rippling water, no wind. His eyes grew heavy.

Not here.

He snapped himself to.

Not here, he told himself. *Not like this.*

He pushed himself up from the ground, but nothing gave. He was spent. He rolled over to his back. His body grew numb, nothing but weariness. He tried to sit up, but could not. He sat still a moment. He heard Barney crashing through the underbrush, getting closer. Coming to finish the job. McCarthy surveyed the area around him. His arm flailed, shushing through the straw, searching like mad for a stick, a stone. The first soft flakes of snow began to fall, slow at first, then quickly taking speed as he heard the crunch of pine cones.

His heartbeat slowed. His breathing shallowed. It was too hard to move. Still, his arm clawed at the underbrush.

The clouds darkened. Any minute, snow would dump all across

the pines, the creek, and the whole damned town.

As he heard the boy approach, McCarthy knew it would be a while before they found him.

After he finished the job, Barney stepped to the creek to clean his knife. The pain in his hand mellowed to a dull thud. He was cold. His jacket, now useless, dripped with blood, both from him and the old man. The old man had bled a lot. Confined to only his left hand, Barney had made a clumsy go of things and been not near as neat as he might have hoped.

A thin layer of white spread over the hollow. Pine branches sagged. Other than the soft sounds of precipitation, everything remained still. The water was too icy and Barney too cumbersome to finish cleaning the knife, so he jammed it into his pocket, still blood-soaked. He didn't dare inspect his wound; he was afraid to look. He climbed back up out of the bottom and took a moment to inspect his handiwork.

"To hell with you," he whispered to McCarthy. The old man's lips were blue. His eyes stared into the Nowhere, still cold and severe, but their urgency long removed. Using his foot, Barney rolled him to the edge of the embankment, then over the side. The body might have rolled all the way down the slope and into Awaneeta Creek, but instead hung up on some brush. Barney scaled the decline to push it again. This time, it rolled a couple more feet before Barney abandoned the effort.

His teeth chattered. He scrambled up the hollow. From up top, he watched the snow dust the body in steady intervals. Barney's chest filled with air. For up until this moment, his life had followed a certain trajectory, as if his destiny had been predetermined long before he had existed or even thought about existing. And nothing ever budged or gave way. It had always looked like things were they way things were and how they would always be.

Until that moment.

The young man wrapped the jacket tighter around his hand and headed out of the woods. Snow fell and the Earth spun. Barney would emerge from those woods a different man than when he entered. For all that hate he'd fostered for so long now lay bleeding out near the bottom of the holler. But Barney knew that, no matter how much he'd hated McCarthy and McCarthy's wall and his damned wife and cursed timber acres, there were others who hated him more—much more.

Enough, in fact, to pay handsomely once they discovered the job was finally finished.

TWO

"When Last We Saw the Bears in Lake Castor"

Frances Mabley bent at the back over the only empty table at the All-Niter Cafe so she could reach the stain on the far corner with a dish rag. It was dinner rush, so she had no time to mind after the cramps festering her feet, no time to sneak that cigarette she felt was long overdue. No time especially for Roy Rains's shit, and she liked to slap him every time he raised his finger to the air and asked for another cup of coffee.

"You got a wooden leg, Roy?" she asked as she zipped past him to fetch the coffeepot.

"Just nervous is all."

"Then don't you reckon coffee is the last thing you ought to hanker after?" She filled his cup, then leaned across the counter until she was inches from his face. "You going to tell me what went on out there?"

"You know I can't say nothing, Frannie," he whispered. "Not until I talk to the sheriff."

"It ain't like folks don't already know about it," she whispered back. "I heard his throat got tore out."

"Don't be ridiculous." Roy sipped his coffee. "Didn't nothing like that happen."

"But he's definitely dead?"

Roy squinted in her direction. Creased the corners of his mouth until it disappeared into the many cracks of his face. He wasn't giving her anything. She arched her eyebrows like she could care less and carried the coffeepot by the crook of her pinky over to the corner booth, where sat Jack Linden and his grandson.

"You need another Coke, sugar?" she asked the grandson. She hovered the coffeepot just over Jack's cup, but he waved her off. "Y'all want anything else today?"

"We're fine," he said, but took hold of her wrist. "Say, what gives with the deputy yonder?"

She slipped free of his grip. "What do you mean, *what gives?*"

"I mean, his get-up."

Frances knew what he meant. Roy normally would roll through the All-Niter in uniform. Wrinkled, maybe, but always in his khakis. Not today. Today he dressed in hunting gear. A bright orange vest over camo fatigues and a stained feed store hat. Badge pinned fast to his chest.

"He's been in the woods all afternoon," she said.

"Ah, so it's true." Jack Linden's voice took on a reverent tone.

"What's true, Grandpa?" asked the kid.

"We don't know nothing right now," said Frances. Rather than deal further with it, she slapped the check face-down onto the table.

She'd come back later for the dishes. Instead, she hustled over to collect payment from Captain Munson, sitting with her brother and Gil Tanner.

"Keep the change, doll." Munson never so much as looked her way as she scooped the bills and coins into her cupped palm. Her brother winked her way, but it was Tanner who leaned forward in the booth.

"Hey, Frannie, when you get a second, can you do me a favor?"

She stuck out a hip. "I won't have a second for a good while, so make it a good one."

"Run ask Roy why he's too good to sit with us tonight." He snickered with the others. "Is it because we ain't wearing our duck hunting gear? Because I can run home and get my waders and my—"

"He's expecting the sheriff," she said. "Y'all say you're his friends, but all y'all do is sit back and laugh when he gets in trouble."

"You ever think we're just laughing," offered up her brother, "and maybe Roy just gets in plenty trouble?"

Frances had more to say, but had used up all the time she'd allotted for bullshit. Instead she took Munson's empty coffee cup and hustled around back to drop it in the dish pit.

There she found old Larry, rinsing chili and ketchup and whatnot off plates before sliding them into the dishwasher. She took the cigarette from his mouth and sucked the last two drags down to the filter.

"It's a mess out there, ain't it?" he asked.

"You're telling me." She dropped the cigarette to the floor tile and stubbed it out with the toe of her shoe. "It's like everybody and their momma is out tonight."

"Can't say I blame them," said Larry. "They been snowed in for three days. They're probably happy to be out of the house."

"They can be happy over at the pizza restaurant for all I care," said Frances. "This is bullshit."

"You think it was murder?" asked Larry.

"I don't think nothing except I got too much to do to sit around and gossip."

Around the corner, she heard the cowbell on the door ring so she sighed, collected herself, and hopped to it. Came around the corner and back into the dining room and stopped suddenly to see Sheriff Lorne Axel standing by the cigarette machine, having sucked all the air out of the room. What forks used to scrape on plates had stopped. Conversation suddenly shuttered and not a soul moved as all eyes in the building were on either the sheriff or the deputy.

Sheriff Axel removed his hat and held it by the brim at his thigh, then scanned the room.

"Howdy, Sheriff," said Roy Rains. He spun his stool when Lorne approached, but didn't get up. "Pull up a stool?"

The sheriff eyed the other men along the counter. "We better get a table, Roy."

Frances felt for Roy. She'd known him nearly all her life, him and her brother running thick as thieves since they wore varsity orange. She'd tell herself he didn't deserve half the shit they heaped on him, but she'd be a liar. A bald-faced liar. So she gave them a minute before stepping up alongside the table and asking could she fetch something for the sheriff.

"Coffee," he said. "Thank you."

"You want a menu, Sheriff?" she asked.

"No, ma'am, thank you."

Rains lifted that fat finger of his again and asked, "You care if I get a warm-up, Frannie?"

Instead of answering, she toddled again toward the kitchen.

"What do you think's going on?" asked Larry as he flipped over one burger with a spatula before pressing it down atop another. "You think Roy's going to catch hell?"

"I think the richest guy in the whole county turned up dead and froze in one of those hollers and somebody's bound to catch it." She crooked her elbow and held the coffee pot about shoulder-high. "Might as well be Roy."

They didn't mind her as she set down the saucer, then the cup, then filled it with brew. They continued on as if she wasn't even there.

Sheriff Axel was in the middle of saying: "—and you ain't spending the day at the deer lease. You're on patrol. You got to dress like it."

"We was on a search-and-rescue in the woods, Sheriff," said Roy. "Sam leases that land out to folks hunting deer and I didn't want nobody squeezing off a shot at me while we was trying to fetch him out the hollow."

The sheriff dropped his head into his hands and said something sounded like, "I need to know you've got this under control, Roy." Frances didn't dare stick around for more. She headed to the far booth to collect Jack Linden's money—no tip—then carried the dirties again to the dish pit.

"Holy shit," she said when she took a moment to breathe.

From that point forward, wouldn't nobody leave her alone. What were they talking about? Did they say it was Old Man McCarthy? Was he dead? If he was dead, had he been killed? She liked to get nothing done on account of everybody'd already heard something.

"I heard he was bled out," said Marge Ricker with a mouth full of french fries.

"My brother-in-law works down at the bank," explained Stella Henry, who drank her iced tea with her goddamn pinky out like high society. Her *iced tea*. "He said the girl who cleans McCarthy's house for him came to work and saw he hadn't been home since Friday last, before the snow fell. Said last she saw him, he was headed out to walk his property. Said his bed ain't been slept in, nor had his dinners been touched."

Gil Tanner had driven the road past the hollows that afternoon. Said wasn't nothing in those woods except for turkey buzzards and county police. "Whoever they found in those hollers," he said, "is dead as nails."

But all of it crashed to a standstill when Sheriff Axel, in yonder booth, stood and motioned for Frances to come over. She held the handle of the coffeepot with both hands as she scuttled across the floor, quilted in silence.

"More coffee, Sheriff?"

"Do me a favor," he said. Instead of looking at her, he stared down Roy, who hung his head, shame-faced. "Seems can't nobody here at the table give me a good reason why anyone in this whole town might kill Sam McCarthy."

"He's dead?"

Sheriff Axel breathed through his nose. Turned his head slow up to look at her. His eyes went soft.

"Yes, ma'am," he said. "He's dead."

"I didn't even know his name was Samuel," she chuckled through her nose. "Since we were kids, we always called him Old Man. Old Man McCarthy."

"Yes, ma'am." Sheriff Axel's hairline hadn't moved an inch in a good sixty years. He scratched at it. "Can you think of anybody that might have cause to kill him?"

"Oh, no, sir."

Sheriff Axel threw another look at his deputy, then again at her. He put a hand on her forearm. Cold hand, but warming.

"If you had to guess…"

Frances nodded. "If I had to guess," she spoke in a low voice, "then it could be near anybody. You see, his wife used to grade even harder during the draft, knowing two points either way would send a boy off to the jungles of Vietnam. Folks like my brother. The other one…name of Danny. You remember him, don't you, Roy? Viet Cong got him in seventy-two, with just a couple months to go."

"I see." The sheriff wiped his mouth with his thumb and forefinger.

"Or maybe folks like the Churchills or the Hergenraders. They got cause too. I mean, how many times have folks asked him to take down that wall at the edge of his property? At the end of the hairpin on Creechville Road? You know which one I'm talking about because folks have asked you time and time again to have him take it down because kids crash their cars into it all the time. Drunk, maybe, joy-riding, sure…but that boneyard on Nokomis is full of folks who met their end at the edge of the McCarthy yard."

It was Sheriff Axel's turn to hang his head.

Frances set the coffeepot on the edge of the table so she could talk with her hands. "It could have been any number of folks who voted some way he didn't like and had to catch hell for it. It could have been his son, who may be a touch queer and unhappy with how his daddy talks in town about him. It could be a drifter, for all I know. Point is," she said, "it could be damn near anybody."

It wasn't until she'd returned the coffeepot to the burner that she realized she'd never filled their cups. She saw the look on everyone's faces—the folks at the counter, in the booths, Larry, who let the eggs on the flat-top burn—and decided it best she took a quick break.

"I'm going outside to smoke," she said, with just as much sass. She grabbed her jacket, because she intended to sit a while.

She hadn't returned through the back door ten seconds before Larry nodded his head toward the booth recently vacated by Jack Linden, where sat Branch Gilmer and his wife. Both keeping their elbows so high off the table as to avoid the mess they so obviously despised. They looked about, as if lost, until Frances showed up to wipe it clean.

"Y'all busy tonight, huh?" asked Branch.

"Something like that," she said, wiping clean the table and scooping crumbs into the palm of her hand. "Y'all know what you want?"

"A couple minutes with the menu would be nice," said Gilmer's wife, all put out.

Frances huffed and thought, *Fine, take all the time you need*, but Gilmer himself held up a finger, pointed it down the row of booths to where sat the two lawmen.

"They say anything about what happened to the Old Man yet?"

"Not to me they didn't, and even if they did, I got a restaurant to run."

Frances cut it short. Stopped at the booth next to them. Stacked the plates and silverware and dirty napkins and asked if they had any room for peach cobbler, made fresh today. They waved a hand to hush her, as they were trying like hell to eavesdrop. She shifted the plates to one hand while fishing out their ticket from her apron pocket with the other. Had just slapped it down when the cowbell on the door rang again.

In walked Deputy Zeke Harris. Folks in town called him "Harmless" on account of they were always saying, "Don't worry about ol' Zeke, *he's harmless.*" He'd enjoyed a reputation as a bit of a thug in his earlier days. A long scar ran the length of his face from some shit he did a long time ago. Few people knew why. He still got in trouble from time to time down at Club 809 where he was known to tie one on and shoot his gun in the air.

"Afternoon, Sheriff," he said as he came alongside their booth. He dusted snow from his hat by slapping it against his thigh. "We turned some stuff out there that ain't looking so good."

The entire room sucked a sigh and Sheriff Axel shushed him. Motioned with his finger for Deputy Rains to scoot over and let Harmless into the booth. From that point forward, they spoke quieter.

"I don't know why they just don't tell us all what's going on," said Larry, back at the dish pit. Frances pulled each plate off the stack and set it into the sink. "It's not like we're a bunch of idiots."

"Don't sound like they know everything that's going on," she said.

"You see Harmless come in?"

"Me and everybody else."

"He's got Sliver outside in his truck."

Frances cocked her head. "Sliver?"

"Lester Foreman's hunting dog," said Larry. "They probably borrowed him and had him down in those hollers looking for the Old Man."

"That's so awful," she whispered, but didn't mean it. Didn't mean

232

it one bit. She wiped mashed potato or something like it off he
fingers and onto her apron and hustled again into the dining room
of the All-Niter.

"If I was them," said her brother, "I'd blame it on a colored boy."

"Shut up, Able," she hissed. "Don't start that talk. Not tonight."

She and the men in the booth didn't take their eyes off the
lawmen. Watched as Harmless reached into his coat pocket and
pulled something out, something in a plastic baggie, and set it in the
middle of the table.

"That's Hank," whispered Gil Tanner.

"Who's Hank?" asked Frances.

"McCarthy's stick."

"His stick?"

Able nodded, not looking away from yonder booth. "His walking
stick," he said. "John Parton gilded a skull and had it put on top of his
mahogany walking stick. Give it to him one Christmas maybe fifteen,
twenty years ago."

"He didn't go nowhere without it," said Captain Munson.

"They say he named it after the singer, you know, Hank Williams."
Able shrugged and scratched his head. "I know different, though. He
named it after brother he had, got snake bit when they was kids."

"Died?" asked Munson.

Able nodded slowly.

"Looks like it's just Hank," said Gil Tanner. "Like maybe the skull
clean broke off."

"Hey, Frannie, maybe you ought to go over and see if you can
find out what's going on," suggested her brother. "Find out maybe
what he's got in that other bag."

"Other bag?"

It's all anyone was looking at. Harmless held this one a little closer to his jacket. Where he'd plain dropped the one holding the head of Hank onto the table, the other one he barely removed from his jacket. Whatever was in it had the sheriff's full attention.

"Be right back," said Frances. She grabbed a cup and filled it with Coke from the fountain. Walked it all the way over to yonder booth. Caught a bit of their hushed conversation as she came closer.

"—wouldn't be the first time we pinned it on a colored boy," Rains was saying. "I say we just do it and get it over with."

Sheriff Axel kept his voice low. "We ain't pinning it on a colored boy. We got two good black families just joined the Methodist church and folks are already screaming end times as it is. We blame this on a colored boy and we'll have a full-blown race riot."

"How about we blame it on a bear?" asked Harmless.

"There ain't been a bear in Lawles County in over fifteen years," said the sheriff. "Best if we—"

Frances set the Coke in front of Harmless and drew a quick breath. She saw it, the thing in the baggie. Purpled and busted and colored with blood.

Fingers. Two bloodied fingers. Busted free, just below the second knuckle.

Sheriff Axel saw the look on her face and motioned with his hand to put the baggie away. Harmless didn't catch on, so he said, "Goddammit, Zeke. Put that away right now."

"Sh-Sh-Sheriff..." Frances had no idea what to say. "Sheriff, you want some more coffee?"

"No, thank you." He stared hate-fire at his two subordinates. "I'm real sorry you had to see that."

Frances could say nothing. She put one foot in front of the other and shuffled back to the kitchen. All the blood had run free from her face. She walked with a hand out in front of her, as if maneuvering the innards of a cavern. All heads turned slowly along with her as she made her way across the room and through the kitchen and, again, out the side door.

She was on her second cigarette when she heard that little cowbell ring and alongside the building came Able, her brother. His mouth wide enough to catch bats and eyes to match. He was already shaking his head when he sat down beside her, careful to keep reasonable distance between the two of them.

"What was it, Frannie?" he asked. "What did you see?"

"I don't care to talk about it."

"I understand," he said. He gave it a minute, then scooched an inch closer. "Maybe you'll feel better if you get it off your chest."

"They'll be looking for me in there." She lighted another cigarette with the end of the one she had going. "I better get back to work."

"Ain't nobody thinking about food right now," said Able. "They'll be fine a minute more."

She didn't move from her spot, except to smoke.

"This town," she said. "It used to be a nice place to live."

Able nodded.

"What do you think happened to it?"

"Still is," he said. "I reckon."

"No, really." She turned to face him. "What do you think happened to it?"

He shrugged. "Mill closed. Lots of folks left. Good ones did, anyway. Left some of the others."

"I'm being serious."

"So am I." He sighed a heavy sigh. Behind them, in the summer, hung a heavy curtain of kudzu, but now was only a wall of leftover snow with nowhere to go. There still was little traffic on the highway out front of the diner. Things were quiet, as things often were after the passing of a winter storm.

"Folks looking out for themselves."

Frances cocked her head. Squinted her eyes. "Huh?"

"That's the culprit, I'd suspect. Folks looking out for themselves. When that damned mill was up and running, we had all kinds of folks moving from all over the country to get in here, because of all the jobs. Folks from places that didn't hold dear the same ideals we got here. Brought in their ways and when it was time for them to move on to the next place, well, they left those ideals behind."

Frances wished the cigarette were longer. She told herself if she lit another, she might as well drop a match down her throat.

Able went on. "I suspect we learned our lesson. Learned all about what happens when you let outsiders in. Learned what happened when you stopped taking care of your own. I know when that mill opens up again, I'll do whatever it takes to make sure them all are kept out, if you know what I'm saying."

"I got to get back in there." Frances dropped the butt to the ground where it hissed in the melting snow.

"Frannie…?"

"What, Able?"

"You going to tell me?"

"Tell you what?"

He wiped his nose with his sleeve. "What was in the baggie. The one Harmless brought in."

"No, Able," she sighed. "I didn't get a good enough look at it."

"That's bullshit and you know it." He stood. Stepped up to her like they were kids again, playing in the yard. "I seen how white you got after you left that table and I know damn well you saw it. Something scared you and you got to tell us what it is."

"Let the police handle it, Able. They—"

"The police?" Able laughed a good one. "Police ain't going to handle shit. Police are those three assholes in there and if any of them ever had a single thought worth a shit, it'd die a lonely death, let me tell you."

"Able, I got to—"

"If somebody killed Old Sam, we have a right to know."

"And if I knew anything," Frances put her hand on the doorknob, "I'd tell you. Now if you don't mind, I got to get back to work."

She certainly did. Someone passing through would have thought a bomb had been dropped in the diner off the highway, things were in such disarray. The telephone rang, would not stop. Larry filled coffee at the counter while eggs smoked on the flat-top behind him. Branch Gilmer and his wife still hadn't ordered and were pretty sore about it. All the while, two poorly-minded children raced each other from one end of the diner to the other. All that and Bruce Springsteen on the juke, which alone would have been enough to drive her crazy. She pulled her apron off the hook and slipped back into it.

"Not a minute too soon," said Larry. "You okay?"

"Let's get this shift over with," she sighed.

The Gilmers were less forgiving. They went on about waiting for a half hour to order, how the table wasn't clean, how this and that, and she had half a mind to rip into them when in came Able—ringing the little bell on the door—and demanding to the sheriff and everybody else in the room that he had a right to know what happened out there in that hollow.

Roy waved off the sheriff, half-stood from his seat in the booth. "Able, I don't think this—"

"You don't think nothing half the time," shouted Able. Shut Roy up and sat him back down in his booth. "Sheriff, you'd better start talking, because this is ridiculous. We all know Old Man McCarthy was found dead. Now we want to know why you got Hank all busted up there and we want to know what's in that other little baggie."

Sheriff Axel slipped out of the booth. He held up both his hands like it was him surrendering to Able. "Mr. Rains," he said, "maybe it's best if you took your seat."

"I ain't taking my seat," said Able. "Not until you tell us the truth. Now, did somebody kill Old Sam?"

"We're investigating every possibility right now."

"Who is?" Able pointed to the deputies. "These two? Shit."

Frances came alongside him and tried to coax him back to his booth. He pushed her aside.

"Lorne, I don't know how y'all do things over in Tucker," Able said, "but around here, we take care of our own. We're perfectly capable."

"Oh, don't I know it." The sheriff dropped his hands. They hung at his side, right one close enough to snatch that revolver, if need be.

"Beg pardon?"

Sheriff said, "Don't I know you folks like to take care of your own. Kind of like when I came into town to see about that cocaine Tucker school kids were buying over here, bringing back into town. Couldn't nobody tell me where it was coming from. Not Roy back there, of course. I expect that from him. But I couldn't find a damn one of you could tell me about that cocaine."

"I don't know nothing about no cocaine," said Able. "I hope you ain't insinuating—"

"No. No, I ain't insinuating nothing. I believe you may not know anything about it. But you might have an idea about who burned that black church ten years back. I had to come over here too, just behind those Richmond news trucks, and couldn't nobody tell me jack shit about that either."

Able knew good and well to shut the hell up.

"And I imagine I can spend a good amount of time knocking on doors and popping in that bar up yonder or hanging out in the barber shops and still won't be anywhere close to finding out anything about who killed Sam McCarthy, will I?"

Didn't nobody say anything. Some hung their heads, some had jaws dropped to the floor. Frances set down the stack of dishes on top of the cigarette machine and fished a couple quarters from her apron. She picked up the receiver to the pay phone and dropped them in.

"All y'all are just as guilty in my book," said the sheriff. "You may not be selling the cocaine or lighting the match, but you all got blood on your hands because you could have done something about it and you didn't. So, no, I ain't got nothing to tell you...*any* of you, because you ain't got nothing to tell me."

If anybody had anything to add to the matter, Sheriff Axel gave them plenty opportunity to add it. He stood there, put his eyes on every single person in the room, whether they looked back or not. When he was good and done, he returned to his seat in his booth as Frances hung up the payphone.

"Frannie," whispered Larry, "these eggs are getting cold."

"They're going to get colder," she said without slowing down. She snatched the coffeepot from the burner and stopped at the sheriff's table.

"Just the check, please," said the sheriff.

"Police don't pay," she said, filling his coffee. She didn't leave. Stood there until finally the Sheriff looked up at her, and that's when she said, "Barney Kerns."

"Do what?"

"Barney Kerns," she said.

"I don't know who that is." He looked across the table. Rains and Harmless shrugged.

"You boys know Barney," she said, disappointed. "Big boy. Hangs out around the 809, I know you seen him out there, Harmless."

Harmless hung his head.

"What about him, Miss Mabley?" The sheriff took a patient, warm tone with her.

"He's the one who done it."

"What?"

"You heard me," she said. "He's the one who killed Old Man McCarthy."

Roy's knees jarred the tabletop from underneath. The spoon rattled in his saucer, the salt shaker toppled.

"You don't know no such thing," he said.

"Sure I do," she said. "I got a friend at Presbyterian over in Deeton. Works the emergency room."

Sheriff shook his head. "Yes, ma'am?"

"Wanda Jacobs." No lights in the faces of the lawmen. Any of them. "Anyway, I called her and asked her if anybody come in missing their…" She nodded toward the baggie in Harmless's jacket pocket. "She said funny thing but yes they did. Barney Kerns. Three days ago in the middle of the snowstorm. Two fingers smashed to shit and couldn't nobody find them."

Sheriff Axel opened his mouth, but could not speak.

"My guess is Old Man McCarthy swung that stick on him, smashed his fingers off. As to why he killed him, I couldn't answer that. I know Barney's momma was Dolores Kerns and she was the receptionist down at Doc Greer's, the dentist. He had her fired what, five, six months back? I'd like to say I don't believe that's motive for killing, but I don't know if that's true anymore. Things being what they are."

Roy Rains opened his mouth, then closed it. Able steadied himself with the back of Branch Gilmer's booth.

"Wanda said Barney left the hospital in the middle of the night," she said. "Said he didn't check out or nothing, just up and left. Three inches of snow and missing two fingers."

She held up the pot. "More coffee, Roy?"

Come ten o'clock, things wound down long enough for Frances to count down her tips, sitting on the stool closest to the register and placing dollar bills into stacks of twenty. Larry flipped two eggs onto a plate and set it steaming in front of her.

"That was quite a night," she said.

"Sure was," he said. He leaned against the pie cooler and sucked on a cup of coffee. "You got plans tonight?"

"I got a frozen pizza and a six-pack," she said, losing her count and having to start over.

"You're a queen in search of a realm."

"Something like that."

Larry made to say something else but stopped shy. The telephone rang. Larry set the coffee down on the counter and walked around to the pay phone. Picked it up. Said, "All-Niter," then listened.

Frances put away the rest of the eggs, then pushed the three stacks of bills closer to the register so Larry could change them for twenties. He hung up the phone and walked real slow to the stool next to Frances.

"Frannie," he said, "I got real bad news for you."

"It's not Beverly, is it?" She looked at her watch. "Goddammit, what is it this time?"

"She said they still ain't plowed her street yet and three times she got stuck in the ice." Larry wiped his lips with his thumb and forefinger. "She said when Frank gets home, he could bring her up. He's got four-wheel drive, but he don't get home for another two hours."

Frances's shoulders slumped.

"This happens way too often," she said.

"I know."

"I'm serious."

Behind them, the little cowbell rang and in came Roger Freidman with a slight limp and a surly disposition. He grumbled something toward them both, then sloughed into a faraway booth. Frances looked from him to Larry, her face a question mark and an exclamation point both. Larry gave her nothing.

"If I could do anything else," she muttered, already on her way to the coffeepot, "I'd be doing it in a heartbeat."

"You're the best, Frannie."

"You're just lucky this is where I ended up."

"I tell myself that very thing on a daily basis," he said, but she didn't hear. She'd already sidled up alongside the table, her thigh touching the metal rim where she asked, sweet as pie, if Roger Friedman knew what he wanted or would he rather see a menu.

THREE

"The Old Service Road"

"Death is a funny thing," said Alexander Stanton. He worked hard to seem at ease with himself, but never stopped scanning the moonlit horizon to see if anyone else were coming. It was midnight, and he sat with Kevin Valentine on the old service road, a cracked and faded, weed-choked half-mile of forgotten and neglected pavement which branched off the highway before dead-ending not too much further past. They were alone, with only the stars for light.

Kevin did not comment. Instead, he wiped the sweat soaking his face.

Alex continued: "Let me tell you, I've looked into it three times in my life. Death, that is. I've looked square into its hungry jaws and all three times, you know what it was that saved me? A couple of inches, that's what. A matter of seconds. All three times, if I had moved a hair to the left or right, I would not be standing right here, right now.

"One time, when I was in college, did you know I nearly got hit by a bus? I was standing on a street corner, waiting for the light to change and talking to a girl, not paying a lick of attention, and I wandered too far off the curb. A big old bus came flying through at sixty miles per hour, came through so fast it blew up my shirt. Missed me by about this much. If that thing had hit me, I'd be hamburger. A couple of inches...

"That's what's so funny about death, in my opinion. There are several decisions we make every single day that lead to us living or us dying and we don't even know that we've made them. These decisions may be as inconsequential as what shoes we choose to wear, or as monumental as whether or not to walk away from a fight. But that little choice made here or there could result in those inches or seconds which make all the difference in the world."

Alexander Stanton did not normally wax so long and rhapsodic, but he was particularly enjoying this. And there had once been a day when Kevin Valentine would not have tolerated such soliloquies. But both men were far removed from such a time, and while Alex relished every moment of it, Valentine wanted only a drink from the flask he knew was kept in Alex's pocket.

But he would not dare ask after it.

Further down the old service road, two silhouettes and the sounds of conversation made their way toward them.

"Ready?" asked Alex.

"Let's get it over with."

As they drew near, the full moon scattered the shadows from the faces of Gene Nash and Barney Kerns. All four men had known each other since grade school, so the formalities they exchanged were brief. A lot of history had passed between them.

"How's the hand?" Alex asked Barney.

Barney held up his bandaged fist and shrugged. "It don't hurt near as much as it did, but it sure ain't pretty."

"You got it to the hospital on time, then?" asked Alex through his teeth.

"I guess so, but the—"

Barney may have finished his thought, he may not have. Valentine made his move. In a single breath, he advanced, drew the shiny black .38 from the pocket of his jeans, and put it to Barney's face. He fired. The report seemed to ricochet from every pine, then bounce into forever.

Barney's head snapped. His knees buckled, and only instinct kept him erect. The rest of him slowly got the news. He fell backwards onto the asphalt...

...and was gone.

Despite knowing it was coming, Gene was plenty startled. He turned away to stare at the moon and wait for his pounding chest to settle. Valentine dropped the gun. He turned to Alex.

"Give me that flask."

Alex spun on him, a finger to his face.

"What did I tell you?" he spat. He did not hand him the flask. Instead, he stepped across Barney's body to put a hand on Gene's shoulder. "You okay?"

Gene nodded. "We're in it now, aren't we?"

"We've been in it, Gene." They stared into the night sky a moment as the silence settled between them. Then, Alex squeezed his shoulder. "Let's finish it."

They turned to Valentine.

"Let's get our stories straight," said Alex. "What are you going to tell them you were doing out here this time of night?"

"I came here to be alone," said Valentine. "I was drinking."

Gene found the gun, then kicked it across the pavement to Valentine's feet.

"Why'd you bring a gun?" he asked.

"I was going to—" Kevin swallowed a lump forming in his throat. "I was going to kill myself."

Asked Gene, "Why?" He plucked a cigarette from his pack and lighted it.

"Go to hell, Nash," muttered Valentine.

"They're all going to want to hear it."

"No, just you." Valentine eyeballed Alex's jeans pocket, the one where he knew the flask was hidden. "Everybody knows why. So do you. You don't have to be a bastard."

Valentine was right: if he were found with a gun in his mouth at the end of the old service road, there'd be little mystery of why he'd done it. He'd fallen leagues since the days when he had been the star quarterback of the Lake Castor High School football team. His rising star had crashed to earth after a ruined scholarship, landing in the bottom of a whiskey bottle. However, they had much further to fall.

Upon returning home from a failed stint at college, Valentine cracked his car by driving into the rear of a parked eighteen-wheeler. He'd been drunk and suffered little more than a faceful of glass from the windshield. His baby brother—in the passenger seat—would not be so lucky. At least, he could tell himself, it had been quick for the boy. The death Valentine suffered was longer, slower.

Valentine got a job for a local electric parts supplier. Too drunk to courier, he stocked parts in the warehouse, day in and day out. A long way from tossing touchdowns…

He'd been approached by Gene and Alex at Club 809, a bar-turned-strip joint kept hidden down the Lake Castor backroads. Used to, he would never have bothered with guys like them. Kids like Gene, who wore secondhand clothes to school, or Alex, who played no sports. The tables, however, had turned.

They played him from the start. Buying him drinks. Trudging down memory lane. Talking about things Valentine could little remember, they felt so long ago.

Remember that game?

Remember that pass you threw?

Nobody's ever taken Lake Castor to the playoffs since.

They had made such a big deal of days gone by, Valentine should have smelled a rat. He could summon no memory of school spirit with either of these boys, nor the slightest interest in athletics. Still, they ordered him another round. Still, there was nary another soul to pay him a simple never mind.

They started talking about how the town wasn't the same since the mill closed. How folks seemed to move away and not come back and it was just all so much better when the Tigers were in the playoffs and Kevin Valentine wore number fourteen. Back when Kevin Valentine was a hero.

"Lake Castor needs another hero, Kevin," Alex had told him. They ordered another round, but had yet to touch their first ones. "This whole business with Barney Kerns and Old Man McCarthy has folks scared."

True. Since Old Man McCarthy had been found in the bottom of Blood Holler, the air around town had been different. Folks moved like everything they touched might electrocute them. Every day there was a new sighting of Barney Kerns somewhere in town. Some new rumor. They'd hear he was in the woods, and a mob of impassioned, civic-minded rednecks would fill a pickup with rifles and six-packs, then take to the woods to find him. Folks drove with their car doors locked and feared Barney might catch them at stop lights. Barney had been blamed for killed or missing livestock.

And somewhere in this conversation about Barney and the state of Lake Castor, Valentine agreed that Barney had to be killed and that he should be the one to do it. Had he argued for this responsibility or had it been foisted upon him? Valentine could not remember. He'd taken whiskeys from Alex and Gene rather than letting them go to waste. The next morning, he'd lain in silence on his floor and could replay nearly the entire conversation, all of it, save for that most important bit.

Valentine understood what he had to gain. For the first time since he wore the Tiger orange, he could get things back on track. He could change the way folks looked at him. He'd often told himself all he had to do was stop drinking. Reapply for housing and return to school. Start working out again and return to his old form. All of this, he'd told himself, could change the narrative, could make folks see him again for who he was instead of the old quarterback who'd killed his baby brother. He could forgive himself, he thought, if people would just stop looking at him like that.

After talking with Alex and Gene, he finally felt there might be a switch to flip which could make all that happen, and his finger had found it.

What he didn't know was what Alex and Gene stood to gain.

"Let's focus instead on what happened," said Alex. Next to him, a misty vapor rose from Barney's cooling body like spirits quitting a corpse. "Kevin is right: the whole town is hip to why he done it. Why don't you tell us instead what happened after you got here."

Valentine took a deep breath. He turned the gun over within his hand. The only bullet they'd loaded had been spent sending Barney to Jesus or wherever, but the little metal revolver felt just as heavy as ever.

"I came out here around eleven," Valentine said with little inflection. "I left a note at my momma's. I was drinking, thinking… getting up the nerve to do it. Then Barney stepped out of the woods. I guess he'd been hiding in there. He saw me, came at me with that knife of his, all crazy and, well…I didn't even think about it. I had the gun in my hand. I turned and shot him. I had only one bullet in the damned gun and that was for me. I used it to put Barney down."

Gene nodded, content. He'd heard the words several times over the past couple weeks, but there on the service road with Barney's body between them, they carried extra weight.

Alex fetched the flask from his pocket. He handed it to Valentine, who stared at it as if it were a handful of rattlesnakes. Angry at the hesitation, Gene snatched it from his friend, unscrewed the cap, and shoved it to Valentine's chest.

"You're going to take this and you are going to drink it," he said. "You're going to drink all of it and when it's done, that's all you get. In the meantime, you are going to get right with whatever God will have you because this is the way things are now. You make peace with it because I don't want you cracking up on us. We all have a job to do and yours is not over. Not by a long piece. And if you start to lose it, then there's nothing we can do for you."

Gene motioned to Barney, as if to punctuate his point.

"So you think hard about Ollie Churchill who used to catch all your passes and how his promise got cut short at McCarthy's wall. You think of your little brother. You think of whatever you have to, because McCarthy needed killing. Barney couldn't keep it together, so he needed killing. We need you to keep it together. So take that drink, Kevin. No…go on and take one. But enjoy it, because you are about to find God. You're going to find redemption and everyone in Lake Castor is going to watch you do it and be inspired by it. Those people you inspire are going to help you run for office and you're going to win, and after that, you won't be drinking for a long, long time."

Valentine swallowed thickly. His eyes flickered from Alex to Gene, from Gene to the flask, from the flask to what had once been Barney. He considered the entire tableau a long moment before he reached across the old service road and took the flask. He followed a quick, furtive sip with a longer, deeper pull. A trickle of whiskey crept down his chin and onto his windbreaker.

"Now take that and get on down the road," said Gene. "It'll be a mile or so before you get to the All-Niter. Somebody there will ring up the sheriff and I suspect you'll have a story to tell. So tell it however many times you have to, but remember, you are a goddamned hero and you save this whole town from Barney Kerns."

Kevin took another pull from the flask. He didn't yet bother to close it.

"We'll be in touch," said Alex. And with that, Valentine knew they were finished talking. His fingers rested at the screw top of the flask, but made little move to close it. He would empty it into himself, even though it was the last thing on earth he wanted anymore. He turned from the others and started the walk down the old service road, disappearing momentarily to the shadows. He would later emerge at the highway, past the partially blockaded entrance to the old service road, where he hiked the mile to the diner. By then, the whiskey would be gone and, after he wildly recounted the story he had rehearsed, folks would forever remember the old quarterback raving half-drunk, half-mad about how he'd gunned down old Barney Kerns in self-defense.

Back at the road, however, Jessup McCarthy watched the old quarterback stagger out onto the highway from a distance, and from inside the heated confines of his father's Cadillac. He waited until his former classmate was up the road and out of sight before he steered the Caddy past the barricades and up the cracked asphalt. He drove with his headlights off, but the night was too still for silence. Alex heard him long before he'd approached.

"How'd it go?" asked Jessup.

Alex nodded toward Barney, lying silent on the chilly pavement. "Went without a hitch. Valentine will be just fine. He's a hero."

"Did you talk to the lawyer?" asked Gene.

"It took some convincing," said Jessup, "but the will won't be a problem. It'll read just the way we want it."

Alex smiled. He backed away from the envelope of heat surrounding the Caddy and looked again to the night sky. A tall stand of trees separated the ruins of the old service road from the McCarthy land. It was on the other side of these pines that Jessup's father had been found stabbed to death. Alex contemplated them for a spell, then—with his head remaining skyward—said:

"You know, pines have a way of telling the future. When a storm's brewing, they'll let you know, even though the system is still a hundred miles or so out. The tops of the pines will rock and sway with the winds, then work their way down. Pines know hours before the big one will get here." He turned his gaze earthward, where the others stood. "What do you think these pines will say about our future if we asked them?"

Said Jessup McCarthy, "As soon as the funeral ends and the money clears, I'll be on my way to Texas and I wouldn't expect those pines or nothing else in Lake Castor to think of me never again. In fact, the only time I'll ever think of this place will be when I cash those checks you'll be sending. After a while, I reckon that to fade as well."

And if the pines could see the future or could they talk, they'd already know that no sooner would Jessup arrive in Dallas before he'd change his name to Jessie and avoid any and all references to his upbringing and ancestry and small town heritage. No one would ask how he kept his lifestyle or from where came these checks or why. For everyone Jessie McCarthy would come to love or care about in his new life would have secrets of their own, and go to great lengths to keep them.

Asked Alexander Stanton to Gene Nash: "Do you think, in the future, the pines see this town building statues of us? Granite statues on marble pedestals…all because of what we're going to do from this moment forth?"

Gene considered the treetops a moment. He knew better. The pines could not see the future, nor tell of it. For, within a month, Gene and Alex would see them torn down to their stumps, then their roots dug plum from the earth, to make way for the new service road. This new thoroughfare would stretch from the highway and provide new points of access directly to the heart of downtown Lake Castor, which had long ago been left to die. Perhaps Gene already contemplated tearing them down, or perhaps he debated the efficacy of an exit on the highway determining the course of a community's future. More likely, he considered their souls and how dark they stood to turn through exchanges they had made and will likely make, necessary or not.

"No," Gene said. "I don't think they'll be building any statues. I don't think so at all."

ACKNOWLEDGMENTS

I could never have written a single word if it weren't for countless people indulging me and enabling me. I could never name them all, but here are those who have left an exceptional impact: Lana Pierce, Natalie Pruitt, Katy Munger, Julie Malone, Bobby Gorman, Jennifer Asbury, David Nemeth, Sam Montgomery-Blinn, Jeff Polish, Piper Kessler and Monique Velasquez, Jedidiah Ayres, Brian Howe, Scott Montgomery, S.W. Lauden, Alex Segura, Benoit LeLeivre, Michael Rollin, Charles Pruitt, Meredith and Paul Snow, Joe Lansdale, Dan Morrison, Victoria Bouloubasis, Mike Bourquin and 106 Main, Anjili Babbar, The Regulator Bookshop in Durham, E.A. Aymar, Captain Tim Horne, Marilyn Hays, Todd Keisling, Tracey Reynolds, Jeffrey Moore, Angel Colon, Michael Howard, Robin Wells-Boerner, Nik Korpon, Sweet Johnny Wesner, Jeremy Stabile, Tim Bryant and The Bosslight, Dr. Emilie Hollville, Zachary Walters, Marietta Miles, Pam Gutlon, Rob Hart, Grant Jerkins, Carlos Alejandro Guajardo-Molina, S.A Cosby, David Nicewicz, Pam Stack, and Max Booth III.

I am eternally grateful for all of the editors who performed the thankless job of helping me find my way into print over the years. I will forever owe them all a drink. Especially Jason Pinter of Polis Books, but also Todd Robinson, Michael Pool, Brian Centrone, Adam Howe, Alec Cizak, Tom Pitts and Joe Clifford, Rob Pierce, Rudy Kraul, Kelly Abbott, Khalid Patel, Eric Campbell, Chris Rhatigan, and David James Keaton. And a big thank you to my agent, Josh Getzler. Thank you all so much.

ABOUT THE AUTHOR

Eryk Pruitt is a screenwriter, author and filmmaker. He wrote and produced the short film *Foodie* which went on to win eight top awards at over sixteen film festivals. His short fiction has appeared in *The Avalon Literary Review, Thuglit, Pulp Modern,* and *Zymbol,* among others, and he was a finalist for the Derringer Award. He is the author of the novels *Dirtbags, Hashtag,* and *What We Reckon,* which was nominated for the Anthony Award (all available from Polis Books). He is the host of the monthly radio show and podcast *The Long Dance.* He lives in Durham, NC with his wife Lana and their cat Busey. Follow him at @ReverendEryk.

CPSIA information can be obtained
at www.ICGtesting.com
Printed in the USA
LVHW03s1401220818
587699LV00001B/1/P